LOVE YOU ALWAYS

A SMALL-TOWN, GRUMPY-SUNSHINE ROMANCE

STACY TRAVIS

LOVE YOU ALWAYS

STACY TRAVIS

Cover Design: Wildheart Graphics

Editing: Emerald Edits

Copyediting: Erica Edits

For the women with hopes and dreams.
Never give up, not for anything. If you give up after five years, you'll
never be able to say it took six to attain them.

CHAPTER 1

rcher

SIXTEEN INCHES HIGH. The stack of growth plans, invoices, and business proposals on my desk is sixteen inches high, and I know this because I measured it. I took valuable time out of my morning to scrounge up a tape measure and measure my goddamn stack of shit rather than tackling any of the things on my to-do list. It's procrastination taken to its highest form.

Closing my eyes and tilting back in my desk chair, I imagine the stack of papers disappearing, like some kind of Jedi mind trick. When I open them, my desk will be empty, and my mind will be clear.

"Ooh, this looks serious." My youngest sister, PJ, short for Penelope June, sounds so cheerful that I almost can't be irritated. But I manage a scowl anyway.

My eyes pop open, and I find her standing in the doorway of my office in the old brown barn at Buttercup Hill, our family winery. I took this office on purpose—so that no one would happen to walk by and feel the urge to stop in and say hello just for the fun of it. The only reason anyone has to come to the end of the hallway is if they need me specifically, and I try to discourage that as much as possible.

I need solitude and focus to manage the wine-making operations, which are the crux of our multimillion-dollar business. My four other siblings are in charge of other areas of business at the winery, but wine making is my domain, which has the power to make or break us financially. Not at all stressful.

"What's up, Peej?" I try to banish the annoyance from my voice, but I can't bring myself to offer a smile. Fortunately, PJ is a straight-shooter and doesn't need me to pretend.

"I like the vibe I just saw. Were you manifesting?"

Running a hand over the scruff on my jaw, I growl at her like a territorial lion. "I don't even know what that means."

PJ winds her mass of blond hair into a knot and perches on the arm of the old leather sofa in the corner. I could point out that I didn't invite her in, but she does what she wants, and as the youngest sibling, she's survived in our type A family because of her fiery, independent streak. "You know, like putting your hopes and dreams out there and getting a little assist from the universe in making them happen."

I roll my eyes. "What makes you think the universe gives a shit? Besides, I don't have hopes or dreams."

"Everyone has hopes and dreams."

"Not me."

"Well, that's just sad."

"Whatever. I can't rely on hoping and dreaming with Dad doing everything he can do to sabotage us."

I'm not being dramatic. Our father's terrible business decisions make optimism nearly impossible. In our dad's defense, he's battling Alzheimer's disease and has a hard time recognizing us, let alone making sensible decisions. We had to take over the business from him, and we're all scrambling to pick up the pieces—

Beatrix designing and running the inn and restaurant, Dash handling hiring, Jax balancing the books, and PJ managing publicity—but the monster job of running the day-to-day operations fell to me, the oldest.

I never aspired to take over from my dad, but it is what it is.

"Have you gotten a chance to talk to him about the fire?" PJ asks, studying her sculpted pink nails. She's talking about the fire that broke out on our property six months ago. The wind blew it toward Autumn Lake, a winery next door owned by Graham Garcia, a half brother we only recently heard about. Twenty-eight years ago, our dad had an affair with Graham's mother. If our mom knew, she never said anything, but their divorce seems awfully well-timed in hindsight.

The first sign of trouble was five hundred million in missing money from the Buttercup Hill coffers. It turned out that Dad had siphoned money from our business to buy the plot of land next door, which he gave to Graham. It's sort of forced us together, united against a common clusterfuck.

"Don't you think if I'd talked to him, I'd tell you all?"

She shrugs. "Not if it didn't go well."

"How could it possibly go well? Not bad enough he nearly bankrupted us in order to buy a vineyard for Graham, but now he may have hired someone to torch everything we have left? It makes no sense."

The fire was just the latest terrible turn for Buttercup Hill, but the vineyards survived. We still aren't producing enough grapes to meet our sales targets, and my sixteen-inch pile is full of unsigned deals and partnerships that might get us there if I'm lucky. Which is why I have no time for my sister and this conversation.

"And no, I haven't talked to him. If his nurse says he's having a lucid hour, I'll rush over, but it's been a bad week. Talking to him when he doesn't recognize me gets us nowhere."

"This is why you should manifest. Tell the universe you need answers from Dad, and you may get what you want, is all I'm saying."

I huff out a breath at her insistence. "When did you get so into all this woo woo stuff?"

"Since I manifested myself a billionaire fiancé. Maybe you should manifest yourself a girlfriend. Or a wife, even. Might make you less of a grump."

"Good one."

I'm not interested. My family depends on me doing my job. The last thing I need is the distraction of a woman. If being my father's son has taught me anything, it's that I shouldn't have a wife. Or kids. It's not in my DNA.

PJ digs into the computer bag dangling from her shoulder and pulls out a spiral notebook with a blue bird on the cover. She taps it with a finger and opens it up to show me a scribbled note at the top of one page. "I've been manifesting getting us a spread in *Town and Country* magazine for months, and I just landed it." She looks like a pixie, grinning at me with her head tilted to the side. In her red lipstick, short skirt, and cowboy boots, she looks like she's ready to pose for a photo shoot on a ranch.

"Yeah? What's the angle?"

Her broad smile reveals a poppy seed in her teeth. I indicate the seed by pointing between my own teeth. "Lemme guess, you had the new lemon poppy seed scone from Sweet Butter?" It's the café here, which doubles as a breakfast stop for most of my siblings, who live in houses around the two-hundred-acre property.

"Guilty." PJ scrubs at the seed and flashes her teeth at me again. I nod that she succeeded. "They're playing up the rustic charm of a third-generation diamond in the rough."

"Translation, please."

"We're rescuing a hidden gem in the wine country from financial ruin and turning it into a wedding destination with the renovated inn. Beatrix has before and after photos of the inn, which readers love. Family-run places are hot right now."

My brain snags on one word. "Ruin?"

Her smile turns into a frown to match mine.

"I had to give them something juicy. They love a comeback story." Teeth gritted, she watches me for a reaction. PJ is one of the few people who's not afraid of my moods. I guess when you're the little sister to three older brothers, you can't be bothered by a mood.

"A comeback story." I take a sip of my lukewarm coffee and consider this. "So they're going to dig around in the disaster of this past year and write about all the things we did wrong? Dad would hate that."

"We're talking about a front-page *Town and Country* magazine story that will have gorgeous photos and will keep us busy and booked for years to come. Relax."

"Yeah, okay. Maybe." I scrub a hand through my hair and try not to think about all the ways this could go south. The reporter could draw attention to our financial problems. Someone could pay too much attention to how things are running under my supervision and start asking questions about our father's declining health. Or some issue I haven't begun to stress about.

I'm tempted to tell her to scrap the whole thing when PJ glances out my window. "Oh, she's here!" It's the kind of reverence reserved for royalty or heads of state.

"Who's here?"

"Ella Fieldstone. She just drove up in that little blue electric car that's all over social media."

If there were a way to roll my eyes farther back into my head, I'd do it. Ella Fieldstone and her dumb car only intensify my headache. Forget the bad ink she gets for being difficult—I didn't like her when I met her years ago. Her diva vibe rubbed me the wrong way back when I lived in LA, and I don't need a second interaction.

"People are so lame. Why do they care what car some celebrity drives?"

"Because it's *her*, and whatever she does gets attention. Did you know that car sales in that color blue spiked twenty percent after she bought hers? She's one of the biggest influencers. She's the reason we got the *Town and Country* spread—having her wedding here is huge. It'll make us the hottest venue in the county, and we can't manufacture that kind of good publicity. Besides, you're the one who's been stressing about how to make ends meet—this will help us."

That annoys me even more. The idea that I should be grateful for Ella Fieldstone's wedding chaps my hide.

I can't even rely on Jax anymore to take my side. Our middle brother will put our balance sheet before my preferences. Before he met his wife, Ruby, his surly, single-dad moods matched my own. Now, he's stupidly happy and in love, leaving me to be the resident baddie in the family.

If I'm honest, sometimes it hurts to be the only one of my siblings who doesn't have a partner, sealed off from being stupidly in love. Then, I remind myself that I'm better off protected from emotions that might derail me. My focus is on business. Numbers. I trust them more than people.

"I'm still in charge of running the winery, so I think I should have a pretty large say." The truth is that I don't have answers for how we'd make up the kind of income that would come from being the hottest wedding venue in the county, assuming PJ is correct.

"Good luck with that. Beatrix says it's a go, and Jax is all about the spreadsheets. It's three against one, dude."

Her phone beeps with a text, and her brow furrows as her thumbs start moving across the screen.

"What's wrong?" I ask.

"Trix says she can't meet with Ella for an hour. She's here on the wrong day or time or something."

"What a shame." I suppress a smile, secretly delighted that the celebrity downstairs isn't going to have red carpets rolled out just because she showed up when she felt like it.

"I have a call with an East Coast editor in five minutes. Can you go down and entertain her until Beatrix can get here?"

"I'm busy." I sneak a look out the window and stand up to get a better view of the small blue car parked crookedly in a space in the gravel lot outside the barn. Figures, she's too fancy to bother parking her car straight. Who cares if she takes up more than one spot? "But I can go down and tell her to take a hike."

The driver's side door swings open, and one bare leg unfolds before a swish of pink floral fabric drops over the limb, obscuring it from view. It's followed by a sweep of wild hair streaked with blond. The wind has its way with the long strands as a slim arm reaches up and swats the hair away, and the woman tucks a handful behind her ear.

Before I can move away from the window, her gaze rises and she looks directly at me, or at least what she can see of me with the harsh morning sun in her eyes. Her hand comes up to shade her forehead, and I move out of view. But not before I get a good look at her face, heart-shaped with delicate cheekbones and bee-stung lips that make me want to search out the offending bee—and thank it.

Shifting her shoulders back, she stares up as though she can look me in the eye. All the work stress must be getting to me because I swear it looks like she's emanating her own light, which I know is impossible. It's also impossible to look away.

Then I grab hold of my senses and take another step back from the window.

Because this is Ella Fieldstone. She's an actress. All manufactured moments and perfect lighting. Nothing I'm imagining can possibly be real.

"Just go down and stall her, please. Act like you care about our winery's future. Manifest something positive for once."

"Right now I'm manifesting you leaving me alone, and Ella Fieldstone getting her little blue car off our property."

I need to sit back down in my chair and do my actual job and let my sisters do theirs. Who the fuck cares about a celebrity wedding and whether it does or does not take place at our vineyard? I'm about to tell PJ as much when a movement outside catches my eye. I look down in time to see Ella Fieldstone step on her skirt and go down like a felled tree.

Huh.

Amid a sprinkling of concern is the thought that maybe I do know how to manifest after all.

CHAPTER 2

lla

I HAVE a bad habit of getting to destinations early. Maybe it's years of morning call times on set, but I hate showing up and finding that everyone has been waiting on me.

Today, I'm a full day early for my meeting with Beatrix Corbett, who offered to walk me through the restaurant at Buttercup Hill and kick off six months of wedding planning. I normally wouldn't show up anyplace twenty-four hours early and unannounced, but I'm here for…reasons.

And I'm really hoping the wedding planning won't take six whole months. It's just a party, after all. A spectacle.

Yes, I know women have been getting excited about their wedding days since the beginning of time, but I'm just not one of them. I'm too practical to get caught up in details like whether to start with a soup course or a plated appetizer. And I spend so much time getting fitted into wardrobe for work that choosing between duchess satin and raw silk dresses feels like a snooze.

Yup, instead of a bridezilla, I'm a bride van winkle—just wake me when it's over.

I'm also a bride who's currently facedown in a dusty parking lot, trying to figure out whether my skirt is caught or the world has just turned upside down. Probably a combination of the two.

A deep sigh escapes me before I even think about turning right side up. So typical.

It's not that I'm naturally clumsy per se, but I do see my fair share of the ground, and I have scars on my knees to prove it. Long story, but let's say it's a good thing I'm not a model because I'd never make it down a runway.

Fortunately, no one saw my latest brush with gravel. I assume this is true because I'm pretty nearsighted. I only hear the faint chirp of birds and a soft rustle of wind through whatever tall trees are dappling me with sunlight and shadows. Taking a long breath, I tug on my skirt, which responds stubbornly, still stuck to whatever caused me to trip.

I tug harder this time, and my ankle twists to the side.

Oh.

I'm actually caught on myself.

My skirt, a flowy thing with little eyelet cutouts along the hem, is stuck in a love affair with the kitten heel of my slip-on mules. I bought the innocent-looking peach-colored pair because they have a low heel. The high ones cause all sorts of balance problems, so I stick to low ones. Not low enough, apparently.

I feel for the edge of the skirt and free the pointy heel from the fabric. The wind billows my skirt up and over my face, and the sides of my shoes grind against the tan gravel as I flail about. Serves me right for not just wearing tennis shoes.

"Make a good impression. Look cute." The perennial instructions from my publicist, Nancy, ring in my ears. She doesn't say these things on repeat because she's a nag. She says them because otherwise, I'll show up in gray sweats with my hair in a pile on top of my head. No makeup. Coffee spilling out of my ceramic mug because I'm too stubborn to use the swag from my last two movies. It feels bougie.

The coffee sits half-spilled in a chipped mug, balancing on a notepad in the center console. I ripped the scrunchie from my hair on the way up the Buttercup Hill driveway, but at least I managed to follow her instructions about the rest, putting on a pale peach sweater, a floral skirt, and the dastardly shoes.

Yanking them off my feet, I chuck them at my Fiat. Checking to make sure no one is watching me with a phone, I roll from my side to a kneeling position, fully aware I just flashed my thong underwear at a bunch of bluebirds and cabernet vines. I hope they won't judge.

My phone rings, so I crawl toward the car to find my purse. My car answers automatically, blasting its caller ID on speakerphone.

"Call from Mom." The British voice I chose for my navigation sounds like my mother is paying me a social call at Downton Abbey.

"Accept." I sit cross-legged on the gravel and look toward the car speakers as though my mother can see me through them. "Hi, Mom."

"Morning, sweetie. Just checking in." The hollow sound of her voice tells me she's driving someplace, and I pray she's actually using the hands-free option because she's already gotten two tickets for being on the phone. I don't think the Department of Motor Vehicles has infinite patience for that sort of thing.

"Are you using speakerphone?"

"What? Oh, yes, yes. I'm in the car. How are you?"

"I'm okay," I say.

"Just okay?'

"No, I'm good. I'm fine. How about you?"

"Well, you know…"

I stifle a laugh and roll my eyes. My mother is the Chicken Little of suburban Los Angeles. She lives in a gated community with my dad in sunny seventy-degree weather and somehow, some way, there's always something dire about to happen.

"Tell me," I prompt. At least it will give me a second to dust myself off before I show up unannounced at the winery where I plan to get married. It's bad enough I came a day early, but now I look like a dusty desert creature with tumbleweed hair.

"I was at Starbucks on Ventura, you know, the one in the mini-mall, not the freestanding one on the corner…" She pauses as though I need to visualize the scene. As though every Starbucks doesn't basically look the same.

"Okay…"

"I'd taken a walk with Victoria around Balboa Park, and then she had to leave to go to work at the furniture place, and I decided to treat myself to one of those coffee drinks you introduced me to. You know, the ones with the vanilla?"

"Vanilla latte," I supply.

"Yes. That. And it was the strangest thing—there was a bird in the store."

I close my eyes. *Here we go…* My mother, a fearless feminist who started marching for women's rights in the sixties and never stopped, does not like "unpredictable wild animals" to come indoors. We are long past the time when I can joke that "predictable" wild animals aren't really a thing. The fear is real, and I've seen my mom cower when a pet hamster was on the loose in the house.

"Someone brought a pet?"

I can hear my mother huffing, which means she's now parked her car and is walking up the driveway carrying a bag of something. She always has a bunch of junk in a bag, whether it's dry cleaning or a few things from the market. "No, from outside. Apparently, it flew in before I got there, and people were standing on chairs trying to shoo it from the store. The baristas were going to call the fire department. I didn't stay to see how it all ended."

"Well, I imagine the fire department got the bird out, given that they have ladders."

"I know I'm being silly. It's just that…" I can almost hear her biting her lip, debating whether to tell me the last part.

"What, Mom? Just say it."

"I'm thinking twice about my idea that you should have a dove release at the wedding. All those birds flying around, even if they are doves. Especially if there's a baby…"

And there it is, the real reason she's calling me. She's been uneasy about my decision to adopt a baby ever since I told her I was going through with it. Her list of reasons is long, starting with the fact that I'm not married and ending with her worry that I'm too busy with my career to parent a child.

When I told her a couple months ago, I did my best to explain my reasoning. At thirty-three, I want to start making plans for my future. My doctor has concerns about some fertility issues that will make getting pregnant unlikely, and I've always wanted to adopt because it breaks my heart to think about kids who need a parent—I want to be that parent.

I've always loved kids, and as each of my friends becomes a parent, I play the favorite aunt. But every time I walk away, it leaves me hollow. I've dreamed about raising a child for a decade, and once I commit to something, I'm all in. And I want this. I really, really want this.

My mom has "thoughts." This isn't new. When I was in the middle of a dating binge of bad choices and big mistakes, she was the first to warn me about getting a bad reputation. Turns out she was right.

That fueled her confidence, so whenever she has a thought about my personal life, I hear about it. Most of her concerns come out as veiled worry about something else—doves, the weather, the migration patterns of birds in general—but at their heart, she's worried about me.

"There's no guarantee the adoption will go through before the wedding, and I wasn't planning on holding a baby up at the ceremony as dove bait," I tell her.

"Okay, well that helps, certainly. And I suppose a lot could happen between now and the wedding date, so I'll stop worrying."

"Spoiler alert. You will *not*."

"You're my daughter. I'm always going to worry about you. Especially when it comes to relationships."

She has a point. I have a trail of bad boyfriends in my wake. If there was a noncommittal, unreliable bad boy within a fifty-mile radius, I probably dated him. It's no secret that my mom wishes I'd fall in love with a fabulous man and deliver her a passel of grandchildren so she can babysit to her heart's content.

My version is proceeding nicely. I've filed my adoption application, cleaned up my image as a serial dater who can't commit, and I'm getting married in six months to a great guy.

Fine. A decent guy.

Okay. A guy.

The wedding has gotten blown up into a spectacle made for *Town and Country* magazine, who arranged a story with my publicist. But…eyes on the prize. There's a baby out there who needs me as a mom, and extra cameras won't kill me. It's just one day, and I'll try to think of it like any other media event—I'll smile and pose in my dress, looking like the America's sweetheart everyone assumes I am in real life.

At least Buttercup Hill is a pretty place for a media circus wedding. Looking up at the towering trees that line the driveway, I inhale the sweet scent of plants and rich soil. It's so beautiful that maybe just being here this morning will convince me I'm doing the right thing by marrying Callum Haywood.

Yes, that Callum Haywood, the country music star, who proposed on stage last year at the Stagecoach Music Festival. The story of the lovelorn princess landing the bad boy rocker was pure publicity gold. I wish I could say I fell hard for him, but…

it's a marriage of convenience, cooked up by our respective public relations teams, that will allow us both to quiet our wild reputations. Mine got particularly bad after an ex with a bruised ego shouted to every social media channel he could find that I'm unstable, reckless, and difficult. Adoption courts don't look fondly on words like that.

Callum's record label told him to clean up his reputation as a cheater or they'll cancel his tour, and my adoption lawyer said my chances of being approved will be better with a stable partner. I'm not proud of the charade, but I'm willing to do it in order to adopt. The fact that I need a man for that bugs the crap out of me, but I pick my battles. He lives in San Francisco and I'm in Los Angeles, but we've made just enough appearances together— me flying to see him on tour and him staying with me and grabbing early morning coffee in LA—that we look every bit the adorable couple. Even I almost believe we're in love sometimes.

But I have a niggling worry that Callum may have gone back to his old ways. A few too many nights when he's been on tour over the past few months when he didn't answer my calls after his shows. He always used to answer my calls.

A few too many times when his tour manager made excuses for why I couldn't come to Callum's house when I was in town. My best friend lives in Oakland, and I love staying with her, but I don't like being told what to do.

Maybe I'm just being paranoid because I don't want anything to derail our wedding.

So I focus on the doves.

"No dove release. Consider it done." I say goodbye to my mom, and the caw of a bird catches my attention. It's no dove. More like an angry starling swooping overhead and disappearing in the grapevines that sprawl into the distance.

I slip my shoes back on and take a deep breath. It will all be fine. As I walk toward the brown barn of Buttercup Hill, I step on the hem of my skirt. Again.

rcher

I START for the door of my office, forcing my sister to trail after me if she wants to keep nagging. Her legs are shorter than mine, and I hear her heels click-clack down the hallway as she tries to keep up.

"Beatrix will murder you if you're not nice to Ella Fieldstone," she calls after me. Her phone rings and she stops following before I make it to the bottom of the stairs. "Hi, yes, put her through." She pantomimes that she has to take her call and points toward the driveway where Ella parked her car. Then she puts her palms together like she's thanking me.

I mime flipping her the bird.

Her voice recedes as I cross the main floor of the barn, which has exposed ceiling beams, pale gray walls, and open shelves containing Buttercup Hill memorabilia—vintage wine labels, old photos of the property, vintner awards. In the time since I took over as winemaker, we haven't been within shouting distance of an award, but I plan to change that.

As I stride past weathered oak tables and leather chairs, the double doors fly open, and there, aglow in the morning sunlight, is Ella Fieldstone. Her untamed hair forms its own halo. Her cheeks flush naturally, no makeup needed. Clear blue eyes open wide like inviting mountain lakes.

Blood floods my veins and my skin tingles. I don't understand why or how, but her presence slams into me like an addiction I won't want to quit. One part irritating, one part extra strength magnet.

This sensation has only come once before. Back in LA. I couldn't explain it then, either.

Same girl, different circumstances. I buried the memory back then, just like I will now.

I can't believe the feeling dares rear up again when I know better. But here it is. Unwelcome, but here. If I doubted it was possible to feel something deeply for a woman I don't even know, now I have double proof.

The air feels like it's been sucked from the room. Sucked from my lungs. I stand there feeling unsure of whether my legs can support my six-foot frame.

I assume it's not just me who feels it because she's built a career as America's sweetheart, making people fall in love with her on a screen. But it's an illusion. It has to be.

It's not just that she's beautiful. I wish it was that because then I could accuse myself of being shallow and get over it. No. She's an impossibly brilliant light. And I'm the unwitting moth, desperate to get closer, even if I burn.

Goddamn.

Just beyond Ella's form in the doorway lies the most beautiful view in all of Napa Valley, acres of cabernet grapevines catching the yellow sun and hills just beyond the miles of rolling land that make up our property. I gaze out there every day and remind myself why I'm working to the bone to save our family business.

But that view—all of it—simply falls away, pale as an ugly fog behind the woman standing there.

Light kisses the bare skin of her arms, hanging gracefully by her sides like a ballet dancer. She tilts her head to the side as her eyes squint and adjust to the dim light indoors. She looks softer and more vulnerable than I expect. Less...sure of herself? Well, she is an actress after all. She owns the goddamn room, even one with a lone man in it.

It's almost like someone ran ahead and adjusted the lighting just so. Arranged the breeze to hit her so that her tangle of wild hair would fly around the soft features of her face, making me strain harder to stare at her pale pink lips.

And I am staring, no doubt about that.

Sixteen inches of paper, I remind myself. I don't have time for nonsense like pitter-pattering hearts. Or celebrities who show up at the wrong time.

I expect to see a bevy of handlers rush through the double doors. Someone carrying her purse or holding her jacket on a hanger so it doesn't wrinkle. Someone asking for an outlet to plug in her blow-dryer or charge her phone. That was my experience with actresses during my stint in Los Angeles.

But she's alone, her pale pink skirt swishing around her legs and making a soft rustle that my ears strain to take in. When the doors finally close behind her, Ella stops a few feet away, regarding me from head to toe before looking down, almost like she's embarrassed.

Ella takes a step closer, and I feel my skin flame hotter. I ignore the sudden urge to wipe a hand over the back of my neck, which feels sweaty. My pulse quickens as she takes the final step closer and extends her hand. I don't want to shake it. I don't want contact with her skin. A warning signal from my brain tells me that if I touch her, life will never be the same.

"Hi, I'm Ella."

I ignore my brain's warning, enveloping her small hand in mine. I expect a soft, breakable grip, but she gives my hand a firm shake like we're closing a business deal. I already know that a business deal is the last thing I want from her, and I swallow hard.

"Archer." My voice is a choked rumble, and I try to repair it by barking out a few more words. "You okay? I saw you fall."

Her cheeks flush like twin red apples. She grimaces and looks down. "Oh, um, yeah. It looked worse than it was."

I notice a few dots of blood seeping through the sheer fabric of her skirt and realize her knee is grazed. "Come. Sit here." I point to one of the brown leather armchairs.

"What? Why?"

"Just…please. Can't have you bleeding all over the vineyards," I grumble, put out about the chore of dealing with her until my sister arrives.

I walk to the staff kitchen behind the tasting room and grab a first aid kit with some antibacterial spray and a bandage. Kneeling in front of her, I tip my head up to indicate she should move the fabric of her skirt. When she does, I swallow hard at the sight of her pale skin, all smooth and perfect except for a bleeding gash on the knee.

I don't want to touch her—can't afford to touch her, given how my heart is thudding in my chest—so I drop the first aid stuff in her lap. "I'm sure you can handle putting on a Band-Aid."

Her brow furrows, but she takes the supplies and quickly plasters on the bandage before standing back up. "Thank you." She looks down at her skirt and dusts it off, but what I'm staring at is the wild disobedient curls, the heart-shaped mouth, the curves that she's trying to hide under an oversized peach sweater. I don't know how to look away, even though I know she's wearing another man's engagement ring. I don't know why she has me so unnerved, and it bugs me.

She clears her throat, but her voice comes out raspy. "I...um, was hoping to find Beatrix Corbett. It's the wrong day, but I was in the area, so..."

"So, you don't have an appointment today? Yeah, that's not gonna work. My sister is probably booked all day, so I'd just come back at the right time. Or call her on the phone." I sound irritable, which is better than dick-whipped.

"Oh. Well, shoot." She looks at the floor again. "Yeah, I guess I should have expected that. I don't know what I was thinking, coming today. I guess...honestly, I wasn't even in the area. I drove up from San Francisco just because I needed some time in the car, you know?"

She trains her eyes on me, and I feel myself flinch. Something in her gaze unnerves me. It's not just the pure deep blue of her eyes, though they conjure impossibly calm waters. There's a playful challenge, daring me to look at her longer. Like some vital question about the universe might be revealed if I do.

And despite myself, I want the answer to that question.

"Yeah. We all need a road trip now and then."

Her gaze softens and I earn the barest hint of a smile. "True."

"Anyhow, sorry I can't help you." I turn to go back to my office, but her hand on my shoulder makes me flinch once more. Only this time, it's because her palm leaves a shock of goose-bumps in its wake. Turning, I see determination in her eyes.

"But you do work here," she affirms.

"Yes, but I have nothing to do with weddings."

She doesn't budge.

"Beatrix is your sister."

I exhale a twinge of annoyance at myself for giving up that information a moment ago. "Yeah."

"Interesting."

I cross my arms and take a step back so I'm outside of touching distance. "Really? I see nothing interesting about the fact that she and I are siblings. Nothing." Her eyes widen at the unwarranted irritation in my voice, but it's my only possible defense against this woman who I should have sent on her way ten minutes ago. I need to be every bit the asshole I have a reputation for being, if only so my brain gets the message—*no good can come to this moth from standing close to her.*

"Regardless, you're the brother I've been dying to meet."

My pulse quickens at that idea, and I forget to take the next breath. I recover and roll my eyes at her overstatement. "No one is ever *dying* to meet me, and once they do, they generally wish they hadn't."

"Why? Your personality?" She smiles, and my traitorous heart starts beating faster. My throat feels thick when I try to swallow.

"I have two other brothers," I desperately choke out, reminding myself that I do not like this woman or anything about her celebrity.

"Is one of them a winemaker?"

"No."

"So, she meant you." She taps a finger against my chest, and I bristle at the ripple of heat that shoots out in all directions from the barest hint of her touch. Then I take a step back and her hand falls. She watches it sink through the air before her eyes return to mine, accusingly. She shrugs, as though my disinterest is irrelevant. "I was hoping..." She twists her fingers and half-smiles like I've made her nervous. "Look, I know I need to pick wines for the reception and all that, but between you and me, I'm a science nerd and I was really hoping to learn about viniculture."

"I—" I shake my head, having no idea what she's talking about. "You want...what?"

"When I come here, I'm so gaga over the vineyards that I can't focus...my brain is dying to know how you turn those beautiful grapes into wine that people talk about a thousand miles from here." Her eyes dance and sparkle, and I want to write her off as an entitled celebrity who wants something we don't provide. And yet...in the time since I took over the wine operations, not a single wedding client has taken an interest in viniculture. Something I love.

A new flutter blooms in my chest. It both pisses me off and rattles my nerves because my heart doesn't flutter at women anymore. Quite the opposite. I need to focus all my attention on keeping the family business going for the sake of my siblings. I need to be the man my father asked me to be, end of story. I can't indulge the whims of a woman who will distract me from everything that's important.

I'm the one who goes gaga over the vineyards. Not her.

"That's not how it works. My job is to run the place, produce the wine we ship all over the country. I'm not a teacher or a performer."

She nodding. "I get that. I don't mean to be a bother. But maybe...I could quietly shadow you sometime? You wouldn't even notice me."

I look at her with her sun-kissed cheeks and rosebud mouth and try to imagine how she could go anywhere without notice. A part of me wants to do whatever she's asking, purely as an excuse to keep looking at her. But my boundaries are there for a reason. I need to stay within them.

"I don't fuck around when it comes to our wine. These are hundred-year-old vines. We grow cabernet in a sought-after appellation that's known around the world. Wine making is a science. It's not an excuse to get drunk and post selfies. I'm not doing some dog-and-pony show for your social media feed."

The barn echoes as my harsh words bounce around in the otherwise silent space. The high ceilings eventually absorb the bark I expected to scare her away, but she doesn't move.

Jutting her hip out to the side, she taps a finger against her lips like she's considering how to answer. Her other hand flexes and balls into a fist as though she might slug me instead. I'm oddly intrigued by the power she seems to wield in her pint-sized frame against a guy who's six-three.

"Okay, then." She wrings her hands and then wipes them on her skirt like they might be sweating. Like I make her a little nervous, which seems impossible. Ella Fieldstone emotes on camera in front of a huge crew for a living. Nothing about this situation compares to that. "Sorry to have bothered you."

She turns to go, the whisp of a skirt flapping behind her as she spins on her heel. Her unruly hair trails down her back and catches whatever light spills into the room through the windows. I feel a sense of relief to be rid of her combined with a near-desperate urge to pull her back that I can't understand.

"Ella!"

We both turn to find Beatrix striding in from the tasting room in her customary dark suit and high heels, which make a staccato sound on the wood floor that feels like nails poking my skin. From the glare she shoots in my direction, I can tell she heard at least part of the conversation, and she's not happy with me.

Ella's skirt swishes as she walks over to my sister and they hug. "I'm sorry I showed up a day early."

"Aw, no worries. Happy to see you."

"That makes one of you," Ella says, shooting me a look.

"Oh, don't mind Archer. He's our resident grump, but he's the key to everything we do here, so we cut him some slack." She's speaking in an upbeat, cheery way that makes her sound like Mary Poppins dosing kids with sugar. Ella laughs, and I roll my eyes, eager to be done with both of them, now that they have each other.

"I've been trying to convince Archer here to teach me about wine making."

I shoot Trix a warning look, a scowl meant to communicate that she should not entertain this bad idea.

"Really?" Beatrix ignores me and flashes a smile at Ella. It bugs me that she's buying into the whole celebrity thing and treating this woman like anything other than what she is—a royal pain.

"I'm sure we could arrange that. Archer knows more than any of us about what we're growing and how that translates into the wines we'll sell all over the world. He's your guy."

I close my eyes in the face of the two-against-one battle and shake my head.

"A lot of what I do is more or less chemistry lab work. It's not wine tasting, if that's what you're thinking." I shrug, ready to see her eyes glaze over at the mention of science. Most visitors to Buttercup Hill are more interested in drinking the wine than looking at it under a microscope.

Her eyes go wide and she starts nodding. "Sounds amazing." She bites down on her bottom lip almost shyly when she smiles. It's the kind of smile that melts solids into liquid and sets fire to entire cities. The woman is good at her job.

Actresses. I shake my head.

"I read all this cool stuff on your website about viticulture and viniculture and the history of the vines here. I guess I just wanted to go further down the rabbit hole," Ella explains, wiping sweat from her hands on her skirt. It's the way I imagine people feel when they meet her.

"I'd venture to guess that very few people read that part of our website," I say. It's one more challenge, daring her to look at the floor and admit she only gave it a passing glance. I spent weeks writing and rewriting that part of our website even though PJ told me I'd drive our guests to drink from sheer boredom with all my farming details.

"I read it all."

I raise an eyebrow, and somewhere in the deep recesses of my brain, I accept that Buttercup Hill needs this wedding, which means I need to toe the line. It's what I vowed to do when I took over from my dad, so if that means letting Ella Fieldstone traipse behind me for an hour, I'll do it. We need the publicity and the money, and I'm out of energy to fight everything and everyone all the time.

"Sounds like you two will have a lot to talk about, then," Trix says, her stern look telling me I'd better not screw this up. "After Ella and I are done with our meeting, why don't I bring her back and you can ply her with wine knowledge?"

"I can't today. I have meetings with a grower off-site, and my day is packed."

"I can come back another time. Whatever suits your schedule," Ella offers, eyes wide and willing. Beatrix taps the toe of her pump on the wood impatiently, and I exhale the last bit of fight.

"Fine. Next week. Same time, same place," I grumble, dreading it and looking forward to it despite myself.

"Great," my sister says, beckoning Ella to follow her out of the barn toward the restaurant where she has her office. I watch as Ella looks down to navigate her way out the door without landing on her ass again. She and Trix move to the door, where there are two steps down to the gravel path.

Slipping past them, I stand next to the door and unobtrusively lift the hem of Ella's skirt so she can walk down without stepping on it. She walks beside my sister, seeming not to notice my interference, which is a relief. Last thing I need is her thinking I care one bit about her.

lla

"He lifted the hem of my skirt so I wouldn't trip," I say, arms akimbo, as though this reveals the meaning of the universe.

Tatum, my college best friend, turns from where she's aiming a watering can at some wilting petunias and squints at me. "What?"

I gesture at the area near my feet where a long skirt would be if I wasn't sitting in a deck chair wearing sweatpants and fuzzy boots. Tatum continues watering the plants on the redwood patio that stretches the length of her house in the hills. One of the best things about leaving LA for the Bay Area is that I get to spend more time with Tatum. I've been splitting my time between Callum's house in San Francisco and Tatum's house drinking coffee or wine, playing with her adorable four-year-old twins, and enjoying the panoramic view. It's also an easier drive to Napa from here.

"He lifted my hem," I say again, pushing my glasses back onto the bridge of my nose.

"Was he being pervy?"

"No! He noticed me stepping down a couple of stairs and just…lifted the hem a couple inches from the ground so I didn't step on it. Didn't say anything, didn't make a whole gesture out of it. He just…did it. Like breathing."

"That's maybe the hottest thing I've ever heard."

"It wasn't hot. It was just…kind." As I say the word it surprises me because all my impressions of Archer Corbett involved words like crabby, arrogant, and gruff. But looking out to make sure I didn't trip was kind. Underneath the grumpy exterior, I think Archer Corbett is a kind human being, and that makes me want to crack a tiny bit of his façade to see more of it.

She puts the watering can down and comes to sit next to me on her own chair, tilting the back to recline.

"Can mine do that?"

She nods, reaching over to help me adjust my chair. Now we both sit at identical angles, looking out at the sun setting over the bay. "Now tell me, was that hot? Me adjusting your chair?"

"No, but that's a weird question."

"I'm only making a comparison. Lifting the hem of your skirt so you don't trip…like breathing…? It's like my regency romance novel where everyone is extending a hand and waltzing and making romantic gestures all over the place."

"You and your romance novels. I don't know how you have so much time to read with your schedule."

"I'm all audiobook these days."

"Still."

"While I drive. I have a commute, remember?"

Tatum works for Vivitech, a billion-dollar tech company in Silicon Valley that makes cutting edge virtual reality games, among other things. It's how she met her husband, Donovan Taylor, a pro soccer star who plays for the San Francisco Strikers. Tatum is a computer programmer and was in charge of building a virtual reality soccer game with Donovan as the star, and let's just say he was not a fan of the project. But he was a big fan of her. The rest is history.

"I know. I'm not judging. I should take a few romance novel recs from you. I could use a little vicarious romantic thrill."

Tatum sits up in her chair and swivels around to face me. "Wait, what? This, from the woman engaged to sexy Callum Haywood, country music's biggest heartthrob?" She hops up from her chair and goes to the rail of the deck, looking all around with exaggerated dramatic gestures. "Okay, coast is clear. No social media stalkers. What's going on with you and Callum? Tell me everything."

Before she sits back down, Tatum goes over to a storage bench in a corner and lifts the lid. She pulls out a silver case and drags a table over, nestling it between our chairs.

I shake my head. "Uh-uh, nope. If you want me to talk, don't you dare pull out those mah jong tiles."

"Oh, come on. We haven't played doubles in forever, and it'll take that squinch out of your forehead if you're distracted hoarding jokers while you tell me about your love life."

I reach up and rub the space between my brows, knowing it's been creased since I left Buttercup Hill. "It's silly. I know I'm being overly sensitive…"

"Spill." Tatum opens the metal case and hands me two racks and dumps the tiles onto the table between us. I join her in flipping them over to their blank side, which has a pink glitter façade that catches the fading sunlight.

"In the year I've been with Callum, he's never anticipated something I'd need—a hug, a foot massage, a grilled cheese sandwich after a long day on set."

"Ooh, the grilled cheese sixth sense is key. Donno gets that, and I have to say our relationship wouldn't be what it is without each of us knowing when the other one needs comfort food."

I nod. "Exactly. Except that Callum is tone-deaf when it comes to the little things."

"Like noticing the hem of your skirt. Noticing when you're about to trip, like breathing," she says. I feel like the skirt hem will be our future barometer for romance, and it irritates me a little bit to associate it with the crabby guy who clearly thinks I'm a diva. But I'll get over it.

"And I know our relationship is just for show, but some-times…I still wish for the real thing." I shrug, smiling at the idea of someone being so in tune with my movements that my steps are his steps. "Maybe I do want someone who notices, and it wasn't until Archer did what he did that I realized it. Go figure, the biggest grump on the planet causes an epiphany about kindness."

"Or maybe it's just him. Maybe you like the grump."

I let out a long breath. "No. I like that he did something nice without looking for acknowledgement. Or without wanting anything in return."

"Those are admirable traits. Does that mean you're having second thoughts about the fake relationship?"

"No, no. It's the right thing to do. I've finally cleared a path to adoption. I'm not backing out now. I'm just pining over some-thing silly."

"Doesn't sound silly to me." Tatum goes to the fridge nestled next to a built-in barbecue and counter space that rivals a high-end kitchen. Pulling out a half-full bottle of rosé, she snags two plastic glasses and comes back to her chair. She pours us each a glass and lifts hers to the light, letting the sun flame up the pink liquid into a deep amber. "This seems like a conversation that would go better with wine."

I take a sip from my glass, and it immediately takes me back to Buttercup Hill and my appointment with Archer Corbett in a few days. A small thrill courses through me, sizzling in my veins and racing straight to my center. My eyes shoot to Tatum, fearful that she notices, but she's moving the tiles around on her two boards.

"I'm engaged. I'm getting married," I say, reminding my body more than I'm explaining to Tatum.

Tatum sips her wine thoughtfully. "Yeah. Famous last words from people who fell head over heels for someone else."

"Why are you pushing so hard for this guy? You don't even know him, and believe me, if you did, you'd push the other way. He's irritable and he thinks I'm an annoying wedding client he has to appease."

"I doubt he thinks that."

"Oh, he basically said as much."

She tosses a tile from her board to start the game. "Three bam."

Having ignored my tiles, I start to rearrange them on my two boards. "Hold on. I'm not ready." Tatum taps a finger against her wineglass, impatient to use her crazy sharp memory to block my every move.

"He *met* you. No one thinks those things once they know you. Even grouchy guys."

"People see what they want to see, and I haven't exactly helped my cause by dating so many people and never having it work out." I pull my knees up and wrap my arms around them, hating that my reputation is cemented in the minds of most people based on a few bad choices.

Okay, maybe more than a few.

"Why did I keep thinking that guys wanted to be with me, Ella, the goofball actress who loves the craft and the deep, nerdy dives into characters, when they really just wanted Ella, the famous person?"

"Because you were a starry-eyed optimist and that's a beautiful thing."

"Yeah, and you know what happens to optimists? They start to believe in the fairy tale—the one with the guy who makes me swoon and fall head over heels. And maybe it doesn't exist. At least I knew enough to cut ties and move on, but then I ended up with the ruined reputation as a girl who can't keep a man? I mean, it's so sexist. Hot, famous men who sleep around are revered like gods, and women get 'reputations.'"

She gestures at my two boards. "Are you going to play or what?"

Growling at her insistence, I pick a tile from the wall and discard it just as quickly. "Five dot." I watch the wheels turn in Tatum's head, already thinking about what hands I might have based on one discard. If I didn't love her so much, she'd annoy me.

"Your reputation isn't ruined. It's just…in need of settling down. And people need to stop judging you. You haven't done anything wrong, but society and the media are hard on women. Try to ignore it and focus on what you want. Didn't your lawyer say things look good for the adoption process?"

"Yes, now that I'm engaged, I'm off the naughty list. And at least I know what I'm getting with Callum. It's not love, but he needs this marriage to work as much as I do, so he's committed. And I filled out the applications in to adopt." I can't suppress a smile at the idea of raising a child.

"Hey, troublemakers," Donovan's voice booms from inside the house, peppered by the jumbled shouts of Lucy and Dennis, the twins. They're tumbling out the door and climbing on Tatum's lap before she has a chance to move her mah jong racks out of the way.

Tiles clatter to the wood deck, and Tatum pushes the racks aside to hug her kids tight. A second later, they're running back into the house, and Donovan peeks through the open sliding door. He grimaces when he sees the mess of tiles and shoves his hands into the pockets of his Strikers sweatpants.

"Sorry. Couldn't hold them back."

"It's really okay," I tell him, scooping my tiles into the carrying case. "Your wife is making me play a double hand of a game I don't like and answer personal questions at the same time. Trust me, I'd have knocked her board over myself if the kids hadn't come in."

"Only because I was winning." Tatum's smug smile would annoy me if she wasn't correct. Plus, I love her like family.

Tatum tips her face up for Donovan to kiss, each of them smiling like newlyweds. I feel a tiny pang in my heart, sadness at the idea that marrying Callum will mean giving up on the fairy tale. I take a sip of wine and try to push away the thought, telling myself I just need a relationship that will allow me to live my life and adopt a baby. I need to stop thinking about men who notice details and perform small gestures without a second thought. I need to stop thinking about Archer Corbett.

And just as soon as I finish telling myself that, I picture myself with Archer—just for a moment, a blip, barely a second. But it's enough. Enough to make me hold out a tiny shred of hope for the sweet gestures. And for love.

I still want it all.

CHAPTER 5

*A*rcher

"WHAT'S your issue with her anyway?" Carson spits the words out between bench presses. I stand over him with my hands lightly grazing the bar, which has one-hundred-pound weights on each end. We both like to lift until failure, which means we need a spotter to stand by and make sure the bar doesn't hit us in the chest when our muscles give way. I'm betting Carson has about three more presses in him until that happens.

I shrug.

There's only one other guy in the gym, probably because it's seven in the evening on a weeknight. All the regular guys with wives and families are probably eating a home-cooked meal and taking their shoes off for the day. I've learned to keep myself busy at that hour, either cooking for myself at home or scheduling a workout with a friend who has just as little going on in his social life as I do. Carson had just pulled up to his house when I called and asked if he felt like a workout. He hesitated for a second—the call of a warm house is hard to turn down in favor of sweating at the gym—but then he said, "Sure. I'll meet you in thirty." He's good that way.

I like working out at this hour because we have our pick of weights and machines, plus we can talk and there's little chance of people overhearing. Gossip spreads like a brush fire around here and I don't need anyone telling tales out of school about me.

Carson eyes me as he grimaces and pushes the bar up again. "I think that's all I've got," he grunts, a vein in his neck bulging purple.

I help him put the bar on the rack, and he swings his legs around to get off the bench. While he wipes down his sweat with a gym towel, I add two more weights to the bar. It's forty pounds more than I usually bench, but that blond pixie has my blood racing in my veins. I need to put my energy somewhere.

While I get into position beneath the bar, Carson stands over me and glares down. "Conversation isn't over."

"It felt over," I say, hefting the bar away. Shit, it's heavy.

"What did she do, turn you down when you asked her out? Ignore you at a party?"

Carson wasn't in Los Angeles with me during the year when I thought I could make a go of things in the big city of shining lights. I had an MBA from Stanford and the arrogance to think I'd take LA by storm. I planned to take my business degree and flair for entrepreneurship down to Lalaland and start something big. What could possibly stop me?

It turned out a lot of things stopped me. "I'm not getting into it, okay?"

"Not okay. Explain. From the way you were talking about her, I thought the bad blood went back a decade or something. I figured she ran over your dog and refused to date you all in the same day."

"No."

I shove the bar away from my chest with a grunt. Hopefully, that signals I'm done talking so we can get back to the workout. Carson stands over me, hands lightly touching the bar, and counts my reps. When I get past ten, my arms start to burn. This is more weight than I usually press. Felt like a good day to push my limits since my testosterone is pumping at high volume and I have nowhere else to put it.

Pushing the bar away again, I feel my arms start to shake. I shoot Carson a look, warning him that he'd better get ready to hold the bar if I can't get through one more rep. He nods. I bring the bar down slowly, watching it wobble as my muscles start to give out.

"One more," Carson says. I push hard and get the bar up, but there's no way I'm bringing it back to my chest without it landing on top of me. "Spot!" I grit out. Carson grabs the bar and lifts it onto the rack.

Sliding out from under the weights, I'm winded but no less agitated. Carson hands me a towel. "You have one more set in you?"

I shrug. "You?"

"I'm good if we stop. Good either way." He wanders over to the free weights and hefts two twenty-pound dumbbells to do a quick set of bicep curls. I walk to the water station and fill up a cup. I'm off my game today, and it doesn't make sense. A million women have walked through Buttercup Hill and none of them have affected me one way or the other. But this woman…I can't get her out of my head.

"Yeah, let's call it." It smells like sweat and mildew in here and I'm just not in the mood.

Carson catches my eye in the mirror and his eyebrows shoot up. "Guess there's a first for everything. You must really be bent outta shape." He comes over to the water station and pours himself a cup. "Let's go to the Dark Horse. First beer's on me."

I want to say no. Carson's like a dog with a juicy rib bone and he's not going to let the Ella thing go. But he did drag his ass down here to keep me company when he didn't have to, so if he wants to go to the bar, I'll go to the bar. Saving grace about the Dark Horse is it's usually full of locals playing pool and watching sports, so it's bound to be loud. Too loud to have a conversation about a girl.

~

"WHERE IS EVERYONE?" I ask, swiveling on my barstool to see if someone—anyone—has come in the door. The place feels dead and hollow like someone called a fire drill and no one's made it back inside yet.

Carson checks the time. "It's early. Give it an hour."

"I'm not giving it anything. In an hour, I'm heading home."

"Fine. So tell me about the actress. What's your beef with her?"

"Jesus, this again?" Maybe if I'm irritable enough he'll leave it alone.

The bartender puts two fresh pints in front of us and only then do I notice I already polished the first one off. He disappears down by the other end of the bar where he starts slicing lemons and limes into wedges.

"This again. Just tell me what happened and get it over with. You know I can't let a thing go."

It's what I love and hate about Carson. He's a contractor by trade, and when I hired him to build a second story on my house, he attended to every detail himself, even when he could have pushed some tasks off to his subcontractors.

My second story was finished ahead of schedule and under budget, which, according to Beatrix, never happens.

He was married once, something he has no problem talking about. "A disaster from moment one," is how he describes it. They were the picture-perfect couple in high school, a football player dating a cheerleader. Prom king and queen. "We didn't know that a marriage needs more to survive than matching high school diplomas." Once they grew up, they grew apart. Carson was the one who called it quits, and his wife left town with their beagle the next day when he was at work. He came home to an empty house and started a new career in carpentry. That's how he ended up in Napa.

Of all the people I know, he's probably the most trustworthy option if I felt like sharing a few details about my time in LA and my initial brush with Ella Fieldstone. It's not like I need to get stuff off my chest, but for the past week, I haven't been able to stop thinking about her.

That's making me feel like talking about her just so I can keep thinking about her.

"I know you can't." Maybe I can't either. Maybe that's why we're such good friends, neither of us letting the other one cut corners.

Carson's eyes dart between the two flat screen TVs on the wall behind the bar, and I vaguely notice that one has some college basketball game, and the other is showing sports high-lights. I can't focus enough to care about either one, but Carson is a stats guy and he's taking in the game recap like he's studying for a test. He's in a few fantasy leagues, so maybe he stands to make some money on the games.

"It was during that year I spent in LA. I met her." I've never admitted it to anyone, but it feels strangely good to get the infor-mation off my chest.

He waggles his eyebrows. "I knew it. Boy meets girl, girl shows no interest in boy, boy hates her until the end of time. Am I close?"

I shake my head. "I'm not that much of a neanderthal. I can handle it if a woman's disinterested."

The bartender pushes fresh pints of beer across the bar top to us. I didn't order them, but Carson nods as though there was some unspoken conversation between them. The cold glass feels good in my palm, and it's not until I rub my hand over the hot back of my neck that I realize I'm sweating just thinking about Ella.

"So what, then?" Carson asks.

I think about how to articulate it after four years of idly letting the incident fester in my brain. "I'd just gotten to LA with big ideas about how I was going to change the world with the app I'd created and the start-up ideas I had. Even though Silicon Valley was right here in my backyard, I was going bigger and bolder, venturing to Los Angeles to live out some sort of dream."

"And get out from under your dad's thumb." Carson tilts his head, assessing my reaction to his blunt statement. I've never admitted as much to him, but maybe in not ever admitting anything, it was as good as laying it out at his feet.

I nod. "What better way to do that than to jet out of town and start my own business?"

"And yet, here you are."

"Yeah, fucker, here I am. My dad's health started declining and I came back here, the ever-obedient son, ready to do the job I never wanted."

"A little dramatic, no?"

I shrug, annoyed. "Just calling it what it is."

"Spare me the self-pity. You get a lot of juice from being the head of a family wine dynasty, even if you bitch about it."

A rueful smile creeps across my face, and I use my pint glass to shield it from Carson. He still sees it. The best thing about him is that he doesn't gloat when he's right about something.

"Uh-huh, don't think I won't call you on your bullshit when it's warranted," he says, wagging a finger.

I nod. "Fair enough. I don't hate it all the time. And I love the vineyards and the art of making good wine. But the less I hate it and the longer I'm here, the more that start-up dream fades away, you know? That's tough to take."

"Yeah, I feel you. My job isn't glamorous, but it's all mine and it's what I'd rather be doing than anything else."

He's never flat out said that about construction, but it heartens me to know he's doing what he likes.

We sip our beers in silence for a moment and I take the opportunity to look at the TVs over the bar. One of them has an Oakland Otters game on and I watch Trix's husband, Ren, narrowly miss scoring a goal. He skates behind the goal and gets back into position, moving faster than I ever have in our league games.

"So what does any of this have to do with Ella Fieldstone?" Carson asks, nudging me with an elbow.

I huff a laugh, acknowledging that the guy never loses track of a conversation. "Oh, that."

"Exactly. That."

Thinking back to the night I had my one brush with Ella, I let the mortification come rolling back. I've done my best to block it, but seeing her again has been a grim reminder of my short-comings.

"I'd only been in LA for a few months, so the bloom was very much still on the rose."

"Meaning?" Carson levels me with a no-nonsense stare.

"I loved it there. I'd lucked into a rent-controlled sublet a few blocks from the beach. Every day, I'd walk down to Ocean Avenue and watch the sunset, all the things that could possibly bother me were behind me, literally. I felt free back then, and LA felt like possibilities."

Carson lets out a long sigh. "Are you going to wax poetic about sunsets or are you gonna get to the good shit? Tell me about Ella."

"Fine. All that's to say I thought I was going to get everything I ever wanted in LA. I had meetings set up with venture capital firms and private investors, and they were all clambering to invest in my start-up." I pause, thinking back to one day in particular and wondering if I'd do things differently if I could rewind the clock. "Until they didn't."

Carson sips his beer and waits patiently for me to continue, not seeming at all shocked that the investors lost interest. "From what I read, investors are fickle. They like the flavor of the month and they back ten of them, hoping one will hit it big and pay for all the losers."

The word *loser* feels like a sucker punch to the gut. It's the idea I've fought against in the years since I moved back to Napa with my tail between my legs. A failure. A loser.

"I guess I was the last to know how the world really works." I grab the hem of my hoodie and hoist it over my head, suddenly feeling ten degrees hotter in here. "Anyhow, the day my last funding source fell through, I went to a party at the friend of a friend's house. Big Hollywood thing with celebs and Maroon 5 playing a private gig in the yard. At least I could enjoy the flashy side of my life in LA, drown my sorrows in expensive vodka next to an infinity pool with a view, hook up with someone beautiful."

I shake my head. It all feels so silly now—those clichés that I thought were actual dreams.

"Lemme guess, the beautiful people in LA gave you the cold shoulder too."

"Just one of them."

"You tried to hit on Ella Fieldstone at a party?" He laughs in disbelief, and I'm tempted to join him. It does seem ludicrous now. After all, who was I? Some nobody who fell out of a grape bin and thought he'd take Los Angeles by storm.

"I had a bit of an ego. Remember, I'd moved to LA after big fancy-pants investors told me I was going to be huge. In college, I'd had my pick of women, so yeah, I figured the women in LA were just waiting for someone like me."

He leans back in his chair like this is the most amusing story —or like it's about to be one. "And?"

"So I was at this party, and this woman caught my eye. I didn't know who she was per se—I'm not exactly a rom-com guy—but I remember thinking she was beautiful in a way I'd never seen before." I also remember that the band was on a break and *Little Wing* was playing. The lyrics felt perfect for the moment, but I keep that tidbit to myself.

"Pretty face, nice rack?" he prods, almost sounding bored.

"Not like that. Something different. She exuded warmth," I say, thinking back. "I know it sounds ridiculous, but something about her drew me in. Like I was supposed to be there talking to her. I felt like it had to be mutual, that's how strong it was. So I walked up to her and tried to introduce myself. But as soon as I got within three feet, two goons in suits and earpieces came up and ran interference like I was trying to assassinate her or something. I figured they had it wrong and tried to catch her eye, let her call off her bodyguards. So I lingered, moved a little closer, and said hello. Finally, she looked at me, and instead of a smile or even an acknowledgement, she squinted like she wasn't even sure I was human. The people she was with asked if she knew me, and this was her response: 'Don't know. Don't wanna know.' Her friends all laughed and one of them tried to tell me off. She said, 'My girl doesn't need one more dude trying to sleep with her, use her, and sell his story to the tabloids, thank you very much. Byeeee.' Then the bodyguards moved between us, and she laughed and turned away like I was some kind of gnat who'd dared to enter her orbit." Thinking about it now, it still stings, but less so. "Or at least that's how it felt. Like I had no business presuming for even a second that I belonged in that crowd or that this beautiful woman would have any interest in me."

Carson clears his throat and nods. I can tell he's getting ready to say something profound, or at least logical, and it's going to piss me off. "Is it possible…" He pauses, takes a sip of his beer, and looks at the ceiling as though this conversation requires serious rumination. He's just taunting me, but glutton for punishment that I am, I hang on every pause and wait to hear all of what he has to say. "Is there a chance that she was with someone that night? Not looking for a hookup? Not interested in meeting random guys at a party? In other words, maybe it had nothing to do with you?"

"That's not how I took it. All I did was try to say hello and I was judged and kicked to the curb."

He gets a rueful expression and rubs his beard like a professor. "Can you blame her? Don't you remember that dudes kept doing that to her? There was a period of time when you couldn't look at *People* magazine without some tell-all from a dude she dated and dumped. You might want to be a little less butt hurt and man up."

"I'm not butt hurt. I just don't like her very much. And I had no idea you were such a fan of gossip magazines."

He shrugs.

"Whatever. It was her, the parties, LA, all of it. All making it clear I had no business there. Obviously, LA didn't want to have anything to do with some kid from a small rural town with a few ideas."

"Was that really the issue? Do you think LA cares one way or another about anyone's hopes and dreams?"

He sounds like my sister. I swear, if he starts talking about manifesting shit, I'm leaving this bar. "Why is everyone so fixated on hopes and dreams?"

"Who's everyone?"

"Nothing. Never mind."

He huffs a laugh and drains his beer. "Sounds like you took it all personally in typical Archer Corbett fashion."

I shrug, not seeing the point of rewinding the past and seeing it differently. "It just summed up everything that was wrong with LA and me trying to make something of myself there. It was all a pretty façade that looked welcoming and beautiful, but when you got up close, it was just a smoke screen. She symbolized everything I hated there."

"Okay, but now, in hindsight, can you sort of see that maybe, possibly, the woman who's here now planning a wedding at Buttercup Hill isn't the demon you've made her out to be? Maybe it was just circumstances and maybe you shouldn't blame her for all the ways you think LA did you dirty?"

I hate how rational he is. Shaking my head at my own stubbornness, I admit, "I guess I hold on to shit."

"Just a little."

"What difference does it make? One year in LA, and I ended up back here. Only difference is that now she shows up here to get married."

A gruff sigh sputters out. I have zero time in my schedule for anything other than making wine and finding new ways to create expensive limited-edition vintages to help us turn a profit.

I just need to show Ella a few things and send her on her way so she can do what every other bride does when planning a wedding here—focus on centerpieces and wedding cakes.

I don't care if she's a closet science nerd looking to make small talk about wine making. She's coming to the wrong guy. Like suggesting the Grinch host a Christmas party. Beatrix knows it, and yet everyone is so cowed by the Hollywood royal that they're bending over backward to grant her every wish.

Problem is I haven't been able to stop thinking about her since she showed up here. It doesn't help that Carson made me dredge up old grudges, which now seem pretty hollow after airing them out. Then again, that never mattered much to me in the past when I grabbed onto some bit of resentment. Once I got mad, I stayed mad.

I signal the bartender for our check and dig my wallet out of my pocket.

"Yeah, that stings a little bit, for sure. But just remember, now she's on your home turf. You make the rules, and if you don't feel like dealing with her, walk away. Let your sisters handle things.

And before you know it, the whole thing will be behind you, and she'll be gone."

I nod, knowing he's right. I'm wondering why the idea of Ella being gone doesn't make me as happy as it should. And I'm realizing a small part of me doesn't hate the idea of giving her a tour in the morning. I try to ignore that part.

CHAPTER 6

lla

Me: It's Ella Fieldstone. Confirming tomorrow

Archer: Yes

Me: Great! I'm excited!

Archer: Ok

Me: Are you excited? Come on, admit it

Archer: See you tomorrow

Me: Can I bring you coffee as a thank you?

Archer: I'm good

Me: What time is good for you?

Archer: 10

Me: Looking forward to it

· · ·

Wow, he's just as grumpy in his texts as he is in person. Nothing I can't handle. He's not the first person I've had to kill with kindness. Jerky directors, irritable key grips—I've given them all the sunshine treatment when necessary, and they've all come around.

I know I'm asking a favor that falls outside of normal wedding planning, but with the amount I'm about to pay for this wedding, I don't feel too bad about him taking an hour out of his day to teach me a few things. He probably thinks I'm a diva. Well, he can get in line.

It's true that I've fired more people than almost anyone in Hollywood, and I always have a rider in my contracts giving me total control over the staffing of whatever movie I'm involved in. That means I can fire the director, the writer, the cinematographer—anyone I see fit, at any time—and the breathless industry media has translated that to mean that I'm difficult to please. But they haven't had to work with jerks who make life miserable for everyone on set.

I only have one real requirement for people who work on my productions—kindness. Anyone who can't adhere to that gets fired. I'm not just talking about people being kind to me. We have a "no assholes" policy on the set and in the production offices. Zero tolerance for bullies.

Archer Corbett's terse texts don't exactly scream friendliness, but I'm giving him the benefit of the doubt. I'm hoping a teddy bear heart beats underneath the grumpy winemaker exterior. And even if not…I really do want to learn about wine making.

That's why I follow behind him as he strides down a winding path behind the barn. His legs are long, much longer than mine since I ditched my shoes in my car. The pair I grabbed in a rush this morning had a two-inch heel, and I worried about toppling over again in front of him.

So I'm rushing behind barefoot, my wide-legged pants

grazing the ground as I speed walk to stay within a yard of him. The tiny rocks in the path sting the bottoms of my feet, but I ignore them.

Archer doesn't bother to turn back to see if he's leaving me in the dust, but that doesn't offend me. I'm on his turf and he's doing me a favor, so he can walk as fast as he wants. I'm busy convincing myself of this when he stops suddenly and whips around. My momentum is too much to slow me down, so I slam into his chest. My hands reach out to break my collision with a wall of muscle that I can feel through the soft flannel of the plaid shirt he wears over a tee.

Pushing myself away, my fingers dig into hard abs, and suck in an unintentional breath. From the smirk that forms on his lips, I know he heard me. I clear my throat, hoping to convince him I'm just suffering from indigestion. I fight the urge to trace the contours of a clear six-pack beneath my hands. One of Archer's palms reaches out to steady me, gripping my shoulder and sending a ripple of heat down my arm. "Sorry," I mumble, listing to the side. His other hand comes out to hold me up at the hip to keep me from toppling over.

I could explain the reason for my lack of balance, but I don't know this man at all, and I don't owe him anything, other than my courtesy as he takes me to wherever he's going to collect grape samples.

"You okay there?" he asks, tilting his head to the side.

I nod. "Yeah. Didn't expect you to stop."

Standing this close to him, I take in his broad shoulders that taper to a slim waist. He's tall, easily over six feet, and solid as an ox—a hot, sexy ox. He has high cheekbones and deep blue eyes like stormy seas. Light creases across his forehead tell me he's not just grumpy—he worries. I wonder what about. His lips press together in a line, but they look soft. He seems like a tumble of contrasts.

He tips his head and regards me, rubbing his chin, skeptical. "Second time you lost your balance. Coincidence?"

I sigh in annoyance. "Fine. I have something called persistent postural perceptual dizziness."

He looks at me blankly. Then shakes his head as though working himself from a trance. "I'm sorry, what?"

"Vertigo, basically. I get dizzy and lose my balance sometimes. And I did not just fall. You stopped and I wasn't expecting that. Okay, Grumpy Grape?"

He almost…*almost* smiles. He removes his hands slowly and watches to make sure I don't tip over. I hold my arms out to the sides as though I'm balancing on a tightrope to prove I'm fine.

"See? Not falling."

He gives me a once-over to assess the veracity of my words. His eyes roam over the length of me the way men have been doing for as long as I can remember. It used to make me feel like an object, but now I know it's more of a reflexive response than anything else and I mostly ignore it. But when Archer does it, I feel a twinge of something I haven't felt in a long time—his gaze feels like a soft caress, and I have the urge for his eyes to linger a bit longer. Each part of my body lights up like a heat-seeking missile as appreciation fills his eyes.

Then he looks down at my feet and his brow furrows.

"Why are you not wearing shoes?"

"I thought I'd be stomping in a vat of grapes like the old *I Love Lucy* episode." I grin at my classic TV reference.

"Great, you're a comedian." His eyes shoot to mine accusingly.

"Fine. I left them in the car. They were…annoying, and I'm more of a barefoot gal anyway."

He shakes his head. "I don't care who you are. You can't go in the vineyards barefoot. Hang on."

Breaking into a jog, he sweeps past me, and I watch the layer of dust swirl behind him as he goes back to the barn. Looking down, I lift the hem of my pant legs off the ground and fan them around my ankles to remove some of the same dust, which forms a small cloud around them.

A moment later, Archer comes jogging toward me with the ease of a natural born athlete, carrying a pair of tall brown boots in one hand and a notebook in the other. Bending down, he puts a knee of his suit pants on the dusty ground and helps me into each boot, having me balance a hand on his shoulder. "Can't have you hurting your feet. Too pretty for that." The irritable grunt of words almost masks their kindness, but not quite. His stern gaze tells me to do as I'm told. I feel like he wants to cling to his grouchy persona, but he can't help being kind.

Bending down, I slip a foot into each boot, which has a soft fleece lining that's so much more comfortable than the ground. Not that I want to give this grump the satisfaction of being right. I nod at him and mutter a quiet "thank you." He responds with something resembling a grunt and starts walking again, a tad slower this time.

With the pain of going barefoot no longer an issue, all of my sensory attention focuses on our surroundings. The sweet smell of lavender bushes. The soft, easy chirp of birds perching high in the trees. The soft glimmer of the sun kissing vine after vine of grape leaves. A gentle breeze stirring up my insides just as it stirs the air around us. "I could live in a place like this." The thought surprises me when it hits because it's the antithesis of my city life, busy with traffic, packed with events and constant peopling.

"It's not all it's cracked up to be." Archer's grumbled words make me realize I uttered the thought out loud.

"What?"

He shakes his head and grunts out a breath. "Lemme guess, you think farm-to-table is a cool trend. You only cook what grows within sixty miles of your house because some earth-mother podcaster told you to drink organically sourced coconut water made with love?"

The words tumble out in such unstoppable succession that

even Archer seems surprised to hear all he has to say. Even though he's snarling like he eats city girls like me for breakfast on the daily, I know that very little of what he's just said has anything to do with me personally. How can it? He doesn't even know me.

This guy has a chip on his shoulder the size of an iceberg. I have no idea where it came from, but despite his jerkiness, I want to know.

"Why are you so cynical?" I strive to keep up with him, but it's hard. I can't get a clear view of his face.

"Cynical? Naw, that's not it."

"What, then?"

He shrugs dismissively like I couldn't possibly understand. I think I catch an eye roll but he's still moving too fast for me to know for sure.

"Go ahead. You ranted at me like I'm the devil, so at least tell me what bug crawled up your pants to make you so crabby."

"You make me crabby."

"Interesting."

"No. Very *not* interesting."

Now it's my turn to shrug. "Seems interesting to me that I can put you in a mood when you barely know me. I don't think I've got a special talent for it. Then again, there are plenty of people who don't like me." My hollow laugh is supposed to sound like I don't care what people think.

"I'm not crying for you, rom-com princess."

I shoot him a side-eye. "Thought you didn't know who I was."

A muscle in his jaw flinches and he blinks. It's not the first time someone has made an extra effort to play it cool around me, going as far as to talk to everyone else in a group I'm standing in and ignore me. I usually feel bad for people who do this, so worried about gawking at a celebrity that they border on rude.

"I said I didn't care who you were. But I know a princess when I see one."

He couldn't be farther from the truth, but I'm not sure I care enough to prove him wrong.

We round the side of the kitchen garden, which is a little bit overgrown in that schoolyard garden project way. Kale plants stand waist-high, and their leaves span four feet in all directions. Squash blossoms trail over trellises and give birth to zucchini and yellow squash that are so ripe and perfect that I have to stop myself from snapping one off and taking a bite.

Then there are tomatoes, yellow ones, cherries, larger beefsteak varieties, all growing in raised beds, one after the other as far as I can see in the distance. The entire food garden is surrounded by fruit trees, some of which have still-green oranges and lemons hanging from the branches.

If we weren't in the middle of such an irritating discussion, I'd ask questions. Beatrix told me that every room at the inn has a bowl of tangerines picked from the orchard on the property, but I don't see tangerines here. Silently, I take everything in, not even pausing long enough to take out my phone and snap photos. But actually, come to think of it...

Fishing my phone from my purse, I activate video mode and sweep around in a circle, taking in everything around us. Everything except that lumberjack of a man still grumping along in front of me. I allow myself to inhale a deep breath of the orange blossoms that still remain on the trees and the sweet earthy scent of tomato vines. I take a few snaps of some particularly photogenic tomatoes and peppers before daring to pluck a cherry tomato and pop it into my mouth.

Almost like he senses that I've just eaten some forbidden fruit, Archer stops walking and stares at me. I take a step closer to him, which also brings me nearer to a vine bursting with tiny yellow tomatoes. I watch him watch me as I slowly reach for a tomato and pluck it from the stem. His eyes stay fixed on my mouth as I open it, drop the tomato onto my tongue, and bite into the sweet, delicious fruit that's still warm from the sun.

Crossing his arms over his chest, he sizes me up. When his hand reaches abruptly toward me, I flinch, unsure whether he'd actually smack a woman across the face. But his touch is gentle as he removes a stray seed from my chin and flicks it away. "Why don't people like you?" His voice is quieter now, and the softer tone draws me in, makes me willing to answer his question.

"Because they don't know me, and they judge me based on things they've read in the media or what they've seen on screen."

Slowly, he nods.

"So you're saying you're different under the surface?" Now the scrape of skepticism is back, the glimmer of softness gone.

"Aren't you?" I stare him down, willing him to crack just a little bit and admit that this bad-boy, grumpy asshole routine is just for show. That underneath, he's a big cinnamon roll softie. Or maybe I've read too many rom-com scripts.

"No."

"I don't believe you."

He huffs his frustration and starts walking again.

"Fine, whatever. Think I'm a good guy pretending to be an asshole. Go ahead and love the views and the pretty purple grapes. Buttercup Hill is awesome, couldn't agree more. Just don't kid yourself. There's a difference between dreams and reality. This here, darlin', this is reality. Just not yours."

I bristle at the endearment.

Darlin'...

In the year I've been with Callum, he's never called me anything but Ella. No nicknames, no sweet, cute ways of telling me I'm special to him. And it's fine. I don't need to be called sweetheart or dear to know I'm his girlfriend. Or fiancée. But hearing the word drip from Archer's tongue does something to my insides that it definitely shouldn't when I'm getting ready to marry another man. I check myself because the feeling, along with all the surprising physical reactions to Archer in the past half hour, is wholly inappropriate. And it needs to be killed and buried right now.

But I'm not letting him off the hook about his cynicism. "Explain, sage winemaker. What's the difference between dreams and reality?"

One corner of Archer's mouth turns down, forming a sneer. Good. It makes his face easier to dislike. He shakes his head and sweeps an arm in front of us. My eyes catch on his strong hand as he gestures at the land around us.

It's just a big hand. Get over it.

"Like I said, people like you who come here and fall all over themselves because it's pretty, and the reality is that what you're looking at is generations of physical labor. It's farming, darlin', plain and simple."

The words are less pointed this time. The earlier diatribe seems to have robbed him of part of his bite. And there it is again, that word. *Darlin'.* I wish that hearing it come out of his mouth didn't have the effect that it did. It's not that I want to be thought of as his darlin'. Or anyone's.

But dammit, I work myself to the bone and that one sweet term of affection gives me the odd impression that someone out there in the world appreciates it. It's nonsense, I know that. Archer doesn't know or appreciate me. If anything, he's just dismissed me. *People like you.* I want to slug him, but that's not how I was raised.

I was raised to answer back.

"It says something about you that you've formed an opinion about me without doing any work whatsoever. I'm just some urbanite who wants to pet a baby chick?" I should be used to it by now. For my entire life, people have looked at the outside package, my dating choices, and my career decisions, and formed opinions. I used to fight against them with my agent, begging her to put me up for dramatic roles, but she refused. "You're America's sweetheart. You need to give people what they want." So I did.

For my entire career, I played to type and had more success than I knew what to do with. But this right here—the idea that a guy who doesn't know me at all thinks I'm just fawning over grapes because it's quaint—it really bugs me.

I feel the anger rise in my chest and know what will happen if I let it build unchecked. I'm going to say something to this man that will tank any hope of having my wedding at this magical place. At the same time, I can't let his incorrect assumption of me go.

"And I didn't form an opinion out of nowhere. I lived in LA for a while. I know what the people there are like."

"Yeah?" I ask, jutting my lower lip forward. "It's a big city. Did you meet every single person there?"

"I met enough."

I'm dying to know how LA did him wrong, or better yet, what woman put a cramp in his swagger because that has to be it. There's someone in particular who ruined it for the rest of us.

"Well, you didn't meet me."

There's cynicism in his bark of a laugh. "Sure didn't."

"Too bad. If you did, you'd know, I spent my first eight years on a farm. I like it here because it reminds me of that. Not because I'm trying to be someone I'm not." I look him dead in the eye to make sure he believes me, then I cock my head to the side. "But if you have baby chicks I can pet, I'm not gonna say no."

He returns my gaze, his eyes just as steely as before. It's some bizarre standoff, each of us daring the other to flinch. Finally, the ticking muscle in his cheek relaxes and his eyes soften a fraction. He nods. "We don't have any chicks here. We have grapes."

rcher

I DON'T KNOW what to make of the woman who's been trailing after me like a lab assistant, writing down notes in my book as I drop samples of grapes into plastic baggies.

We've moved from the vineyard closest to the tasting room and the kitchen garden to the most distant parcel of vines on the Buttercup Hill property. I normally hop in my truck to come out here, but Ella insisted she didn't mind walking the mile to get out here. Maybe she wants to get her steps in or something.

Once again, I didn't have time for my workout, so I don't entirely mind walking the vineyards on foot. The stack of papers in my office moves to the back of my mind as I inhale a few deep breaths of fresh air. That's the reason I go out for my daily run—to remember to breathe deeper than I do when I'm indoors at my desk.

The sky is that impossible blue color that looks like it came from a box of crayons, somewhere between pale blue and periwinkle. Not a cloud anywhere. The tops of the oak trees sway in the breeze, but otherwise, the air is still. All I see for a clear mile in any direction is rows of grapevines laden with dark purple cabernet grapes, some of the best in Napa.

The vines are so heavy with fruit that some list forward as if begging to be relieved of the weight. I've been over here every day for the past week, plucking grapes and taking them back to the lab outside the wine cellar. And each day, I end up deciding the grapes aren't quite ready for picking. So the vines take in a little more sun, pull in a little more water from their deep roots. And I come back, thinking maybe today's the day.

"You're going to let me see the lab, right?" Ella says, squinting up from the notebook and not bothering to shade her eyes from the strong mid-morning sun. In every direction, rows of cabernet vines span out on trellises. Guests at Buttercup Hill never come out here, which is why it's one of my favorite places on the property. The only sounds are birds and the distant hum of cars on Silverado Trail. Now I regret mentioning that we have a lab. This woman doesn't miss a thing.

"Don't you have places to be today?" I ask.

She grins. "Nope. No place better than this."

I half expected her to get bored after twenty minutes of walking down yet another row of vines and waiting for me to choose a solitary grape to test. I also half hoped she'd decide that having her wedding here might be more trouble than it's worth once she saw that it's basically farmwork everywhere except the inn and restaurant where Beatrix throws the most elegant events in three counties.

If anything, she seems more invested now.

I slap a hand across the back of my neck, which feels hot in the blazing sun. I wish she was the irritating diva I expected because this woman, with her outsized enthusiasm for viticulture and her gawking interest in seeing my lab makes me almost like her, and there's no point in that. After today, I don't plan on seeing her again.

"I just hope I can read your chicken scratch," I grumble, as she makes note of which land parcel and which type of grape I've just picked. I try to look over her shoulder to see what she's written down, but she hides my own notebook from me as though I'm trying to cheat on an exam. It's exasperating, and I wish I didn't find it a little bit charming.

"Are most of the grapes here cabernet?" she asks, scribbling in the notebook. "It seems like about eighty percent of the ones you've picked are cabs."

She's not wrong. In fact, my plan today was to sample eighty percent cabernet grapes and twenty percent sauvignon blanc. "Lemme guess, back on that farm, someone taught you math?"

"Not on the farm. But I did manage to get a college degree, so percentages came into play somewhere along the way." She saunters along beside me in her too-long pants and muddy boots which have picked up a layer of grass on the bottom.

She looks right at home out here, and I figure that her years of acting have given her that ability to blend into whatever setting she arrives in for a movie. I can picture her as an American expat who lands in Tuscany without knowing a soul. She's supposed to get married, but her fiancé dumps her. So she goes to Italy and takes the only job she can at a vineyard, falls in love with the son of the property owner. Some shit like that…

My brow instantly furrows when I notice her staring at me with a curious grin on her face. I wish I didn't like the look of it because the last thing I need is to have any sort of interest in a woman at all. Let alone one who's marrying another man. "What?" I gripe.

"You were smiling."

"Was not."

"Oh, yeah, you were."

"Better get you out of the hot sun because you're imagining

things, darlin'." I indicate she should walk back in the direction of the old brown barn, which we can't really see in the distance because of the angle of the sun.

"I didn't imagine a thing," she says, her grin widening into a full smile. I don't get out of the way in time because the force of that smile—her straight teeth with a tiny space between the front two, her pillowy lips coated in the palest pink gloss, the apples of her cheeks which frame her heart-shaped face—it just about does me in. "And I'm going to find out the reason for it, mark my words."

Shaking my head, I turn away from her and head back toward the barn. No point in arguing. I just need to do a better job of keeping my thoughts to myself and stop imagining her falling in love in vineyards—in movies.

"For fuck's sake," I mutter, more to myself than at her. Looking over my shoulder to make sure she's following, I see that she's still smiling. Great. Gotta find the one person in the world who's immune to my moods and have her trailing around after me like a puppy after a nap. Sounds about right for my luck.

She also seems unable or unwilling to stop talking. Her voice sounds like a goddamn song as she narrates our walk to the building with the fermentation tanks. "Are these oaks? I should know from the shape of the leaves, but I'll admit I was kind of a Girl Scout dropout, so I don't know my plants. I don't picture you in a Boy Scout uniform, but I guess if you grow up in a place with plants and trees and nature, you don't need to join a club to learn what's what. So…are they oaks? I don't see any acorns on the ground," she twitters, somehow oblivious to the fact that I'm only punctuating her observations with the occasional grunt.

"Yes. Oaks."

"Ah, so I haven't lost all the farm girl in me." I sneak a look in her direction and see the blissed-out joy she seems to feel just being here. I used to feel the same way when it felt like being here was a choice, not a family obligation.

After twenty minutes of her yammering on with that silky voice, we reach the lab. I hold the door open and motion for her to walk inside.

"Ooh, I feel like I'm being invited into the inner sanctum," she whispers, stepping quietly so the boots don't make noise on the cement floor.

"I'm still not sure why I agreed to show you all this," I say, and it's the God's honest truth. I'm not in the practice of bringing guests to the lab to show them how I determine when the grapes are ready to be picked. Sure, there are probably some who'd get a kick out of knowing the inner workings of Buttercup Hill, but we keep a tight wrap on what's open to the public and what's kept behind closed doors. Any competitor could come on a wine-tasting tour and learn far too much about our process if we let just anyone peek behind the screen.

"Because I asked nicely," she says, eyes darting around the room. I watch her take in the clean white countertops, the assorted beakers and pipettes on neat shelves, the microscopes that make the place look like a science classroom. Ella studies the large wall where a map shows all of our vineyards, marked in different colors depending on what types of grapes are grown there. Next to that, whiteboards have lists of which grapes have been picked already and where they are now—the casks and barrels where they're fermenting.

Ella takes it all in as I pull out the small plastic bags from the larger burlap bag. She doesn't ask questions, making me think the way everything is laid out is self-explanatory. That fills me with an odd sense of pride, even though I shouldn't give a rat's ass what she thinks.

"Can I have my notebook?"

She opens it to the page where she's neatly written down everything I rattled off in the vineyards, all the numbers and names that correspond to the grapes in the bags. I look it over and nod.

"Did I do okay, Grumpy Grape?"

"Don't call me that." I look over her list and take the first grapes out of their bags and drop them into test tubes. I use a glass rod to crush the grapes. Standing close to me, she watches over my shoulder, like a student memorizing every step in order to get an A.

"Deal, as long as you explain what you're doing." She leans on the counter and folds her hands under her chin. "We're measuring Brix, right?"

I turn my head, surprised. "Yeah. How do you know about Brix?" I find her face inches from mine. The rush of heat I feel in my chest startles me and my eyes dart to hers. I never expected to find a woman's wine knowledge such a turn on.

We stand frozen for a beat, something passing between us that I can't identify. I clear my throat and glance away from the intensity of her gaze.

I pull two rolling stools over and place them a foot apart from each other. We each take a seat.

She shrugs. "Doesn't everyone? One degree of Brix is one gram of sugar per hundred milliliters of solution. What's the solution?" She cocks her head with such a matter-of-fact look of boredom that I almost think that everyone does know what Brix means. But…no.

Cocking my head to the side, I return her stare, my eyes tracing the lines of her face while I wait. By the time they land on her lips, she flinches. "Fine. I did some research. I'm kind of a science nerd, you might as well know."

None of this tracks with what I know about Ella Fieldstone the actress, which is admittedly not much. I have to own the fact that I've made some sweeping generalizations about her based on one interaction with her and the splashy gossip rag stories no one can avoid without living in a cave.

"You are?"

"Totally."

I nod, brow furrowing again as I turn back to the test tubes. "So if you already know about Brix, why are we here?"

"Oh, well, I read up on wine making a little bit, but only the broad strokes. There's nothing like seeing it in person."

"And you require this in order to pick wines for your wedding?" I'm still not understanding why this whole charade is necessary to throw a few bottles of cabernet at her guests. We have many vintages of wine at Buttercup Hill, but knowing about Brix doesn't make them a better pairing with fish or meat.

"Not exactly. The wedding part is a party. But this—getting to spend time here learning about how everything works, getting down into the science of wine, that's what gets my juices flowing. It's what'll make the rest of the wedding planning bearable, just between you and me."

There's so much to unpack. She isn't excited about the wedding planning? It flies in the face of nearly everything I know about engaged couples and destination weddings. And her. I took a deep dive into social media and found way too many instances of her crowing about her wedding to that country star.

But before I can broach the subject of why she needs to make wedding planning more bearable, a veil of concern drops over her face. She waves her hands between us. "Please forget I said that. I'm excited about the wedding. And the planning. I'm just…like I said, I like science more. Got a little carried away, is all."

Wheeling my stool a few feet away, I cross my arms and take her in, confounded by the study in contrasts.

"You find the wedding planning unbearable?" I can't let it go.

"Forget. It."

"I can't."

"That's your problem, not mine." Her mouth forms a stiff line, and all her prior joy disappears behind a mask of seriousness.

I wait, thinking maybe she'll reconsider and spill some tea if I give her the opening. Some people are uncomfortable enough with silence that they talk just to fill it. I'm not one of them. Apparently, neither is she.

"Fine." I open a drawer in the lab table. "This is a refractometer. Should I bother telling you what it does, or do you already know?"

Her stoic expression cracks slightly but I don't get anywhere close to a smile. "You should tell me."

"It measures the sugar levels. The Brix. I'm looking for something between fourteen and sixteen."

Her eyes blaze to life. "Cool."

"Yeah? Is that a science nerd term?"

She shrugs. "It does the job. Do you have a sense just by tasting them, or is it hard to tell?"

"Depends. I should've taken a few grapes of each sample so you could taste them before I put them under the refractometer." Out in the vineyards, I was just trying to get my job done and get rid of my inquisitive sidekick, but her interest is reminding me of the few things I like about this job.

"Next time."

I shoot her a side-eye. "This is the one and only time. We had a deal, remember?"

"We'll see about that," she says, standing from her stool. The swiveling seat moves along with her and she grabs the lab table with both hands to steady herself, but the motion sends her tipping toward me. I steady her with a hand on her shoulder, acutely aware of the warmth of her skin and the fact that I don't want to let go yet. She looks down at my steady grip and up at me. Her eyes are unreadable, but her lips part and she lets out a quiet exhale that sounds like a sigh.

"You okay there?"

"Fine as fuck." She swallows and blinks a few times.

I suppress a smile. She's an unfiltered, slightly clumsy nerd. I like it.

Her breath hitches when I remove my hand, and she stays there, still as a stone. Then she licks her goddamn lips.

Our faces are inches apart. It would be so easy to lean closer, to taste those lips I've been staring at all morning. But I'm not about to make a pass at an engaged woman.

"When's your wedding date?" I rasp. She startles and backs away.

"April ninth." A rendition of "Here Comes the Sun" starts playing in her purse, and she fishes around in the oversized blue bag. "Speak of the devil," she says, letting out a sigh that seems directed at her phone.

She answers the phone by punching at it with her index finger. "Hi, Callum…yeah. Hold on—*what?*… We need to talk about this… Okay, sure…I'm coming." She hangs up and shoves the phone back into her purse. I pick up the next test tube, but she shakes her head. "I can't do this now. I'm sorry." Her whole demeanor has shifted in a matter of seconds. Her smile disappears. The sparkle of interest in her eyes is gone. "I have to go."

Before I can ask her anything, she's moving for the door. Doesn't matter. There's no way I'm leaving that conversation unfinished, even if I have to dig into tabloid news to find out what she meant.

"Bye," I call after her.

And she's gone, leaving a cold void where there was warmth and joy a moment ago. Leaving me with a sense that everything I thought I knew about life has changed, even if I can't say exactly how. But now that she's gone, the wild mess of her hair blowing in the breeze behind her as she heads toward the parking lot, all I can think is that I want her to come back.

CHAPTER 8

lla

"I THOUGHT we pushed the fitting to next week," I tell Pippa, my stylist and queen of my closet. If not for her, I'd own stacks of sweatpants and tees. That's it.

Okay, I do have stacks of sweatshirts and tees, thanks to a sponsorship deal with an athleisure company, but if not for Pippa, that's all I'd wear.

"Originally, we did, but then the dresses came in for the Met Gala, so I figured we should do it all in one go. They're absolutely stunning, by the way," Pippa's clipped English accent chirps from the speakerphone of my car as I speed back to San Francisco.

"Wait, I'm not going to the Met Gala."

Pippa laughs. "Better check the Style section of the paper because Callum was in there crowing about walking the red carpet with you."

I huff out a breath. Typical of him to make a decision and tell the media before he asks me about it. One more thing I'll remind him of when I see him in a half hour. "Great. And when is it, exactly?"

"In two weeks. And don't kill me, but I went ahead and gave Christian the go-ahead to make your gown. Are we good with that?"

Whenever Pippa refers to me as "we," she means "me." And she's telling me that I had better get on board with her idea.

"Okay, sure, you had me at 'all in one go.' I'll be back in LA tomorrow. Can we do it then?"

"Of course, love. Tomorrow it is."

I hang up the call and watch the scenery whiz by, all the beauty of Napa Valley fading in the distance as I barrel down the freeway to the city.

A short drive later, I'm in San Francisco, striding through the door of a coffee shop around the corner from Callum's Pacific Heights house. "We might have a problem," he says, standing up from a white leather couch where he's been drinking a fancy coffee in a tall glass with a handle. His arm circles around my neck and he kisses the top of my head. My eyes immediately dart around to see if anyone has captured the moment on a cell phone.

It's not like I'm surprised when people snap surreptitious photos and sell them to *People* magazine, but I like to at least have some awareness when it's happening. The few people in the place seem to be watching us, but I don't see any cell phones.

"You mentioned." I keep my voice low and shuttle him to the couch farthest from the other people in the room. "When did you find out about the tour getting extended?"

He sits back down, leans back, and puts his arms behind his head, his longish brown hair falling into his eyes before he flips it away with a sexy toss of his head. The tattoos on the insides of his biceps stretch when his arms flex. I take a seat in a chair next to the couch and stare at the images of a python wrapped around one arm and a bleeding heart on the other, and then my eyes trail to his pecs visible through a skin-tight black tee. He's every bit as hot as he was the day we were introduced, and my mind wanders to our first few dates at hole-in-the-wall restaurants, outside of public view.

I'm not in love with him, but I do like him well enough. He's sexy and fun and sometimes sweet. We're compatible because he understands my lifestyle, schedule, and time constraints. He knows how to play the media game. When we first started dating, I allowed the same hopes to flourish that I always feel with someone new. Maybe he could be my great love.

I kept looking for a spark, hanging on little touches and gestures that could be the beginning of something, but there was no real heat between us. That is, until our publicists stepped in and reminded us each that we could benefit from making our relationship into something more. Then, we created heat for the sake of good press.

Everything we do these days is fit for public consumption, another chapter in the tale of a Hollywood couple. All fancy dresses, photo ops, and magazine spreads. And the moments in my lawyer's office, where my focus is on what we can have together—the family I've always wanted. Eyes on the prize.

"It was always a possibility, but since I've sold out the last sixteen shows, it's basically a slam dunk. Here, come sit closer," he says, patting the empty space on the couch next to him. Obediently, I move over, and he puts his arm around me, tugging me close.

Maybe it's the effect of spending several hours with Archer Corbett, but I feel like I need somebody to touch me. I'm especially grateful for the muscular warmth of Callum's body and his easy affection. I snuggle in and try to work through the news he just gave me.

"So…you'll be gone for…how long?"

He bites his bottom lip, the only indication that he's not quite as cocky as he seems. It's the side of him I like, the man behind the mega touring star. Unfortunately, I rarely see it. He *is* a mega touring star, after all.

"It could be four months or so." He holds up his hands. "I'd come back for the wedding, no question, but then I might have to leave again, depending on the tour dates."

My heart sinks. "It's not that. Four months is a long time, and we're supposed to be acting like a couple." My mind fights against the fear that he's gone back to his old cheating ways. That he might want to be away from me for months at a time so he can be with other women. It's not so much that I'm offended, so much as saddened. I feel like I can't even hold on to a man enough for a fake relationship, let alone a real one. Our whole arrangement could unravel if he's caught on camera by even one onlooker. It would make me look weak in the eyes of the public, and it would put the whole adoption in jeopardy.

He turns toward me, lighting up like a puppy spying a pillow to shred. "Come with me."

It's sweet, but I don't want to be there because he feels guilty. And honestly, I don't want to be there at all. Our relationship of convenience feels so much more complicated than it did when we both agreed to it.

"Oh gosh, I don't know." My brain spins with what that would look like, weeks on the road, late nights, hotels.

"Think about it, okay? I'd really like to have you there." He taps my nose with his finger and leans in for a kiss. It's sweet, discreet. He's equally aware of potential cell phone cameras, and I appreciate that. "So why'd it take you so long to get here? Where were you?"

"Oh, that. I was at Buttercup Hill. Which reminds me, we have a walk-through there next week." I feel a zing of excitement at the idea of going back there.

Because I love the location. Not because I like a certain grumpy lumberjack winemaker.

"Where?"

"Hello…our wedding location? We're supposed to taste the food, see everything. You have it on your calendar, right?"

He nods. "Sure, sure. Yes. When is that again?"

"In a week. One week from today." I've only told him eleventeen times.

He doesn't answer because a country music fan has spied him and sidled up for a selfie. She wants me in it too. I'm America's sweetheart. How can I possibly say no?

rcher

I TAKE the stairs two at a time, my heart beating out of my chest. I know I should calm the hell down before I barge into my dad's bedroom, but today is the day his nurse called me to say he's somewhat lucid. If I'm going to get anywhere with him, I need to strike while the iron is hot.

I'm holding a report from the marshal and there's no way to interpret it other than as tangible fact—the fire that burned part of Buttercup Hill and Graham's land was arson.

Investigators have no leads because the cameras on our property just happen to have a blind spot in the area where the fire started, but I have my suspicions. After the big Napa fire a few years ago, my dad made an offhand comment to me about that blind spot.

"Not bad to have a corner where you can do a little dirty work if you need to," he'd said. At the time, I didn't make much of it. But now that the dirty work has been done...it's hard not to make a connection. It's hard to imagine my dad setting fire to the vineyard he grew into a three-generation family fortune, but none of his actions in the past year make sense. Even being non compos mentis—not of sound mind—doesn't explain it to us, his kids, who are trying to keep the place running.

Betsy, Dad's nurse, hears my feet on the stairs and opens the door to his room, already shushing me before I make it down the hallway. "He's resting."

Normally, I take everything the nurse says as gospel. I tiptoe around the house I grew up in and only come up to the wing of the house where my dad lives when she tells me he's lucid. But I need answers. It makes me less patient with his current state.

"Can you wake him up, please?"

The nurse, a gray-haired woman in her fifties with the patience of a saint, shakes her head and rests a hand on my forearm. She never overreacts, never yells. Just calmly attends to my dad's needs, just like she has for the two years since he was diagnosed with Alzheimer's disease. He gets confused more and more, forgets my name, mixes me up with my siblings. And then there are the business mistakes that have cost our family millions of dollars and jeopardized the very land this house was built on by my grandfather.

Betsy studies me, her cool gaze not bothering with any part of me except my eyes, judging my level of seriousness. And annoyance.

"He's awake, just resting. Having his breakfast. I don't want you to agitate him and you seem…frazzled."

"I'm fine. Can I see him, please?"

I shouldn't have to ask for permission to see my own father. I hear her talking to my dad in hushed tones, and then I hear his booming baritone barking at her, mostly complaining about how the newspaper is from the wrong day and that there are no sports on the TV. He loves sports, always has, and one of the few positive memories I have of my childhood is him coming to watch me play hockey.

That was a long time ago.

She peeks her head out and motions me inside. I find my dad sitting at the desk at the far end of his room, where a breakfast tray sits untouched with toast, berries, juice, and eggs. He has the *New York Times* and the *Financial Times* spread out on the desk, and he sits with his hands holding down the pages as if they might fly away.

"Hi, Dad."

He looks up and squints at me, and I wait for signs he recognizes who I am. "Jackson?"

I sigh and look at Betsy, who nods, bright-eyed, as though my dad calling me by my younger brother's name is a positive sign. She ushers me closer to my dad with a wave of her hand and goes about straightening up the room, fluffing pillows on the bed, emptying trash cans that aren't full.

"No, Dad. It's Archer."

"Who?" The harsh rumble of his voice hits differently today. I realize how much we sound the same, accusing and irritable, no matter who's on the other side of the conversation. His brutal stare says that no matter what I've come to say it will only irritate him and create more problems. Again, it's familiar. Guess he succeeded in making me in his image despite my efforts to be different.

"Your son. Jackson's older brother."

He wags a finger. "Don't try to trick me."

My heart sinks, watching my own father insist I'm someone else, not the son who's dutifully taken over his job for the past two years. "Dad," I say, taking a step closer. He reacts like a frightened animal, holding his hand up and shaking his head.

"You're not Jackson."

"No. I'm Archer, your older son."

For a split second, I see a flicker of recognition. "Take care of the business, Arch. Take care of the family." It's the same refrain since I took over, and the source of the weight I carry on my shoulders.

"I will, Dad. Don't worry."

Just as quickly, the sharpness in my dad's eyes disappears, and I watch the vein of confusion settle in. "Worry? About what?"

I shouldn't have come. I should have waited for "a good day," but I fear there won't be any of those. Maybe not ever again.

He looks off into the distance like the information he's seeking is somewhere in the wallpaper design. Then his eyes scan the room, and I watch the confusion take over. My dad's brow furrows and his mouth turns down into a scowl as he searches for a touchstone. Betsy moves toward us and his eyes flicker with recognition. "Judy, I'd like a glass of water."

Betsy pours a glass of water but doesn't correct him when he calls her by my mother's name. Maybe I should've let him call me Jackson. Either way, I can see that he's not in any state to give me the information I'm seeking, but I figure I don't have anything to lose by asking.

"Dad, someone set fire to Buttercup Hill."

Slowly, his gaze returns to me. "Really?" His face bears a tiny trace of a smile.

"Yes. Do you know something about that? The blind spot?"

The smile evaporates and his brow furrows again. "Judy, I asked you for water."

Betsy pushes the still-full glass toward my dad and wraps his hand around it. "Here you go." He doesn't drink it. She tilts her head toward the bedroom door, her signal that I'm just agitating him and I'm probably not going to get what I want. But I'm a determined son of a bitch, so I try once more to make small talk. Sometimes when my dad relaxes, his cognitive function returns.

"It's a pretty day today. Do you feel like getting out?"

He shakes his head. "I need some water. That's what I want."

I blink hard and nod. "Okay."

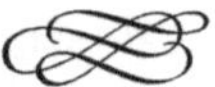

lla

"It won't take that long, I promise." I shuttle Callum along, looking over my shoulder every thirty seconds.

Next to me, I hear Callum inhale a deep breath and let it out slowly. I know him well enough to understand that it's just the way he breathes, rather than some appreciation for the scents in the air. Other than that, the only sound is the crunch of our feet on the gravel and the chirp of bluebirds in the vineyard. I can picture them perched on the houses Archer pointed out to me the last time we walked among the vines. Callum inhales again, reminding me I need to keep my focus on him—on our wedding—and not the nervous twinge in my heart over the winemaker who seems to be occupying more and more of my thoughts.

That needs to stop. I'm probably just nervous about the wedding, thinking about all that has to go right in order to clear the way to adoption. I haven't gotten to where I have in my career by losing focus when it matters. And right now, all that matters is being able to walk into that courtroom with a husband on my arm and proof of a stable home life for a child.

Beatrix drives up in a golf cart and offers to shuttle us to the restaurant. "Oh, that's not necessary. I like the walk, and that way I can show Callum around."

"Ella, if we're being offered a ride, I'll take it. No reason to walk if we can ride in style." He's in the golf cart before I have time to argue. I take a casual glance around before I slide onto the seat next to him, but Beatrix leans in and hands us each a printed menu, blocking my view. It's just as well because I should not be looking for a certain winemaker who treated me to the best day I've had in months.

Beatrix hops into the front of the cart and steers us along the path toward the restaurant. "Your guests will enter along this drive, and we'll direct them past the vineyards to the restaurant. It gives people a sense of the winery and the relaxed vibe here, so they'll arrive at the wedding location with a mood already set," she tells Callum, who's barely listening. His thumbs move across the screen of his phone, but he has the good sense to grunt occasionally, so Beatrix thinks he's listening.

I nudge him. "Do you want to look around?"

"Not really. This is your show."

"It's not a show. It's our wedding, and you were the one who insisted we invite the press," I whisper, throwing an irritated glance his way. He's oblivious.

Turning away from him, I take a deep breath of the lavender field Beatrix is gesturing at. "So pretty," I acknowledge, compensating for my fiancé who couldn't care less.

My eyes snag on the kitchen garden, where Archer and I were walking when he called me a rom-com princess. "Do you think I'm a rom-com princess?" I ask Callum with a smile, trying to rekindle a connection.

"What?" At least he looks up from his phone.

"Someone called me a rom-com princess, which I thought was kind of funny. Do you see me that way?"

"What way?" He's back on his phone tapping away.

"Never mind." I try to quell my jittery pulse and the nervous anticipation of seeing Archer. It's ridiculous. I shouldn't be craving sweet gestures from a grouchy man who isn't my fiancé.

A minute later, the cart sweeps past the lake, and I look out for the swans that seemed to be keeping watch over Archer while he walked along the other day. No swans. No Archer.

Stop looking for him. You're here with your fiancé. To plan your wedding.

Maybe if I tell myself enough times I'll feel more excited about it. Beatrix pulls the cart into a parking spot outside Butter and Rosemary, a white, sprawling two-story farmhouse with ivy-covered trellises running along the path that leads to the red double doors at the front. Rosemary hedges and wide planters filled with more lavender and succulents flank the gravel pathway. I inhale a deep breath that makes me feel like I've entered a spa.

I think about how lucky the Corbett family is to live here and experience this every day. My eyes close for a moment and I imagine myself waking up here in the morning and walking onto the balcony of my bedroom, looking at the sun rising over the vineyards and inhaling lavender and rosemary in near silence.

"I could live in a place like this." I sigh and tip my head against Callum's shoulder, willing him to be a better guy. I know it's not fair to want or expect it when that's not what our relationship is. Grabbing his hand, I play the part of selling our relationship, the idea that all of this is real. I know Callum likes me, but I feel myself willing him to pretend to love me, at least in front of other people.

"Seriously? Out here in the sticks?" Callum says while pointing a finger toward the vineyards where the grapes hang in the shade of the vines.

"See how the grapes are growing beneath the canopy of leaves? That way, the fruit is shaded from the sun."

"Um, okay." He goes back to his phone.

"Do you not find it a little bit interesting?" I glare at his busy fingers tapping on the screen, not even caring that they have the talent to play a guitar.

He looks up. "Sorry, but no. I don't have a hard-on for grapes." He puts an arm around me. "Just have one for you."

He flashes me that country boy grin that has women around the world throwing their cowboy hats at his feet. It moves a of piece my heart. How could it not? At the end of the day, I'm the girl with the bad reputation who believes in love, even if I can't find it and only have a fake fiancé to show for it.

I let errant thoughts of Archer fade away and try to focus on what's in front of me—my wedding and my future. And then adoption.

"Works for me."

CHAPTER 11

rcher

FOR THE FIRST time in weeks, I slept like a felled redwood. I don't know what to make of that because I stayed up later than I should have reading everything I could find about a certain actress, but sometime after midnight, I must've drifted off with my light on.

The sunlight woke me up just after six, and I rolled out of bed like a soldier on duty. Slipped on my running shorts, stuffed my feet into my shoes, put on the rest of my gear. I was out the door within ten minutes without thinking about whether I feel like hitting the pavement or not. Running always tells me for sure whether I'm worn out or whether I have enough juice to make it through the day. A mile in, I was feeling pretty good, so I picked up my pace and finished the six-mile loop in about forty-five minutes. I promised Carson I'd join him later for "shoulder day" at the gym, so I guess today will be a double workout day.

Walking the path past the pond on our property, I swing by

Sweet Butter for a latte and sip it on the way back to my office. In the distance, I hear the rumble of tractors in the far vineyard, where the grapes are ready to be picked. I hop onto a forklift truck and drive out there to watch the pickers.

"Hey, boss," Elma says, looking briefly away from the vines but never missing a single grape. She's the best picker we have, and it's no accident. She learned from her father, who worked for my father. Her family has lived in Calistoga for almost as long as my family has been in the area, and since I took over the wine making, she's taught more than a dozen pickers how to do their jobs better.

Bunches of grapes drop into a bin at her feet as she slips a sharp pair of sheers through the vines. Then, like she has an instinct for inefficiency, she stops and winds around one of the trellises to talk to another picker. "You're leaving too much fruit behind."

They normally chat among themselves in Spanish, so I assume she's using English to make it extra clear to me that she's on top of her game. I lean down to inspect the vines she's already picked clean and notice only a couple of lone grapes that didn't make it into the bin. When she comes back over, she tips her head up at my inspection, knowing her technique is above reproach but wanting me to tell her so anyway.

"You're the best of the best," I say, appreciative of her skill. I'm never annoyed to dole out praise to our workers when it's warranted, and I want our employees to be happy.

"We're getting every dollar out of this harvest. How my daddy taught me." She goes back to slicing through the vines and the purple bunches of grapes soon fill the bin. I haul it to the truck and slide it into the back, where several other pickers have already deposited their full bins.

When the truck is fully loaded, I start the engine and drive back to the winery. It's my favorite time of day—late enough that workers are already here, and the winery feels productive, but not so late that day drinkers have arrived, and Buttercup Hill turns into a tourist destination. Not that I don't like and appreciate the guests who we depend on to keep buzz going, but it's not my area of expertise and I'm just as likely to offend someone with my mood as I am to say the right thing, according to PJ or Beatrix.

Backing the truck up to the de-stemming machine, I throw an arm over the passenger headrest to guide me. Unfortunately, my path is blocked by a certain light-haired pixie I can't seem to get rid of. I hit the brake and turn off the engine. Hopping out of the truck, I glare at her. "Standing behind a moving vehicle isn't smart, princess. Good way to get run over." I step out of the truck and slam the door.

She puts her hands on her hips like Wonder Woman. "You wouldn't hit me."

I shake my head, as exasperated by her as I am glad to see her. My eyes rake over every part of her, taking in the sassy jut of her hip, the tiny nip of her waist, the rolled-up jeans and purple hoodie that make her look like a college student, and the flip-flops that leave her a full foot shorter than me. "Don't make it easy, then."

"Can we start, boss?" Elma asks. I nod and the workers start emptying the bins from the back of the truck and lining them up in front of the de-stemmer.

"Why are you here?"

"All charm, as usual, Archer. Would it kill you to be friendly?" She turns and leans against my truck, arms crossed.

If she only knew how hard I'm trying to be aloof when I want to be more than friendly. To cage her in between my forearms against my truck, inhale the sweet scent of her skin, and see if her lips taste as good as I imagine. But showing her the gruff asshole in me will do a better job of pushing her away, and then maybe I'll be able to stop thinking about her all the fucking time.

I swallow hard and run a hand over my face. "Sorry. To what do I owe the pleasure?"

"I just had a meeting with Beatrix to go over some things."

A part of me feels annoyed that I don't already know this, but I'm also aware that if I keep meddling, Beatrix will think I'm trying to tank this dream wedding, so I've been observing from afar.

"What's happening here?" She points to where the bins are being dumped into the machine.

"De-stemmer. Before they go into the vats." I gesture to where clumps of grapes ride up a conveyor belt to where a mechanism removes the stems and deposits the grapes into a clean bin. The stems end up in the composter. Her wide eyes take everything in, following the grapes as they go up the belt.

"Cool." She laughs. "I know that's not a proper wine term. But still, I find it cool."

Watching her geeky fascination, I try to reconcile the public image of Ella Fieldstone—America's sweetheart, the rom-com queen with a long string of hot-mess relationships—and the calm, inquisitive woman who keeps showing up here wanting to talk about grapes.

We stand side by side for a few minutes longer, watching the machine do its thing, before I ask the question I still want answered. "Did you come here to finish our tour?"

I could be imagining that her cheeks pink up at the suggestion she's here to see me. Implicit in my question is the moment left hanging between us when she seemed as drawn to me as I am to her.

She looks down, her long lashes feathering over her cheeks, and once again I'm struck by how good she is at making men fall for her. I won't be one of them, but I can see her appeal to the poor suckers who never saw it coming. They're no match for the sparkle of her bright eyes that make it seem like she's never seen anything as fascinating as the person directly in front of her.

"I, um, I'm not gonna lie. I'd love to." She bites her lip, reluctant. "I mean, I don't want to take up your time. If there's someone else you want to send me with…totally okay." She stalls and stammers and I don't understand why she's asking for someone else. Not to mention the shift in enthusiasm from the last time she was here. She looks over her shoulder, and when her gaze returns to me, I see conflict in her furrowed brow.

I should welcome her reluctance. I have a hundred things on my plate today and I've been neglecting a critical deal to buy the grapes we need to meet our overseas wine quota. Giving her a tour is the last thing I should be doing. This ridiculous crush or whatever it is that has me utterly distracted by Ella Fieldstone needs to die on the vine, so to speak. I should take her cue and outsource this task to any one of our employees who knows our wine-making process backward and forward. But I can't resist her.

"I can do it. We have a few different types of fermentation tanks, and—"

"Good God, are you really talking about fermentation? You must've finished the fascinating lecture on mold spores and gas." Beatrix sidles up next to me and elbows me in the ribs. She thinks she's being funny, but I'm hardly laughing when I see who's next to her—Callum Haywood. Tall, musclebound, tattooed. He looks me over with steely impatience, as though I have no right to talk to his fiancée. It makes me flex my alpha male just to prove him wrong.

"Some people actually find it interesting. We're a winery. It's what we do," I remind my sister.

"It's what *you* do. I help our guests plan their weddings. And design stuff and oversee the hospitality—"

I put up my hands to stop my sister from listing all of her accomplishments and duties. "I get it, Trix. You do a lot. We all appreciate you." It takes all my self-restraint not to roll my eyes, and I exert that modicum of restraint because I'm aware of Ella watching me.

In two strides, Callum is next to Ella, tugging her into his side, possessively. He kisses her cheek like a wolf sampling his first course. "It's nice." I cringe at his disinterest in a wedding to the woman he's lucky enough to be manhandling right now.

Is it my imagination, or does she flinch a tiny bit when his lips touch her skin?

Ella looks at her phone. "You saw everything in fifteen minutes?"

"We walked through the restaurant and looked out at the garden from the roof, but I didn't show him all the photos of how it looks when we set up the space. And we have a tasting menu prepared so you can decide what you'd like," Beatrix explains.

Callum shakes his head. "I don't need all that. Whatever you want is fine." He turns toward Ella and surveys her face as though searching for imperfections. I don't like it. He grabs hold of the loose strands of hair that catch the sunlight like gold threads and shoves them behind her shoulders. Patting her hair down, he tries to tame it. My hands ball at my sides, itching to reach out and undo his straightening.

"We toured the garden behind Butter and Rosemary, but we haven't gone over to the inn yet," Beatrix says, tucking a stray strand of hair back into the ponytail that's her signature look. She's dressed in a pencil skirt and heels, looking much more professional than I do in my worn jeans with holes in the knees. Like she just reminded me, I don't work much with the guests—I work where there's dirt and plants and science.

Beatrix taps a pen against a page in her binder and looks at her phone. For a while, I thought she'd mellowed out when she and her college ex fell hard for each other all these years later. But now that she's a mom, she runs her life on a schedule like no one I've ever met. Still, she seems happier than ever with her fiancé Ren, the pro hockey star who became one of my friends in the process.

Turning back to look at Ella and Callum, I feel fucking ill. While Ren and my sister became better versions of themselves when they got together, I can't help thinking that Ella doesn't look like her best self, standing under the possessive arm of her fiancé. I don't know him from Adam, but there's something about the guy I just don't like. His swagger, his inked neck, his dark jeans that are so tight there's no question about the bulge of his dick.

I like the woman I've gotten to know a little bit, with her wild hair, sharp gaze, and unfortunate dizziness, and it doesn't take a genius to see that Callum isn't good enough for her.

Yeah, I'm jealous as fuck, and it's a hundred percent inappropriate because I have no claim on her. I'm just a guy who can offer her science nerd side a little distraction from the wedding planning she seems to loathe. Well, fine. As long as she wants to keep learning about wine making, I won't begrudge her the chance to tag along with me at work. She is the client, after all.

"You ready to see the scene of the crime—or the future one, anyway?" Callum pulls Ella in a little tighter. I want her to squirm away, but she doesn't. I watch for signs she hates it, but she gives nothing away.

"You're calling your wedding a crime?" I grit out, hating this guy more than I have any right to when he's not doing anything particularly wrong.

Callum's head swivels and he blinks at me as though he's just taking note of my existence. He chuckles and runs his hand up and down Ella's arm before kissing the top of her head. "What we do after the wedding might be a crime in a few states." He shrugs, so fucking smug. I have to stuff my hands in my pockets to keep them from reaching for his thick neck and squeezing until the tattoos pop off.

Ella laughs uncomfortably and Beatrix looks from the happy

couple to me. Her head tilt tells me to chill the hell out, but I can't.

"Sure, I'm ready to see the inn. Most of our people will be coming from out of town, so they'll be staying for the weekend. We should probably reserve all the rooms," Ella says.

My stomach lurches. Somehow all the touring and talk about the wedding still seemed hypothetical until the mention of guests.

"Sure," he says, tipping his head toward my sister, who starts leading them in the direction of the inn. I walk along with them, ready with an excuse about needing to meet with our foreman in the vineyard nearest the inn if questioned. But no one raises the issue.

"Do people send invitations five months out?" I ask.

Beatrix shoots me a questioning stare, but I return it with innocence.

"Oh, um, more of a save the date with lodging info and stuff. The actual invitations will go out two months ahead," Ella answers, walking next to my sister and delighting at everything in our path. Callum galumphs behind them, eyes fixed on his phone.

Beatrix looks questioningly at me more than once as I tag along after the group. It's true that I should be in my office—I should have closed that grape deal yesterday—but Ella in the grip of her fiancé is like a car crash I can't ignore. Even if it causes a pit to form in my stomach each time he puts his hands on her.

When we reach the inn, the first stop is the honeymoon suite, which is a luxe cottage, complete with a chef's kitchen and a massive living room. Beatrix feels like it's the showpiece of the newly-renovated inn, and even I can admit that it sells the place better than anything we could put on our website. Ella oohs and aahs over the giant stone fireplace, the pale brown couches over-stuffed with feathers, the white-tiled kitchen where our staff sets up an omelet bar and coffee station for guests.

Callum moves ahead of us to the bedroom and whistles at what I know is a king-sized bed under a smooth white duvet cover. Large fluffed pillows. Sunlight streaming in from the paned windows. Panoramic views of vineyards. "Ella, come see the bedroom," he beckons. She shakes her hair out and follows him into the room. My gaze stays fixed on her until she disappears.

"What are you doing?" Beatrix's harsh whisper matches her scowl.

"Nothing."

She motions me farther away from the bedroom, walking us out onto the porch of the free-standing suite. "Not nothing. I'm pretty sure you've never accompanied me on a tour of the wedding facilities before."

I shrug. "There's a first for everything."

She blinks at me, unconvinced. "I swear, Archer, if you derail this wedding, I will not forgive you. We need this. The exposure will keep this place booked for years. That's income. It's a no-brainer."

"I'm not derailing anything." I do my best to make my expression a mask of disinterest as she studies me. "Anyway, I should get back to the cellars. We have a big yield of cab today. Can't waste more time here." I leave with the sound of Ella's laughter following me from the bedroom. It sounds like silver fucking bells.

CHAPTER 12

lla

CALLUM HAS the patience of a gnat. Once he'd checked out the honeymoon suite, he had no interest in seeing anything else at Buttercup Hill and took an Uber back to the city. It took a lot of pleading to get him up here today, so maybe I should count myself lucky that he saw the venue at all. I guess guys aren't as into all the wedding details—or maybe just this guy.

After confirming that I want to rent the entire inn for the wedding weekend, I leave Beatrix's office and walk back to my car. At least, that's what I should do.

I should not wander over to the winery and see if Archer will make good on his willingness to show me the rest of the wine-making process.

I shouldn't.

But I do.

Archer is standing outside the wine cave deep in conversation with two men in wide-brimmed straw hats. As I draw near, I overhear that they're speaking in Spanish, but I only recognize every third word or so from my rudimentary high school classes. I don't know why it surprises me that Archer seems fluent.

It's so freaking hot hearing him roll his Rs that I feel a searing flash of heat shoot through my body. Which absolutely should not be happening. Not when I'm engaged to another man. Even if it's fake, we have a deal, and I'm not about to jeopardize the adoption process by letting my lady parts run the show. But oh, how they want just a taste of Archer Corbett.

Before Archer notices me, I take him in from a distance. He has that rugged strength that doesn't come from hours in a gym —or at least not only from that. He works with his hands, hefting bins of grapes from his truck, just as easily as he handles delicate glass beakers and looks at minute differences in sugar levels.

He pushes his hair back from his face with strong fingers and his muscles flex—all of them, from the bicep I can see to the shoulder muscles under his worn tee. The sun hits his face, kissing the sharp angles of his cheekbones and the hard line of his jaw. Nothing about him helps stop the ripple of desire I feel spreading from my chest to my limbs. And lower, to my aching core, where it has no business going.

I'm engaged, I remind my parts.

Archer turns and catches me gawking. The corner of his mouth quirks up into a half grin, the closest thing I've seen to a smile thus far.

Finishing up his conversation with a few quick directives, he leaves the men behind and strides over to where I feel rooted to the earth. "You're still here."

"Yeah," I say, dizzy at the nearness of him. I blink and let out a long breath, mentally talking myself down. "I thought if the offer for a tour still stood…but you're probably busy."

Glancing back at the men working forklifts outside the cellars, he shakes his head. "No, I'm good."

"Really? I don't want to be a waste of time when you have a winery to run."

The blue of his eyes deepens, and he looks almost angry. "Nothing about you is a waste of time." The intensity of his words seems to surprise him, and he looks away.

I want to just roll with it. I'm used to people who are awkward around celebrities and it's easy enough to flash the America's sweetheart side of my personality to put them at ease. But a part of me doesn't want to put Archer Corbett at ease. I like his intensity, especially when it's directed at me.

"Okay, then. Show me what you've got, slugger." I flash him a smile and take two exaggerated steps toward the cellar before his expression relaxes and he catches up.

"You're trouble, you know that? I really should be working, but this is more fun," he admits.

I nod. "How often do you allow yourself to have fun?"

"Almost never," he admits.

"Shocking. Okay, I feel better about distracting you, then."

On our way into the cellar, we pass a shed full of buckets and tools. Archer grabs two clean glasses from a tray on a metal countertop similar to the one in the lab. I follow him up a set of stairs to a massive cellar, where the air temperature drops a good twenty degrees from outside. A narrow wooden plank floor runs between rows of giant round metal vats under the slanted roof of the cellar.

Archer opens one of the vats, its lid lifting to reveal a swirl of dark red grapes fermenting in their own juices. He waves some of the vapors toward us with one hand. "Have a sniff, but don't get too close because there's a lot of gas in there and you'll get a face full."

I don't back far enough away, so I'm assaulted by the intense scent of something between ripe and rotten fruit. It takes effort not to gag. "Smells...good."

Archer's low chuckle echoes under the bare beams of the ceiling. "Not yet it doesn't. At least to most people, and I'm sorry to say, darlin', you don't have much of a poker face."

"Fine. It's awful. Do you disagree?"

"I'm just used to it. Smells like bacterial progress to me, and this one with the high intensity and heat coming off the top is nice and ripe."

"Yeah, it's ripe all right."

Archer closes that vat and opens a few more as we make our way down the row. Each one smells slightly different, or maybe I'm just getting used to the smell of fermenting grapes. When we reach the far end of the room, another staircase takes us down to the cellar, where massive metal tanks stand floor-to-ceiling. Each one has a tiny spout on the front, and Archer wastes no time opening a tap and pouring some wine into each of our glasses.

He waits as I take a large sip. I immediately wince at the sickly sweet liquid and can't force myself to swallow it. I stand there, cheeks inflated with the too-large sip of awfulness. His eyes dance in amusement as I decide whether it's appropriate to pour what's left of my wine on his head. "You can spit it into the glass. It's okay."

I let the wine dribble from my mouth indelicately. "What *was* that?" I ask.

"Very young wine. Nearly all sugar."

"You think?" I wince at the layer of sugar still coating my tongue. Archer walks to one end of the room and comes back with a bottle of water, twisting off the cap before handing it to me. I gratefully slug down a gulp of water, then another, but it's not lost on me that he bothered to loosen the cap. Something Callum would never do. Then I admonish myself for comparing them.

"Sorry. I should've warned you before you tasted that one, but the look on your face was priceless." He takes the bottle from my hand and shoves it into the front pocket of his jeans.

"I will find a way to exact revenge." I stand tall, but that still puts me at a foot shorter than his muscled frame, and I doubt I look very imposing.

He smirks. "The rest of these are more mature, taste like the wine you're used to." We walk to the next tank and Archer pours out the wine that was in our glasses without sipping the vile sweet wine himself.

When he puts them aside and pulls out two fresh glasses, I stop him. "You don't need to waste two glasses. I'm happy to share to save someone washing them, I mean, if you're okay sharing a glass with me."

A muscle ticks in his jaw, and he nods, putting one glass down and pouring a few ounces of white wine into one glass. He swirls it around and lifts it up to what little light beams down from the bare overhead bulbs. "I think you'll like this one better."

He holds it out to me, and our fingers brush as I take the glass by the stem. A jolt of awareness hits my skin at the contact with his, and when I lift my eyes to his, it's clear he felt it too.

"Oh no, you don't. Not falling for that. You drink it first." I put the glass down so there's no chance of additional hand interaction.

He picks the glass up and takes a sip, rolling the liquid around on his tongue before swallowing. My insides nearly melt watching him. All thought is funneled to the image of his tongue sweeping across my skin, and it's all I can do to suppress a moan. My eyes briefly drift shut, and I find him watching me intently when they open. "You okay there?"

I nod, unable to find words, and carefully take the glass from him. I move it to my lips, pressing them to the exact spot where his were only moments before. I don't know what possessed me to do that, but I don't regret it. I also don't regret that I'm suddenly sweating in a chilly room. I take a sip, then another one. "I like this one. It's the opposite, very alcoholic, not at all sweet."

Archer takes the glass back from me and takes a sip. I stare as he swishes the liquid inside his mouth, moving his tongue around. It's the most sensual thing I've ever experienced. I feel the urge to videotape him to preserve this erotic moment. Then I come to my senses, remind myself I'm here to taste wine before my *wedding*, and talk my hormones down. It's just wedding jitters, surely.

Right. Keep telling yourself that.

While it's true that Callum has never made me feel even a smidgeon of the heat that's radiating from Archer, I tell myself that's unimportant in a future husband. What I need is rationality, a partner who doesn't make my skin heat, my pulse pound, or other parts of my body flood with a tsunami of pheromones.

Again, keep on perpetuating lies.

I look longingly as Archer pours the remains of his wine into a trough beneath the vats. I need something to cool me down, and almost like he senses that, Archer takes the bottle of water from his pocket and hands it to me. I accept it gratefully and drink down about half of it.

"Better?" he asks.

"Parched," I say lamely, listing to the side. His hand reaches out to prop me up as though we're mentally connected and he knows where my body is headed before I do. I feel a zing of electricity along the surface of my skin where he's touching me, and my eyes drop to his hand.

"I think I'm steady now," I say. My throat suddenly is dry, despite the ample flow of wine. "It's a little warm in here is all."

He looks down as well but doesn't move his hand. Pulling out his phone and tapping the screen, he nods. "Yeah. It's a toasty forty-eight, princess." His chuckle lodges inside my bones. This is where I get myself into trouble—not reading the signs of what men want, not having a firm enough grasp on what I want. I wobble again and he holds tight.

"I'm good. Really." I take a step back, forcing him to let go. I immediately wish he hadn't.

"Want to try another?"

I nod enthusiastically. I can't possibly be drunk from the little tastes of wine, so maybe it's the proximity to this lumberjack winemaker making me feel like I'm walking on clouds.

We taste a few more, some sweeter, some more acidic, none ready for bottling. "How do you decide when it's ready?" I ask, leaning against a cool metal tank for its cooling properties. I also need it to hold me up because of all the wine.

He taps on the side of a tank. "It's like a watermelon. If it sounds hollow, it's good."

"Seriously?"

He studies me, maybe gauging whether I'm a serious enough wine student to merit information. "Why are you so interested in this?" His deep voice reverberates in the cavernous space.

It also reverberates in me, and I wish it didn't.

It can't.

It still does.

This is why my reputation was in shambles when I met Callum. Flitting from one man to the next, never finding what I wanted, letting one relationship die after a few dates and picking up with the next tempting man a few weeks later. None of it spelled stability. None of it made it seem like I was holding out for love. None of it made anyone think I'd make a very good mother.

But that is all in the past. Now I have goals, real goals, that stretch far beyond a fling with a hot guy. I want to raise a child and pour everything I have into the health and happiness of someone else. There's no room for distractions that will take me off course.

Distractions like Archer.

And despite my vague suspicions about Callum's fidelity, they're just suspicions. Things have been good between us, and my adoption lawyer seems optimistic that we'll find a match sooner rather than later.

I need to stay focused on that.

Archer guides me to a different building that's filled with what look like big green eggs. And by "guides," I mean that he holds on to my elbow and I hold on to his forearm as I totter across the gravel and focus on not falling. I cock my head, unsure what I'm looking at, even though stacks of wine barrels throughout the space should give me a clue.

"The eggs are a different look but same process. They lend a different flavor profile—we mostly use them for the small-batch, higher-end wines we produce."

"Ah, and now we've come full circle. Maybe those are the ones I should serve at the wedding. With a bespoke label. Is that at all doable?"

At the mention of the wedding, Archer's eyes narrow and his mouth flattens into a hard line. "Sure."

I say nothing, waiting for him to explain what has his bloomers in a bunch all of a sudden, but he doesn't elaborate. "Okay, great."

"Great."

"You might want to at least taste them before you decide. We could do that now or set up another time, maybe when you're deciding on the menu. I can have Beatrix take it from here."

It feels like a dismissal, and even though I just told myself to stay focused on Callum and my future, I can't help but feel like he's shutting me down. And I know why—the mention of my wedding to another man.

It sends a warm flood of emotion through my heart that he's honorable and has enough integrity to control himself around someone who's supposedly taken.

"I ought to get back to work," Archer says, his tone flat. Despite what I thought felt like flirtation a few minutes ago, he's all business now.

"Of course. Thank you so much for showing me everything."

"My pleasure." He hesitates, his eyes roaming slowly over my face, tracing every contour with such intensity that I feel it in my bones. Then he extends his hand. It's awkward.

"Oh, come on. I think we're at least at the hug stage," I say, flashing him my America's sweetheart grin, cute but meaningless. I reach my arms toward him, but he hesitates before taking a step closer to me.

I'm expecting the kind of hug I get daily from guys I work with on set or husbands of friends—one step up from a handshake, friendly, easy.

Archer's hug is nothing like that. He envelops me in a hug that I feel in every part of my body. It's warm, protective, off the charts with sensory overload. I find myself unable to let go.

In each place that his hard planes of muscle meet my softer curves, we fit like the lost puzzle piece in a picture that's been sitting unfinished.

Holy shit.

This was not a good idea. If this is what it feels like to get a gentle hug from Archer Corbett, all I can think about is what it would feel like to have more of him. *All* of him.

I push him away with both hands, which land on his abs, and my brain does a quick calculation that there is indeed a six-pack under his soft shirt. Dammit.

"Thanks for…just thanks," I sputter, backing away as though I'm touching lava. He cocks an eyebrow quizzically, but I don't have an explanation for what I just experienced. I only know I need to get out of here before I launch myself at him and climb him like a tree.

You are engaged.

"I know!"

Realizing I've just answered my subconscious out loud, I blink hard. If I didn't already seem like a loon, I'm a lost cause now.

"I mean…" I fumble, turning toward where I think the exit is. "I need to go." I practically run from the room. "Thank you. Thank you so much."

I don't give him a chance to answer.

CHAPTER 13

rcher

FINALLY, I feel like I'm making some headway on the giant stack of papers in my office. Orders from sixteen new California wine shops confirmed. One new overseas distributor secured. Most of our numbers for the month look like they'll add up, as long as we don't have an unexpected cold snap that could freeze the vines overnight. I cross my fingers under my desk, newly open to things like manifesting and hoping.

I don't want to think too hard about why I might have a slightly less gloomy outlook on the world, but I know. Just spending a little bit of time with the sunny Ella Fieldstone has been like sprinkling fairy dust around Buttercup Hill. I may be grouchy, but I'm not made of stone. My mood is lighter from the sheer delight she seemed to take in every aspect of the job I inherited and normally see as a chore. In a couple hours, she had me remembering what I used to find fascinating about the wine-making process before it became a daily grind.

Surprising myself, I pick up my phone, pull up my social media account, and enter Ella's name like the stalker I've become. The usual string of photos pop up, most of them candids of Ella and Callum at one event or another. But this time, I zoom in, analyzing her expression, trying to find evidence that she's as joyful with him as what I experienced with her in the wine cave. In most of the pictures, even though they're not posed, she seems aware of the camera, tipping her head against Callum or giving her characteristic pixie grin.

But in a couple of the photos, she looks less guarded, more resigned to walking next to him hand in hand, like it's a job. I'm clearly reading into the situation, but when I compare them to photos of Ella on her own, there seems to be a veil of something I can't pinpoint when she's with Callum, an effort to plaster on a smile. It looks like acting. And like a movie-goer who suspends disbelief for the sake of a story, I'm seeing what I want to see.

On that note, I go back to my pile. Enough daydreaming about another man's fiancée.

I put in a call to Graham, making sure he's growing enough sauvignon blanc grapes to supplement what we have so we can collaborate on a special edition next year. He assures me that we'll be good to go, so I pencil that into my planner. Next month, next year—it's all a blur of projections.

I skip lunch, feeling good about the groove I'm in. Maybe I can even finish early today and get out for a hike before dark. But that's when Beatrix calls me with an urgent S.O.S. She's talking into the phone before I even say hello.

"I know you're up to your eyeballs, but I can't reach anyone else with a truck, and it's sensitive because it's her."

"Slow down, Trix. I missed half of that. Who is *her*?"

She covers the receiver, and I hear a muffled directive to someone else before she starts repeating whatever she said before. "Ella. She was meeting with the florist in St. Helena and got a flat. There's already paparazzi buzzing around, so she ducked into a shop to buy a hat. She's been trying to get roadside assistance from Fiat, but they can't get a tow truck here for two hours. Do you think you can tow her car to a shop on your truck hitch?"

Slapping a hand against my cheek, I look at my pile of papers. So close, yet so far…

"Why's she need a tow? Doesn't she have a spare?"

"I don't know, Archer." A frustrated sigh tells me Trix doesn't have the bandwidth for this.

"Fine. I'll get her. Tell her to text me her location."

"Perfect. Thank you. I owe you," she says. I nod, not entirely unhappy about the errand and still willing to collect on whatever Trix thinks she owes me.

ELLA GREETS me with one tanned leg in the street and a hand in the air like she's hailing a taxi. Why does it have to be a hundred-degree day so that Ella is out here in a tank top and shorts? I almost swerve into a parked car after staring too long at her leg, bare under a pair of denim cut-offs that make my mouth water like a goddamn pervert.

Jesus. Tow the car and get back to work.

I park behind her little blue powder puff of a car, which has one very flat rear tire. She comes over to the driver's side of my truck, nearly getting side-swiped by a passing car in the process. I reach for her shoulder through my open window and pull her toward my truck. "Let's not add a hospital visit today, yeah?" Her bare skin feels so good under my hand, so right, and I pull back from it like a lit match.

"Yeah. Good plan."

She takes a step back, so I exit my truck and follow her to the sidewalk, where she points at the offending tire. "That's the one." In a baseball hat and dark sunglasses, with her hair tamed into a knot, she's unrecognizable unless someone is really staring. I look around. Nope, just me.

"Yes, I see that. Do you have a spare? Easier to just change it instead of dragging it to a service station."

A look of confusion pulls her mouth into a frown. She takes a step closer to the car and pats at the tire, as if testing its temperature. "I don't know how to change it."

"I can help you with it, darlin'. But do you have a spare?" Music hums from the car speaker, so I open the door and turn off the ignition, but I notice her tank is on empty and shake my head.

She pops the trunk and peers inside, hands on her cheeks with concern. I see a tennis racquet and a yoga mat, but no spare. "Does this lift up?" I point as I lift the floor of the trunk, revealing an unblemished tire and some tools. Ella's hands drop from her face, and she pats my forearm.

"Oh, that's a relief."

I wrestle it out from its harness and retrieve a tire iron she probably never knew she had. "Okay, princess. You're going to learn to change a tire. I'm fully aware you probably have 'people' to do things like this, but I was raised to believe everyone should be able to change a tire."

"I believe that too. I just didn't find anyone willing to teach me. Until you." I feel a strange twinge of pride at being her first—even if just to pop her tire-changing cherry. Her happy, willing face is all the encouragement I need to motion her to sit next to me on the sidewalk as I walk her through the steps.

It takes a few tries to get the jack positioned right under the chassis, but she insists on doing it herself. When I lean in to move it over an inch, she mock-glares at me and slaps my hand away. "Use your words. Let me do the work."

"Move it over an inch or you'll crank right through the flimsy plastic this car is made of."

"Hey, I like this flimsy plastic car. It's much more me than the

Beemer the studio bought me after my last film. I like to fly under the radar."

Looking at the partial face visible beneath the hat and glasses, I start to appreciate the effort that takes. "Yeah, I'm sure all you mega-stars say that, trying to seem humble and all," I tease.

"Yup. It's in the mega-star manual." Her laugh sounds like fine crystal glasses welcoming everyone within earshot. It lets loose something inside me, the final bit of resistance to admitting to myself that I like her.

And that I'm in deep trouble because of it.

She moves the jack to the proper spot, and I show her how to turn the crank. A big stripe of grease marks one of her legs and her hands are covered in black exhaust residue, but she never complains, never implies she's too pristine to get a little dirty. I find myself wishing she'd be just a tad less adorable through the process so I'd have a reason not to like her. But she's giving me no reason not to find her utterly charming.

Despite my fierce insistence that she's just another client of Buttercup Hill, I feel my resistance slipping. I like her.

Once Ella gets the car cranked off the ground, she admires her handiwork. "Pretty good for a newbie," she says, standing up. She immediately pitches forward, and I reach out to steady her. She puts a hand on mine like it's nothing, like we're in synch now, me knowing when she needs steadying, me reaching out almost without thinking. "Thanks."

I nod. "Now we need to get these lug nuts off. And if you've had your tires rotated recently, they're probably on pretty tight." I give one a test turn with the wrench. "Do you have a rag or towel or something? Might help your grip." While she searches her yoga bag for a towel, I quickly loosen all the nuts and hand her the wrench. While she uses it to twist each of the five nuts, I sit on the sidewalk next to her, giving her quiet encouragement. "You've got this, princess."

She nods and keeps working. I see the side of her that must

show up at work in long hours on the set. I appreciate her focus as a dribble of sweat runs down her cheek. I blot it away with my finger and wipe it on the hem of my shirt.

People mostly ignore us as they walk by on the sidewalk.

"Are you one of those Zero Club people," I ask, crossing my arms.

"I have no idea what that is."

"People who drive until their tank has zero miles left and then keep going to see how far they can go without running out of gas. It's a thing."

"That's the dumbest club I've ever heard of. No, I'm just the regular kind of busy person who puts off getting gas until the last minute. Is there a club for that?"

"Prolly not. Membership would get too big."

"Ah, see? You understand. I'm glad you're not judging."

"Who says I'm not judging? You're outta gas with a flat tire in the middle of nowhere."

"I tried to get gas at this place out of town, but it turned out to be only a self-serve carwash. Then I got sidetracked." She pops her head up and looks around to where there are, admittedly, plenty of shops and people. "And we're hardly nowhere. It's almost as busy as San Francisco."

And yet...she's here in my neighborhood, yet again, without her fiancé. And here I am, yet again, warming to her when I had no intention of doing so. Only now, I've stopped resisting it.

With the bolts loosened, we pull off the damaged tire, which has a large nail deep in the tread. "This may be able to be patched," I say, picking up the tire and stowing it back in the trunk.

"Cool." Ella lifts the new tire on, and I watch her do everything in reverse, putting the lug nuts back and cranking down the jack. When she's done, I stand up and help her to her feet, holding onto her hand and looking to see if she's wobbly. But her wide grin is all I see. "I changed a tire," she whispers. It feels like a secret between the two of us, so I keep my voice equally low.

"You crushed it."

"I did." She brushes a strand of hair from her cheek, leaving a grease smudge on her cheek. Using the hem of my shirt, I wipe it away. "Can't have you looking like you work in a garage or someone's liable to hire you."

I retrieve a container of wet wipes from my truck and wipe down her hands. With her new tire and a promise to hit up the gas station just outside of town, Ella thanks me with a hug that somehow manages to make me half hard. Fuck me. I need to send her on her way.

"You good?" I take a step back. She looks as startled as I am by the wild electricity that passes between us with every touch.

"I'm good." Her voice is a quiet rasp.

"You going home by way of a nice, safe freeway at a reasonable speed? No driving through construction sites or fields of broken glass."

She holds up a hand. "Scout's honor, Grumpy Grape."

I nod and she slides into the driver's seat. I close the door, trying to hide my smile at the nickname I don't entirely hate. Her smirk tells me she sees it anyway.

Trouble. Deep, deep trouble.

rcher

"Is it weird to miss a person when they're not a rightful part of your life? Wait, don't answer that. I don't want to know."

Stopping at a lookout point on the hill that gives our winery its name, Colin holds up one of the hiking poles he insists on using. "What if I want to answer?"

I groan. "I still don't want to know."

It's been a couple weeks since I helped Ella fix her tire, and she's been an obsessive thought on my mind ever since. The image of her in those tiny shorts—and without the shorts or any clothes at all—continues to haunt me, growing stronger each day that I don't see her. The way she reacted when I held her up to keep her from wobbling. Her surprised look after she hugged me. I refuse to believe she felt nothing. But the idea that she felt *something* haunts me even more.

Then what?

It's a bluebird sky day, not even a hint of a cloud, and no one's on the trail. Feels like a gift. Colin and I take this hike about once a week, a habit we got into when he moved to Buttercup Hill to get out of the spotlight after making a poorly-timed statement to the media and tanking his company's stock.

He and PJ started dating on the sly, but I've managed to get over it now that it's clear to me they're meant for each other. Not to mention that he's the one who stepped in to save us from our first round of financial ruin a couple years back, so I don't rib him nearly as much about being with my sister as I'd like to.

"I assume we're talking about the actress."

I use the hem of my shirt to wipe the sweat from my face. It leaves a stain in the gray fabric, but Colin's the last guy who'd judge. Looking out at the view—miles of grapevines in orderly lines, a little residual burn from the fire that burned part of Buttercup Hill and a lot of Graham's land, and all the various homes of my siblings fanned out on the property—I always feel calm. Perspective. Literal perspective.

"Yeah. Ella. How'd you know?"

"It's all PJ can talk about. Ella this, Ella that. You'd think the royal family was having a wedding here."

Colin famously keeps his head in the sand when it comes to celebrity culture. I've never heard him relay a piece of gossip and frankly, I'm surprised he's heard about Ella. The guy really does only care about space.

"Apparently she and Callum whatever-his-name-is are considered Hollywood royalty." I spit the words out, still annoyed by how disinterested Callum seemed in his own wedding. "Though he's kind of a douchebag if you ask me."

"Not a country music fan, then?"

"Nope."

Colin bends down to stretch his calves before we hike down. It's part of the ritual of hiking—waiting for him to go through a series of stretches before we start, halfway through, and at the end. He's the best-stretched hiker I've ever met, and knowing him, there's some science behind it. I don't stretch after I run, so I don't bother after hiking either. It's never been a problem.

"You like her."

"She's fine. She's a client."

Colin chuckles and shakes his head. "Keep telling yourself that, but you don't talk about clients, and you haven't been able to shut up about her. If you think you don't have a thing for her, you're in denial."

Looking out over Napa Valley, I take a moment to notice how quiet it is up here. It's normally where I go for some peace and quiet, but today I can't escape my best friend yammering in my ear. Or my own thoughts.

Maybe he's right. Even if I wish it wasn't true. "I don't want to have a thing for her, trust me. Even if her fiancé is an asshat who clearly doesn't deserve her, she's engaged to him. That's a line in the sand I'd never think of crossing."

Annoyed, I look out at the view. Why does the sky have to be so damn blue? I could use a few clouds and a storm right now to match my miserable mood.

"I don't *want* to like her," I admit.

"I get it. That's what's mysterious about the human heart. It kind of does what it wants without our heads being involved."

I roll my eyes. "Is that some mystery of the universe you discovered while you were looking at Saturn one day? Jesus."

"It's common sense," he says. "And it was Jupiter, asshole."

"Yeah, well, you've got that right about the heart going rogue. I can't figure out what she sees in him. I saw the two of them together and I swear, there was zero chemistry."

He laughs. "Is there a tiny chance you only saw what you wanted to see?"

"Um, yeah, genius."

"Not an insult." Done with his stretches, Colin eyes the trail that will take us back to Buttercup Hill and plants his poles in the dirt. "Ready?"

"Sure."

We take a last look at the view from the top.

"Here's what I'm loving," Colin says, pulling off his baseball cap, ruffling his hair, and putting it back on facing backward.

I let out a sigh. "Oh, here we go. What is it, some kind of interplanetary connection you saw through your telescope last night?"

He chuckles and I appreciate that I can still give my billionaire former college roommate shit about his nerdy love for space. In some ways, Ella reminds me of him, which is nuts because they couldn't be more different. Except that they're both pathologically nice, extremely successful at what they do, and a little misunderstood by the rest of the world.

"This is the first time in years I've seen you excited about something. Anything. And you deserve to be excited. Even if she's engaged, it's the start of you getting in touch with that organ beating in your chest that you've ignored for half your dumb life. Maybe it's a sign you can finally get out from under your dad's thumb and live your own life."

I start hiking down, not wanting to get into my "dad baggage," as Colin calls it. He's known me long enough to remember how hard I worked to impress my dad in college and how little acknowledgement I got for it. Football player? A shrug. A 4.0 GPA? To be expected. The only thing I've ever done that made my dad seem even a tiny bit impressed was learn about wine making. And that was before his dementia took away his ability to run the winery he built from nothing into the powerhouse it is today.

"I'm living my life. I'm just doing it within the constraints of a job I didn't ask for because my siblings are all pulling their weight and I need to pull mine."

"Not really the same thing when you do it with constraints."

A jogger blows past us going uphill and we both shake our heads at the try-hard. "So getting back to your question, the issue isn't that you miss her—that's awesome. The issue is that you don't think she's a rightful part of your life. How can you change that?"

It's why I like Colin so much. Where most people see roadblocks, he sees challenges.

"She'd have to break up with her fiancé." I can't believe I'm even saying the words. They're an impossibility.

Colin nods gamely, not seeming to see the problem. "Great. I know you, and you wouldn't even say the words out loud if some part of you didn't believe in the possibility."

I think about that. Maybe he's right. Maybe I should utter the thought that's been bouncing in my head since I saw Callum and Ella together and had to restrain myself from punching his lights out just to put some daylight between them.

"What if she doesn't love him? What if it's some kind of publicity stunt or something she'd walk away from if she met the right guy?" I suggest.

Colin picks up his pace, which he only does when he likes an idea.

"Then I think you need to do everything in your power to find out."

It's lucky for me that PJ's office is down the hall from mine, so I overheard it when she scheduled a photo shoot for today with *Town and Country* magazine. From my office window, I see the convoy of cars arrive at noon and I hear the tromp of feet downstairs as PJ shows everyone around. But I see no small blue car, and my heart sinks.

It's just as well, I remind myself. The more time I spend with Ella, the more time I want to spend with her and that has to stop. Like Jax and Carson said, it's not healthy to spend this much time thinking about a woman I can never have. At best, it's a distraction. At worst, it will derail me from doing my job. I can't afford either one.

The voices fade away as PJ leads the group outside, and I refocus my attention on the pile of papers on my desk. Maybe somewhere in the mess is an explanation for what my father was thinking when he decided it made sense to torch our winery.

An hour later, I'm nearing the bottom of the pile—mostly financial reports and contracts with vendors who will sell our wine nationwide. I need to update all of them and make sure the terms are more favorable next year or we'll never turn a profit. Right now the margins are so small, that if even one wine distributor decides not to carry Buttercup Hill wine next year, our numbers will tank.

I pick up the phone and dial one of the reps who's been dodging my calls. It could be that he's just busy, but he could also be avoiding confrontation. He answers on the first ring, a good sign.

"Hey Joe, it's Archer at Buttercup Hill."

"I'm terrible. I owe you a call."

He owes me six, but I won't split hairs. "No worries. I'm working on next year's contracts with Wine House and More Wines, and I want to make sure you get in on this year's reserve wines before they're all accounted for." I sound as friendly as I can manage while holding my breath, half expecting him to level me with bad news.

"Right, right. That's what I've been meaning to talk to you about. I need to reduce our quantities for next year. I'm sure you know, there's less demand industry-wide. Millennials are drinking hard kombucha and mocktails."

It feels like a stone bottoming out in my gut. It's one thing to lose business from one distributor, but I hate to think it's an industry-wide trend. This could be the blow that kills our numbers unless I can find someone else to buy the wine he doesn't want.

I see Ella walk out of the tasting room and say goodbye to the photographers and journalists who PJ is herding in the other direction. Realizing she's probably about to leave, my adrenaline shoots through the sky. "Fine, fine. Whatever quantity you need. We'll work it out."

Poor business decisions, rushed negotiations…is this what it means to crave another person from the depths of your soul? Fuck me, because I'm already past the point of no return.

I manage to slow my roll by the time I get outside, wandering over to where Ella still stands on the gravel drive.

"Did the rom-com princess lose her car?"

She rolls her eyes, but I don't miss how the flush colors her cheeks or the way she smiles—her real smile, not the one she saves for the screen. "The magazine sent a town car to drive me. And why do you keep calling me that?"

I study her pursed, heart-shaped mouth, the high rosy cheek-bones and mass of wild hair that begs to be twisted around a man's hand while he ravishes those lips, and shake my head. "What do you want me to call you?"

"Ella is fine."

"Okay, princess." I'm like the schoolyard punk who can't stop pulling the hair of the girl he likes.

She huffs a laugh. "Seems like you don't wait for permission to do what you want."

We walk in silence past the lake on the property where two swans are out today, puffing their feathers as though they know Ella is important. I want to tell them to relax. But I'm finding it a bit hard to relax myself as she strides next to me. The light floral scent of her perfume dances around us like a fairy cloud and the golden highlights of her hair keep catching the sun.

"It suits you," I mutter to myself.

"Sorry, what?"

"Nothing." Guess I need to watch my volume when I'm muttering near someone with perfect hearing.

"I heard you." She says it like a warning, one I'll ignore.

"So why'd you ask what I said?"

Another eye roll. "I'm not some diva who makes demands on other people and has to be waited on."

I point out the swans, who are sailing along next to us as we round the last curve in the path next to the lake. They seem to be keeping pace, as though they're in on the conversation.

"Didn't say you were. You just look like a princess to me."

She makes a disgusted noise that has the swans turning around and heading the other way.

"Problem?"

"Um, yeah. You don't even know me and you're forming opinions based on, what? A job I have that you know nothing about? Seems like you're the princess."

I huff a laugh at that. "First person who's ever called me a princess."

She shrugs. "Maybe I'm the first one who's been honest."

I should have a retort, but the comment is so surprising that I'm left with thoughts instead of words. Namely that she's not afraid of me, which puts her in a very small category of mostly family members, and even some of them steer clear.

"Okay, I'll bite. Since you're being honest, what do you hate about being called a rom-com princess? Isn't that kind of your bread and butter?"

"At work, sure. But people assume I'm just like the characters I play—sweet but clueless, can't keep a man, too naïve to understand the vagaries of the real world. America's sweetheart. But it's just a role, and frankly, I'm tired of it." She looks at me, as if daring me to say I've made no such assumptions about her, but I can't.

"Come on," I say. "Let's tour the tasting room. It's the only thing you haven't seen yet. You can tell me how you became America's sweetheart, and I'll pour you wine and make you forget about it for a while."

I should have my head examined. If wine shops are scaling back, I need to put my head down and figure out how to make up the shortfall. But that's been the story of my life for longer than I can remember, and I'm damn tired. Even if she is engaged, Ella is the first person in a long time who's made me want to work less. Drinking wine with her instead of working will surely bite me in the ass, but I can't make myself say no to this woman.

Can't.

Won't.

lla

IT's cool in the tasting room. I like it.

Exposed beams on the ceiling, wall sconces, brown leather armchairs with low tables topped in sheets of gray zinc. The lighting is intentionally low, giving the room the feel of an old western steakhouse with hanging plants and vineyard views.

And because it's a beautiful day and most guests are tasting wine outside, we're alone.

It makes me feel like I've entered another world, one where science and farming meld to create a really nice place to sit and sample wine. Magical. I don't dare say as much to Archer because he'd probably laugh. So I tell him what he asked about.

"Somehow I fell into the role of America's sweetheart, who makes men fall for her and women want to be her friend. I didn't seek it out. In fact, but you know…people like to typecast. I look the part and those were the roles my agent sent me to audition for. And those were the roles I landed."

"Makes sense."

"I thought so too until I realized I was getting further and further from my goal."

"Which was?"

"I'm a theater nerd. Even with the rom-com roles I get, I do deep dives into characters and research everything I can. It's like science to me. I studied drama because I fell in love with Shakespeare in college."

"You're kidding, right?"

"I know, I know. Everyone thinks Shakespeare is something you just have to get through in order to graduate, but if you read it closely, he's actually—"

"Hilarious," he interrupts. For a second, I'm not sure if his conclusion is directed at me. The way he grouches around, I assume he thinks my love for Shakespeare is ridiculous, if not hilarious. But he doesn't give me a chance to question him.

"Actually, yeah. Shakespeare is a fucking riot. Why don't people realize that? He had the best possible insults in the world of literature. 'I am pigeon-livered and lack gall.'"

"*Hamlet,*" I say, dumbfounded.

He nods. "'Thou cream-faced loon.'"

I shake my head. "I don't remember where that's from."

"Ah. *Macbeth.* It's a good one."

"Almost as good as 'thou lump of foul deformity.'"

He holds up a hand. "Call me that and the science lesson is done, princess."

I laugh, my eyes settling on his face and noticing for the first time that he's not frowning. It makes me want to keep looking, and I take in his angular cheekbones and slanted nose. The stubble from a couple days without shaving. It softens the hard line of his jaw. Then there are his eyes, like blue lasers that miss nothing, leave nothing to chance. Lips that make me wonder...

I startle when I realize I've been staring longer than I should be. And he's staring back, daring me not to look away. I don't want to, but I should.

My lids drop closed for a moment, breaking the bond between us. It's necessary. I don't know what I'm doing, staring into the eyes of a man who isn't Callum, the man I've committed to marry.

"Hold that thought." Archer disappears into a back room and returns with a half dozen bottles of wine on a tray, along with glasses and what looks like a hunk of cheese. He pulls a box of crackers from his back pocket. "Full service," he says, laying the tray on the table next to us and presenting me with a glass. The bottles are all open with corks in them, and he spins them around so I can see their labels.

"What looks good to you? Red, white? Or dealer's choice?"

The only problem is that I can't see. "I, um, think you should decide." I fish around in my purse for my glasses, but I'm pretty sure I won't find them. "I didn't bring my glasses because of all the media hoopla with the magazine, and since I didn't drive, I don't need them. Which means I can't read the labels too well."

"What do you mean? What does the magazine have to do with you wearing glasses?"

"I prefer not to see all those people so clearly when they're fussing and taking photos."

"So, you can't see? Right now?"

I shake my head. "Not well. It's a thing I do when I go places with big crowds. Mostly it's when there's paparazzi around or people yelling my name. It completely overwhelms me to the point of feeling nauseous and actually starting to freak out a little. So I started going without my lenses and realized it helps. It forces me to focus only on whoever is directly in front of me. I can handle one conversation, one person."

The one person I can see clearly is staring at me with his jaw open as though he's learned something profound.

"So you never even saw me." His gruff words are so quiet I barely hear them, and I'm confused even then.

"Never saw you where?"

He blinks a couple times and shakes his head. "In LA."

"What?"

"I was at a party in LA, and I tried to meet you."

"Wait, when?" Holding up both hands, I try to temper my shock with some sort of recall. My confused brain tries to rewind history because I have no recollection of Archer Corbett before I walked into the barn at Buttercup Hill.

"Maybe four years ago. It was a pool party in some fancy yard in the Hollywood Hills with huge views of all of LA, and I saw you and just…wanted to meet you. But your bodyguards told me to take a hike."

My face goes hot at the thought that I came off like the kind of diva I swore I'd never be when I was offered my first movie role. I hate the idea that people I paid to work for me kept me away from someone like Archer Corbett.

I'm halfway through my second glass of wine, and I already feel buzzed. It's not the right time to reveal the brewing feelings I have for Archer. I'm sober enough to realize that. But I can't have him thinking I'm the kind of person who'd ignore someone I didn't know if he tried to meet me.

"I vaguely remember a party. Or a dozen. There were a lot of pool parties, a lot of places I had to be when I'd have rather been home in sweats with a book. Most of the time, I stayed in my little bubble, talked to as few people as possible, took the photos my publicists wanted, and got out of there."

He nods. "I should have known that." He scrubs a hand over the back of his neck, looking like a guilty child. "It wasn't you. It was me feeling like a failure in LA, and trying to talk to you just convinced me I had no reason to be there. Maybe I was looking for proof I didn't belong. Anyway, that's maybe why I came off a little frosty at first when we met here."

I can't help it. I burst out laughing. "A little frosty? That's how you'd describe it?"

He hangs his head in mock shame. It's adorable. When he looks up at me, there's something different in his eyes. They're clear, unencumbered by doubt. They're also hooded and deep blue. It's like he's asking permission, but I'm not sure for what. And I'm not sure what I can give him permission to do.

I know what I want him to do. I want him to kiss me. But…I can't.

I can absolve him of any doubt about what happened back in LA. "Archer, I can assure you that if I saw you at a party, I'd want to meet you. And now that I have, I'm very glad it was here in Napa and not in LA."

His eyes drop closed for a moment, and I watch him suck air into his lungs. When he opens his eyes, he nods. "Let's get some fresh air. We can taste the rest outside. I want to give you the whole wine-tasting experience."

"Wow. A 'wine-tasting experience,'" I say, mocking. "Sounds serious."

He shakes his head and leans his forehead on his fingertips, blocking part of his face. But I can still see him clearly enough.

I love that I've just made Archer Corbett blush.

rcher

THE DAY COULDN'T BE NICER for wine tasting, and the property is humming with activity. Ringed by a stand of oak trees, one group of visitors tours the kitchen gardens and learns about the farm-to-table philosophy of our restaurants. The tour will end at Butter and Rosemary, our Michelin-starred restaurant, where guests can either take a cooking class with one of the chefs or sit down for a four-course tasting menu of seasonal dishes paired with wines. It's one of the "experiences" Beatrix has been working on, and she has a two-month waiting list to get a spot.

In the other direction, guides set out with groups of guests on tours through the wine caves, where our in-house sommeliers will give presentations on our varietals and sell limited quantities of our special edition wines. Every wine-tasting slot throughout the day is filled, and a handful of guests have shown up on the off chance someone cancels. If they can't get in for a tasting, they'll tour the grounds and buy a bottle or two to have a picnic on their own.

"Wow, it's bustling here," Ella says as I walk her down a path lined with lavender and rosemary bushes next to the wine-tasting patio, where every table is filled. Our employees bustle through, setting out clean glasses and bringing the next in a procession of wines for tasting, starting with tender whites and ending with the bolder reds. Some of them eye me as I walk past.

"I think you make people nervous with the whole gruff and angry thing," Ella observes.

"It's not just me. They're probably just nervous in front of a Corbett family member."

"Really? Because I've walked through here with your sister, and no one scurries around in fear like they're doing now."

I look around us and see no scurrying. Everyone looks the way they always do when I'm around—serious about their jobs, as they should. Then again, I've never done anything to make them feel less nervous, so today I try to nod and smile.

"Now you just look constipated," Ella says, her laugh ringing out like a bell across the patio. I notice I'm not the only one who heeds the call, as several guests look in our direction, and a few whisper to the people they're with and try to gesture inconspicuously. A couple pull out their phones and snap quick shots. It's then that I remember Ella Fieldstone is widely recognized, and I shouldn't be parading her through the middle of the patio.

"Sorry. Didn't mean to attract unwanted attention for you," I say, guiding her toward a separate patio off the back of the wine cave. As soon as we round the bend, the chatter of the crowd dies down, replaced by the chirp of birds and the quiet I crave.

"It's fine. I'm used to it by now."

"Yeah?"

"Yeah. No glasses, remember?" She points to her unadorned eyes. I feel sad that she seems more resigned to this part of her fame than thrilled about it, and it makes me think back to that night at the party in LA with even more understanding about why she was surrounded by protectors. I doubt I'd even have approached her back then if I understood this aspect of her life better.

I walk us over to a smaller tasting room with a high counter and barstools on one side. I gesture for Ella to take a seat on one of them, and I go around to the other side of the bar to line up the varietals I want her to try.

"Tell me more," I say, pulling a bottle of Pebble and Clay sauvignon blanc from the fridge and wiping down the condensation on the label. I had Ruby, Jax's wife, give me the list of wines she recommended for the wedding. Ruby's the best sommelier we have, and she talked my ear off last night about each of the wines. By the end of an hour, I had sixteen pages of notes and was in over my head, but I'm a determined son of a bitch, and I stayed up late studying everything Ruby told me.

"More of what?"

"What that's like, the celebrity. It doesn't bother you to have people point at you and sneak pictures for their social media accounts? That would drive me crazy."

She laughs. "Now, why am I not surprised that Archer the Grouch doesn't like people?"

"I don't dislike all people," I clarify. "Just most people."

Ella shakes her head and points to the bottle. "That label's pretty." I take a look at the silver letters etched on a pale, cream-colored label with the Buttercup Hill flower underneath. It floats over a faint outline of the old brown barn. If you glance quickly, the barn doesn't stand out, but the longer you stare, the more details emerge. It really is a work of art.

I lean an elbow on the bar and gaze at the label in my hand. "Isn't it? I remember my dad telling me how he came up with the idea for the logo and the barn behind it. He said it all starts with family. Hence, the barn. And from that, the fruit of the vine can grow."

Ella puts her chin on her hand and listens as I speak, her eyes flitting from the logo to my face. It's intoxicating being this close to her in the intimate space, somehow even more so than when we were in the wine cave. Out here, dozens of people sit just a few yards away, but we're alone here, almost like we're insulated in a bubble, suspended in time.

"I like that," she says quietly.

The sharp ring of Ella's cell phone startles us both. She leans away from the bar top and searches her purse for her phone, and I go back to wiping down the bottle, which has a new layer of condensation on it. She checks the screen, where I can see Callum's album cover mugshot smiling through fog. If the ringing phone didn't jar me out of my fantasy—the one where Ella and I are meant for each other, and this is the moment she realizes it—the appearance of her fiancé's face is the record scratch that sends me back to reality.

Ella sends the call to voicemail, which surprises me. "Feel free to get that. I can wait."

"No, it's fine." Her brow creases, and she looks at the phone screen again. The call has already gone to voicemail, but she hesitates before putting it back into her purse. She opens her mouth, then shakes her head and looks down at the counter.

"Doesn't seem fine."

She inhales a slow breath and blows it out again, equally slowly. "It is."

I wait, hoping she'll say more, but she blinks a few times and forces a smile. "Where were we?" She reaches over and taps the bottle in my hand. "Tell me about this one."

Carefully cutting the foil capsule from the top, I recite Ruby's list of tasting notes and insert some of my knowledge from the growing side. "This one is unusual for the Rutherford area because it's a sauvignon blanc grape that behaves like a cab. It's slightly more finicky than the other whites we grow, and we think that's because it was grafted onto old vines that probably have cabernet origins. The grapes are a bit more fragile than the other whites, so we only grow a limited amount, hence the private reserve. We only produce a few dozen bottles in the years when we produce at all. So this one that you're about to taste is pretty special."

"I feel like a wine snob considering something so valuable for my wedding day."

"What better occasion?"

She flattens her lips into a forced smile and nods, but something's off. "Guess you're right. That's the whole reason I'm here, after all." And just like that, the whiff of real emotion is replaced by a movie-set version, where everything is suddenly kissed by a golden glow. Ella wraps her delicate fingers around the stem of a glass and tips it toward me. "Let's open 'em up."

It's not my place to ask about her relationship, especially as an owner of Buttercup Hill. My job is to play the professional, help my family hang onto a celebrity client, and make sure her wedding is every bit as worthy of the social register as possible. That's how we'll grow our business in the face of dwindling wine orders. That's how I'll ensure my family's legacy. Not by intruding on the personal details of a client or her feelings about her fiancé.

I keep that in mind as I plunge the spiral screw into the cork, only letting my imagination veer slightly to where the cork is instead wedged in Callum's carotid artery. Pulling out the cork with a clean pop, I lay it on the counter with the moist end facing Ella. "You should test to make sure it's not dry. Means it's been stored right."

"Oh, I trust you know what you're doing," she says, tapping the wet end with her index finger. "Yep, it's wet."

I hold the bottle up to the light, so the sun's rays are refracted by the pale yellow liquid, making rainbows dance on the countertop. "The color's a little darker than a lot of sauv blancs because of the fruit. It's a green grape with pink flesh."

I keep thinking back to the day when she was here with Callum and the way she almost flinched when he put his arm around her. The way he barely seemed interested in the wedding—to *her*. My hands ball into fists and I fight to unclench them.

I should find something to talk about, tell her more about the wine, teach her something. She always wants to learn. But we've spent time together over the past weeks, and I'm feeling honest with myself about how much I like her. And I want honesty from her.

"I'm sorry," I say, putting my glass down. "I'm just not seeing it. I know it's none of my business, but I don't give a shit. If I don't ask about it, I'll regret it." I grind my teeth and suck in a breath as though I can retract the words.

"What?" She looks up from studying the labels, and her eyes bore into me like lasers.

"You…Callum. As a couple. I don't see it." And there goes my chance.

She goes absolutely still and looks up from the bottles. "Archer…"

I wait for the rest. Her defense of how much she loves him. Her explanation of all I can't possibly know about the depth of their love. But she doesn't finish her sentence. She shakes her head and looks at the ground.

I start pacing in a circle, needing to move my body to give the pent-up energy and irritation someplace to go because I feel like hitting a punching bag, and last I checked, we don't have one in the tasting room. At the high table where the wine bottles are lined up, Ella sits motionless like a statue. Her inertia acts like a vacuum, forcing me to stop moving.

I stand across the room from her, intensely aware of each one of my senses. Eyes flooding with the sheer beauty of this woman who has no idea she's been the subject of every goddamn dream I've had for two months. Ears aware of the hollow silence in the room, that pregnant beat before she crushes my dreams forever by telling me to go to hell.

I can almost taste what I know would be berry-flavored kisses leading to my tongue roaming across every inch of her skin, each bit tasting more like honey than the one before it. My skin feels hot, prickling like I'm about to break a sweat, even though it's ice cold in the tasting room.

"He's not good enough for you. I know I barely know him, but I know that down to my bones. When I saw you together, I didn't see anything remotely close to what I'd feel if I were your fiancé." I can't help the possessive growl that overtakes the last few words.

Her jaw goes slack, and her brow furrows. "What do you mean?"

I opened this Pandora's box, and it comes with fear. I'm intensely aware of this moment and what I say next marking a line between where we are and what we could be. Except that maybe we can't be anything. I just need to know.

"If you were mine, I'd feel…like I'd won. Like I'd never have to ask the universe for anything again."

She swallows hard, but this time she doesn't look down. The pink in her cheeks duels the piercing blue of her eyes.

"Archer, you have to understand that it's complicated." Her voice is quiet, but at least she's still here. I half expected her to walk away or slug me.

"That's what people say when it's really uncomplicated and they just don't want to accept it." I take a step closer to her, hemming her in between my knees and leaning close because this is important. "Do you love him?"

Blinking, she seems to be considering what she wants to say. I wait, hoping my patience will pay off.

Finally, she bites her lip and utters the only word that makes a damn difference to me. "No."

The breath enters my lungs in a jagged rush of vital need, as though it's the first time I've had enough oxygen in weeks. She holds up a hand.

"This stays between us." She hesitates again then lets out a sharp exhale. "It's not a real engagement. I mean it is, in that we're getting married, but it's for the sake of our careers…and other things. We both need damage control. Him for his record label and his tour, and I need to prove to an adoption court that I'm responsible and able to be a good parent. I know it's not what you'd expect. I mean, most people marry for love. And there's affection there, it's just… Like I said, it's complicated."

Of all the explanations for how her love for Callum is complicated, a marriage of convenience for the sake of adoption was not on my radar. It makes me glad, on one hand, that she's not wildly in love because somehow my befuddled brain thinks it gives me a chance with her. But then I allow what she's just told me to sink in. *Adoption court?*

"You're adopting a baby with him?"

She nods slowly. "I've always wanted to be a mom. I want it more than anything, but there were so many things written about me, so many things people believe about me being unstable. There was a whole thing with some of my exes saying I was unstable…"

"Assholes. You've been dating the wrong guys, darlin'."

Her eyes soften. "Yes. Anyway, I'm in the process with a lawyer of trying to adopt, and the engagement to Callum quieted all the outside noise. Things are moving ahead, and I need Callum to play his part. I need to play mine."

"Oh." I wish I had a better, more eloquent response. I have so many questions, all mixed with confusion and relief that I was correct about what I saw. Even if it doesn't change anything. "Okay, then. When did you decide you wanted to adopt?"

She looks down. "When I found out my chances of conceiving naturally are very low. I've had a lot of tests. It's basically about the shape of my uterus, if that's not TMI. And there are so many babies in need. I could do something really good for one sweet, innocent little human. I want that."

"No, it's…" My mouth feels dry. "That's great that you figured out a way to make it work. With Callum." I can't tell her that I wish it was me in Callum's place. I can't say anything about how my thoughts have been consumed with her when I can't give what he's offering.

"Not everybody marries for love. It's not conventional, but nothing about my life is conventional. I do know what I want, though, and I'm not going to do anything to jeopardize it."

"A baby," I confirm. It's something I can't give her. I don't want kids. Simple fact.

"Yeah. It's what I want." She clears her throat and points at me. "And how about you? Great love? Wife? Girlfriend?"

"Nope. Negative."

"Come on, Grumpy Grape. You're a catch. You could have any woman in nine counties. Why not?"

The compliment sends a river of heat down my spine, but as much as I want to pull her close and crush my mouth to hers, I know it would only make me a selfish asshole after what she's just said, even if she does feel an attraction to me.

"Not for me. I'm the opposite of you. I don't want kids, and I don't have much need for a relationship. Work is all I need to fulfill my every need," I deadpan.

"Yeah, I can see that." She laughs. "All you need is work. Isn't that what the Beatles said?"

"Exactly. So you get it."

"Honestly, not really. Why are you so opposed to a family or kids?"

Exhaling, I push a hand through my hair. "How much time do you have?" I try to punctuate the question with a laugh, but it comes out more like a wheeze. "I didn't have great role models for that, and I don't want to make some kid miserable when I can't offer the right stuff to be a parent. That's the short answer."

She gives me a sad smile that says we'll agree to disagree about the kinds of futures we envision. "Not my place to say, but I bet you have the right stuff in you somewhere."

Her assessment of me makes me sad because of how wrong she is, just as it warms me from the inside that she sees something better in me than I've got.

I put a hand on her shoulder. "I guess it would be easier to take if I knew it was true love. If I thought he was so head over fucking heels in love with you that he's waiting for you to come home so he gives you everything you deserve. Knowing it's not real makes it harder not to kiss you. But not impossible."

Her eyes close and she gives me a small smile. "Thank you for hearing me and respecting that Callum and I are engaged and we're getting married and that my plans mean something to me." Our eyes lock and I see the anguish. The acceptance of lost opportunities.

I nod. "I get it. I understand." The worst part is that I really do understand. I don't want her to sacrifice the security of knowing she'll be able to adopt a child.

I feel something pull at me inside my chest, an ache that comes from inertia. I wish I could be the guy she needs in her life —the husband—who will show the twisted, mistaken world that Ella Fieldstone can offer a child the stability it needs, but I can't do it. Not that she's asking in any shape or form.

"I should go. That town car driver's been waiting around all afternoon." She stands and tests her balance. After a small wobble, she takes a step away from me and smiles. "Thank you for the tour."

"Best part of my day." It's no exaggeration. I shouldn't be playing hooky from work responsibilities, but it feels damn good for a change.

Her eyes widen and the corners of her mouth pull into the hint of a smile. "Mine too," she admits quietly, sneaking a look to the side as though someone might have heard. But we're alone.

My eyes rake over her, noting the uncertainty in her eyes that slowly settles into purpose as she meets my gaze with confidence. Like a fire ignites behind them. Her cheeks flush. Her lips look ripe and full.

It would be so easy to close the gap between us. So easy to take what I've started to believe is rightfully mine even though I have no goddamn reason to think it.

But she doesn't allow it. Instead, she turns and walks away.

rcher

I DON'T EVEN MAKE it back to my office before my phone starts blowing up.

"Hey," I bark at Graham, who goes on to tell me that the grower we've been negotiating with just sold the majority of his cabernet grapes to a competitor. So while I've been pursuing a futile romance with a Buttercup Hill client, even more of our business has gone to shit. Another piece of evidence why I should never distract myself with anything other than work. Especially women.

My heart feels like it's been hollowed out and laughed at. For the second time, I actually believed I might have a chance with Ella Fieldstone. What a joke.

"You need to get laid, and quick," Colin says, commandeering my truck toward the Dark Horse pub at the outskirts of Napa a couple hours later. I hear a quick succession of "heck yeah" and "seriously" from the peanut gallery behind me, aka my brothers and Ren, Beatrix's fiancé. They've all but kidnapped me after I told them I'd be skipping their guys' night out in favor of reading a book.

"I need to be left alone," I grumble, looking out the window and knowing there's not a chance of these guys staying out of my business when they think they know better than me. The dark hills to the left are scarred from fires a few years back, reminding me that I still don't have any idea why my father would hire someone to torch our own land. I know he's not making sound decisions, but this goes beyond moving numbers around on a balance sheet. He had to have thought things through, and it makes me sad and angry that I may never know what he was thinking. If he was thinking at all.

"I call bullshit on that," Dash says, surprising me because he's always game for an adventure but he rarely goes on the attack. "I mean, get laid or don't, but you definitely need to be out with us instead of brooding at home."

No one says anything specific about Ella, which is probably because they all know me well enough to understand that I'd jump out of a moving vehicle rather than talk about catching feelings for another man's fiancée. It's only because they've shown that bit of sensibility that I decided to throw on a hoodie and leave the house. That, and they showed up, let themselves in with Jackson's spare key, and commandeered my truck. Assholes.

We reach the bar in fifteen minutes, and I follow them inside, taking a quick scan of the room to see if there's anyone here I know. I recognize a few women sitting at the bar because they were friends with someone I dated years ago, but if they remember me, they probably won't have nice things to say. Their friend called me a litany of names, all involving fear of commitment and general bad behavior, and hell, she was probably right.

I duck behind Colin and move toward the corner of the bar. "I'll grab us a table."

"What do you want? Beer? Shot?"

"Beer." I make my way to the table and slide into the seat facing the wall. A few minutes later, everyone joins me and we get into an intense conversation about hockey and the Oakland Otters, where Ren is an impact player. They've been having a good season, despite a rough beginning, but they're a long-shot prospect for the playoffs. "It might take another year before we have the chemistry to get there," he admits before downing half his pint in one slug.

"But it's coming together. I can see a difference in this half of the season." I'm not blowing smoke. The team's record is better, sure, but ever since my sister got back together with Ren, I've seen every game and studied the team like it's my job.

"We're better, yeah, but we lost too many games early on. We'll get there."

I finally start to relax, at home in the dark space with guys who have my back, talking about sports. I only look over my shoulder once to see who else is in the bar. Otherwise, I'm focused on the guys who are here to help me forget about Ella for a few hours.

Ironically, after thirty minutes, I'm the only one who's still sober. Sitting at our table in the corner of the dark bar, I have a perfect view of the mating rituals that define the human race. Boy are they pathetic.

Men sauntering up to women who are here with girlfriends—and clearly not interested. Women laughing and flipping their hair, trying to get Ren's attention—and he's clearly not interested. It's a wonder we pair up and date at all.

Meanwhile, my brothers are acting like competitive, hormonal middle-schoolers, fake-fighting each other with pool cues. *And I'm the one who's still single*, I think, shaking my head.

"You're so full of shit, Dash. I'm the one who taught you to play in the first place," Jax says, swaggering over to the pool table and putting his name on the chalkboard for next game.

"Doesn't mean you're better now. I actually play on the regular."

"Not sure I'd brag about that. You're just admitting you have no life." Jax draws a slash on the board and puts Dash's name on the opposite side as his opponent. They've been like this their entire lives. Dash, as the youngest brother, is always trying to prove he's bigger and tougher than the rest of us, and Jax, in the middle, can't resist taking the bait.

Colin and Ren come from the bar with a new round of drinks. I take mine and slide it onto a coaster on the sideboard next to the pool table. They won't even notice if I don't drink it, and after being here for an hour, I have less interest in drinking away my misery than I did when I got here.

"You two having a throwdown? I'm in for next game," Colin says, always competitive, no matter the sport or situation. That leaves me alone without a partner, right when my old and very drunk friend Alicia totters over. We've known each other for years, never dated. I never wanted to, and I always assumed the feeling was mutual.

Tonight's the night her inhibitions are low enough that she decides to set me straight. "I always wanted you, Archer. Why didn't you want me?" she asks, slurring her words and almost missing the barstool she tries to sit on.

"Aw, Alicia, we're too good of friends to ruin it by hooking up, we both know it."

She nods and smiles, showing some lipstick on her front teeth. "You're a good guy, Archer Corbett, telling me lies. Don't worry. I don't hold any grudges." She pats at my chest.

"I'm glad. And if I hurt your feelings, I apologize."

She looks up at me with a drunken grin, her eyes blinking slowly as she tries to focus. "I see three of you. Thass not a good sign." Her hand remains on my chest, one finger drawing circles on the front of my hoodie.

"Nope. I'd say not." I look around for her friends. It's time for them to take care of her and it's time for me to get home. I'm the only one sober enough to drive, and it's my truck, so if the guys want to keep playing pool, they can call an Uber later.

Problem is that I don't see the women she was with earlier. I stand up from the barstool and Alicia lurches forward. Apparently she was using me for balance. I catch her before she falls off the stool and rearrange her so she's leaning against the bar. The bartender shoots me a look of sympathy.

"Did you see where her friends went?" I ask.

He points to the exit. "They left about a half hour ago with a group of guys. Looks like they made her your problem."

"Of course they did."

"It's fine. I'll get her home. She's a friend." He doesn't get off work for another hour, and I'm ready to go.

I let the guys know I'm leaving. They're in the middle of a heated game of pool, so they barely seem to notice. "Ruby's at a girls' dinner in the area. She said she'll drive us if you wanna take off," Jax says, always looking out for Dash, who always assumes someone is looking out for him. As to the other guys, they're just along for the ride.

I help Alicia off her barstool, and she leans heavily against my side as we walk toward the door of the bar. Jax nods his approval, knowing she needs help home. I'm sort of happy to have an excuse to leave this place. I'm all for a night out with my brothers and friends, but the idea of hooking up with someone depresses me.

Alicia is halfway to passing out by the time we reach my truck. I manage to get her into the passenger seat, but then I notice she doesn't have her purse. "Alicia, where's your purse?"

"What?" Her eyes are bleary and barely open.

"Your purse. Do you have keys to your apartment?"

Her eyes drift closed, and she hums something unintelligible. I jog back to the bar and look around the area where she was sitting. Nothing. I have no idea if she even had a purse with her or if her friends took it when they left. But now I'm stuck with a drunk woman who I'm not about to leave sitting in front of her apartment building alone on a cold night.

Guess she'll be sleeping on my couch.

Just what I need.

CHAPTER 18

lla

I TAKE the stairs two at a time. My legs burn from the hour-plus I put in at the gym and I should probably calm down, take a breath, not jump to conclusions.

But I know the car that's parked in my fiancé's guest spot beneath his building. I also know the woman who drives it.

I reach the top of the stairs and let out a deep sigh. It's a moment when I'm acutely aware of a before and an after.

And also a choice.

Callum gave me a key to his San Francisco house so I could "come crawl in bed" with him when I'm in town. Even though I've been mostly staying with Tatum, I've spent a few nights here. Guess he wasn't planning on seeing me tonight.

The implicit understanding in his invitation was that he'd be in bed alone, and on all the other times when I'd finished up at a movie premiere or publicity event, there he'd be, clad in silky boxer briefs, his broad chest naked and muscled from hours at the gym. All of those times, I'd appreciated his attention to detail —from the time he spent honing his physical form into something anatomy professors could have used for a lesson, to the time he spent perfecting guitar solos in between tours.

I can turn back around and pretend that the press junket went late instead of ending early, allowing me to slip through his front door unannounced. Or I can confront my fate, even if I already hate that it's been changed without my permission.

It's not like turning around will undo the transgression if he's in bed with another woman. It will just keep me from knowing about it for a little longer. But I've never been one to run away from my life, so I grab the doorknob.

Before I wedge it open, I hear the sounds of what can only be described as frantic, desperate humping on the eve of the apocalypse. How else to explain the guttural panting and moaning that makes what they're doing sound like both ecstasy and pain?

Flinging the door wide, I find the lights on and clothing strewn all over the white carpet. Callum is such a neat-freak, prone to unbuttoning his shirts and hanging pants over a chair even in the heat of passion, that for a moment I convince myself the man grunting his way through an orgasm must not be the man I'm planning to marry in a few months. Through the fog of my revulsion and anger, I can't help but note that Callum has never made me feel something so good that I sounded like that. Is it weird that I feel offended?

I've never been at a loss for words until this moment. Nope, scratch that. The words are here. "Callum, seriously. What the fuck?"

The grunting stops. The sheets flutter around, body parts untangle, and two surprised faces stare at me beneath just-fucked hair. Callum squints at me because he's nearsighted.

Jenny, Callum's tour manager, blinks long eyelashes that look like mini awnings that I can see from across the room. Her hair clip is askew, red lipstick smeared around her mouth, pale skin streaked with pink blotches in the shape of Callum's fingers.

She's normally the one who calls to tell me Callum has last-minute plans and can't see me. I suspected she was covering for some tour bunny. Guess I should have looked closer to home.

And the worst thing about the whole situation is that I convinced myself that I could be satisfied with a marriage of convenience. I told myself I didn't need real love as long as I stayed focused on the child I want to adopt. But this feels awful. Even if the tabloids haven't discovered him cheating yet, I'll always be worried about people finding out. Worried it will make my reputation look even worse. Worried it will jeopardize the adoption.

Worried I can't go through with a magazine-perfect dream wedding four months from now. How can I pretend it's a festive, happy event instead of a farce? Even I'm not that good of an actor.

lla

"Don't do this," Callum pleads, sounding genuinely sorry, as I methodically go through the drawers and cabinets where I've left a few things over the past year that we've been together.

The bedroom overlooks the Pacific Ocean, which glimmers under moonlight through a wall of windows. He's owned the place for longer than I've known him, but it barely shows any signs of wear. White leather armchairs at the foot of the bed sit uncreased. The white carpet always looks freshly vacuumed, and the low wood table contains three arthouse books, arranged at a right angle to the bed.

Jenny is long gone, having thrown on her clothes and scurried out of the condo as soon as she saw my face. She knew Callum wasn't going to ask her to stick around. Guess that's what makes her a good manager—knowing what her boss wants. And giving it to him.

"Cal, I'm doing it." Yanking open a drawer, I realize I don't know what I'm doing exactly. I'm also unsure what he's asking me *not* to do, so I stop. "Don't do what?"

"End us."

Forehead resting against his fist, he sits on the bed where hours before he was thrusting his dick into his tour manager. The sheets are no longer in disarray, but I can still smell the sickly pungent scent of sex. I probably always will.

Exhaling a long breath, I stand with my arms crossed and wait for him to look at me. He does, eyes red from rubbing them, hair still askew, mouth pulled down into an anguished frown. "Don't go," he pleads, tilting his head in that way that lets a long lock of hair fall across his cheek. I always liked that. His dark eyes look bottomless, smoldering for me. I liked that too. So many times, I've looked into those eyes and seen our future. Now, I see a manufactured fairy tale I was dumb enough to believe. I'm not as mad at him as I am at myself for thinking he could be better than his reputation.

Callum Haywood had been linked with several different A-list stars in the two years before we met. But then, so had I.

Our manufactured love story was the kind of epic fodder that social media lives for. We were photographed at every turn. We were called Hollywood royalty. Our names were blended together so people could refer to us simply as Ellum.

And I do like him. Or, I did. Now, I don't know what I feel except that I need to get out of his condo and think.

"I can't be here with you. I can't even look at you," I tell him, shoving my toiletries into the bathroom trash can.

"Are you taking my trash can?"

"Were you fucking your tour manager?!" It's the first time I've raised my voice and it feels good.

He holds up his hands in surrender. "Fine. Take the trash can."

"I just need to get away from you so I can think."

He stands up from the bed and walks over to me, hands drawn together like a prayer. I try not to notice how his biceps flex when he does it. "Okay. Take the time you need. Just know that this was a one-time slip. We had some drinks…it was stupid. Purely physical. And I'll fire her, never see her again." His eyes plead. He bites his bottom lip, looking vulnerable.

"God, Callum. That is such utter bullshit. Did you get that out of a book of things to say after you cheat on your fiancée?"

He takes a step closer and I take a step back. "You're the one I love. And I know you love me. We can get past this, can't we?"

I shake my head, hating conflict but unwilling to roll over. "I don't know. Probably not," I admit. I don't see how I can ever look at him the way I did before.

He nods and hangs his head. I open a drawer and grab the bras and panties I stashed there months ago. Looking around the room, I can't think of anything else I want. Taking all this stuff is hardly the point, but I feel the need to do something, make my exit from this place feel like something to him. So rifling through his drawers is apparently the way I will do that.

But now there's nothing left to grab and no reason to stay, so I head for the door.

"What about the adoption?" Callum's voice echoes in the hallway behind me. I turn and my eyes blink shut.

It's not that I've forgotten about it—to the contrary, it's all I think about. But do I need Callum Haywood for that? Do I need to accept his apology so I can keep my court date in the spring, a month after our wedding?

"Just give me time to think."

"Take all the time you need. I'll be here. I really do love you."

I roll my eyes as the sex stench follows me downstairs.

"Let's face it. This relationship was a farce from the beginning. We were just a Hollywood couple, made for the tabloids. It was never going to work," I say, mostly to avoid taking responsibility for jumping at the first guy who seemed willing to be my husband.

An almost-smile tugs at the corner of Callum's pretty-boy face. "That mean you don't blame me for stepping out on you?"

I fly at him and push his chest with both hands. Unfortunately, due to his beefy build, it has the effect of a fly hitting a window. "No, you imbecile. Even if we weren't perfect, I'd expect my *fiancé* to be faithful. Jesus, Callum, don't you have any morals at all?"

He shrugs. Maybe he doesn't know the meaning of the word.

I think about what could have happened with Archer on the patio outside the wine cave. How every part of my body ached for it to happen. It sure seemed like Archer wanted it to happen. But like I told him, I'm engaged. That has to mean something, or what's the point?

I continue throwing items into a bag, whirling around looking for who knows what in my attempt to clear my life of all things Callum.

"Am I just a fool? Am I the only one who thinks that a commitment is sacred?"

Callum, who's been watching me with his arms crossed and a confused expression, relents. His cocky posture sags a little and his mouth turns down. "No." He shakes his head. "You're right. It should be sacred. I guess that's just one of the many reasons why you're too good for me."

I've been hearing that excuse for ages, how no one can introduce me to their single guy friends because I'm "too good" for them. It just strikes me as one more way that what people see when they look at me isn't who I am.

"I'm sick of people telling me I'm too good. I'm just...normal good."

He extends his arms to hug me, and despite how angry and betrayed I still feel, I consider patching things over and embracing him.

Then I come to my senses. "But yeah, you're right. I am too good for you."

I take my things and walk out the door.

CHAPTER 20

Ella

I can't stay here. I can't even stay in the same city as him. So I start driving.

The problem is that I don't know many people in the Bay Area, and as much as Tatum loves me, I don't think she'll appreciate me showing up at four-thirty in the morning. So I drive north, my foot on the gas and my hands on the wheel knowing what my brain hasn't managed to process—I'm going to Napa. It's the one place I've been in the area with the kind of wide-open spaces I need to think.

Not that there's much to think about. I'm not going back to a guy who cheated on me, no matter how sorry he says he is.

But I don't know what I'm doing instead.

The scenery slips past me under a half moon and a dark sky. I barely notice any of it. When I reach Vallejo, still thirty miles south of Napa, I pull off and find my way to a coffee shop that's open and serving hot coffee and whatever else I want from the all-day menu. I want a huge stack of pancakes, a scoop of butter melting on the top, and a lot of syrup. It's strange that Callum makes me sick at the same time that I have a huge appetite, but I'm too worn out to question it.

A tired-looking woman with a pink diner dress under a white apron sidles up to my table with a menu, but I shake my head and give her my order. "Cream in the coffee?" She writes everything down on a little pad with a tiny pencil, which she tucks into the apron pocket and makes her way to the kitchen. Her white clunky tennis shoes squeak as she goes.

Thumbing through the address book on my phone, I locate the number for my lawyer, who I can't call at this hour. Even if I did, she won't be in the office. I continue down the alphabetical list of everyone I know, ultimately deciding that the people who live in time zones where they'll be awake aren't the ones I want to tell about Callum. So I sip the coffee when it arrives and lean my forehead on my hand, trying to figure out something resembling a plan.

An hour later, I'm no closer to a plan, but my stomach aches from downing three mammoth pancakes and enough coffee to supercharge a rhino. That's when I get back into my car, which seems to be on autopilot bound for Buttercup Hill.

I shouldn't be here. I'm just a future wedding guest with no wedding now, and none of the people there owe me any of their time. Least of all Archer. Which is why I'm about to get back into my car and head for the Oakland airport when Archer's front door swings open. Shirtless in a pair of low-slung sweatpants, he looks awake but tired. The smooth muscles of his chest and abs catch the pale light from his outdoor sconces, and my mouth waters. I don't even try to look away. When my eyes land back on his face, I see him squinting but hardly scowling. He looks confused but pleased to see me.

Archer blinks into the relaxed, dim light of early morning—

it's maybe half past six—and cocks his head when he sees me standing between my car and his front door.

"What's up?"

I open my mouth, but no words come out. His question is too big to answer.

"Did we have an appointment?" he asks, raking a hand through his hair and taking a step toward me.

Shaking my head, I take a step backward. "No. Sorry."

What am I doing here?

I turn toward my car and yank open the door, but Archer's long stride has him standing next to my car, blocking my access to the front seat. He's pulling a shirt over his head, and my brain is a muddle of regret for coming here, disappointment as his naked chest disappears, and lust over his perfectly mussed hair and the intensity in his gaze.

"Wait. Would you just hang on a second?"

"You're in my way."

"Yeah, that's intentional."

"You're a big oaf and I need you to move."

A hazy, sleepy grin creeps across his face. "I'm an oaf?"

"Like Shrek, only a little less green."

"Shrek was an ogre," he says, smirking now and hanging his arm on the top of my car door. I wish he didn't look quite so damn handsome when I feel like a mess, but it's comforting to have something nice to look at, at least.

"Are we really splitting hairs over which word I should use to insult you?"

"Funny, I'm not insulted." He definitely doesn't seem insulted. In fact, he seems almost…content. If I didn't know better—i.e., that it's a horrific hour to wake a person on a Saturday, unannounced—I might even think he's glad to see me.

"Why are you smiling?"

The smile fades and I worry I've scared it off.

"Wait, no. You were almost happy. I don't want to ruin that."

"Almost?" The crease in his brow is proof I've offended him, though I'd think the oaf comment would've dealt a heavier blow to his ego.

I shrug. "I just mean…I liked the smile." Slowly, it returns, lips turning up at the corners, cheeks pulling upward, even if he seems to be fighting it.

"Why are you here, darlin'?"

As usual, being called darlin' by the gruffest man in Northern California melts my resistance.

"I…" Shaking my head, I tell myself to ask the oaf in front of me to move aside because I don't have an answer to his question, at least not an answer I'm ready to tell him.

"Talk to me." His voice is a quiet rasp that sends chills over the back of my neck and down my spine. If this man has the power to do that to my body with one word, I imagine what he could do to the rest of me if he just reached out and—

No.

I'm torn between wanting to tell him about Callum, admitting that everything he saw in him was correct, or keeping my failings to myself out of embarrassment that I'm in this situation.

It's not that I don't want to give him the satisfaction of being right—I don't want the disappointment of being wrong.

Archer brushes a finger under my chin, enough to ignite my skin and make me suck in a small breath. Tipping my chin up, he lets his gaze linger on my face, moving from my eyes to my mouth, which starts to water under the strength of his stare, and back to my eyes, which are locked on him. His pupils dilate and he lets out a long, slow breath.

"Why?" It's almost a plea. The muscles in Archer's face have gone slack. His eyes are soft and welcoming, communicating that I can trust him.

I feel weightless, shaky in anticipation of what will happen when I tell him. Archer's other hand, strong and steady, comes out to grip my hip. Like he knows the barest wind could blow me over.

"I walked in on Callum and his tour manager last night." My throat feels tight as the awkward words wedge their way out. "In bed," I add as though the first part wasn't clear.

The softness in Archer's expression disappears in an instant. His jaw tightens and a muscle starts ticking in his cheek. His eyes, which looked so gentle and calm a moment ago, now look charged and ready for battle.

"That fucker."

Archer drops his hand from under my chin, but his other one still grips my hip. He looks like he just ate something that tasted putrid.

"There may be more to it that I don't know, something going on with him, or maybe I freaked him out with all the wedding plans," I start to protest, to tell him that Callum isn't a bad guy. All my fears that somehow this is my fault bubble to the surface. Maybe Callum just did a bad thing, but…*wait, why is my knee-jerk response to defend him?*

Archer shakes his head. "No. Don't do that. Not for a second. This isn't on you. Him cheating has nothing to do with you and everything to do with him being a grade-A piece of shit." He takes a deep breath and lets it out slowly. "I'd like to drive back down there with you and tell him to his smarmy face."

"That would be a waste of a good road trip."

Deeper lines crease Archer's forehead. One side of his mouth pulls down. "I'm going to ask you again. Why're you here, darlin'?"

It's a fair question. After telling him I intended to go through with a fake marriage for the sake of the adoption, I know I look like I'm just here on the rebound after being betrayed. "It's where I want to be."

He nods, but his expression doesn't change. "Because you need a shoulder to cry on? I can be that, I suppose."

"No." I take a step closer.

"Why, then? I don't do rebounds with other men's women."

I shake my head. "No. That's not it. I had hopes for a relationship with Callum, but as you know, it was for specific reasons. The wrong reasons. And I never felt for him what I'm starting to feel for you."

His eyes soften, and he swallows hard but doesn't move.

"This isn't a rebound," I continue. "It's what I've been wanting since I met you. And now I need to know what it's like to have your hands on my skin."

His hand, which had been balled into a fist by his side, unclenches. He raises it and slowly traces the side of my face, from my temple down to my chin.

"This feels like the beginning of something that could get very, very good." His voice is a sexy rasp.

The beautiful, searing heat of his touch reminds me that the last thing I want is to leave this place or do anything to detract from this, his hands touching me.

I reach my own hand to touch his and hold it against my cheek where it rests. He sucks in a sharp breath. I wonder if his heart is beating out of his chest like mine is. I reach for the soft fabric of the worn band t-shirt he's wearing and gingerly place my hand against his chest, over his heart. I feel it's steady beat and imagine the blood rushing through his veins the same way mine is making me lightheaded now. I also feel a hard plane of muscle beneath my hand that makes me want to strip the shirt right off his body and touch his skin.

His hand moves from my hip, slowly grazing before lifting my hand from his heart and bringing it to his lips. His warm breath feathers over my skin, sending a chill across mine. My shoulders relax. I feel myself lean closer to him, heart hammering in my chest. My skin vibrates with my pulse, and I feel more alive than I have in my life and he's barely touching my skin.

Our eyes stay locked in an unbreakable acknowledgement of

the before and after. Before we kiss, life comes with all of its mistakes and regrets.

After…it's the great leap, the first steps on the dusty surface of the moon, uncharted and magical. I want to linger in this in-between state for one more moment because I can already tell that after Archer's lips meet mine, there will be no going back.

As a shaky breath of air enters my lungs, I also know that I don't want to go back. I've been fighting against the feeling of wanting this man from the day I walked into the old barn and saw him staring at me in the doorway.

I almost didn't even recognize the moment as significant because it felt like the film sets where I spend half my time. The lighting perfect. The air still. Everything about the moment felt like a curated movie designed to signal a romantic moment instead of what it really was—the beginning of something that could change the trajectory of my life. Something that already has.

Archer tips his forehead against mine and I feel the weight of his inhale, as though he's wrestling with his conscience like he was the last time I saw him, trying to talk himself down.

"I want you more than I've wanted anything in my life, but I'm worried it's not right…" His words sound choked and regretful. His eyes meet mine, assessing whether I agree.

"Stop worrying. It's right."

"Yeah?" There's still sadness in his eyes, but his hands curl around mine, holding me in place.

I nod against his forehead. "I wouldn't have come here otherwise."

His chest rises and falls with another strangled breath. His hands slowly work their way up my arms, leaving goose bumps in their wake, until they roam over my shoulders and he's cupping my chin in his hands.

"I'm glad you did." His voice has that morning gruffness, though I suspect he wasn't sleeping when I pulled up. "I just…"

He closes his eyes and presses his lips together. "I know you came here out of a rough situation, and I don't want to mistake that for something else." His throat works as he swallows hard. "I don't want you to regret anything that…might happen."

I nod, more certain than anything of what I want. "I'll only regret it if it doesn't happen."

His whole body shudders like I've set off a firestorm. He takes one more slow breath, eyes fixed on mine. They glow with a feral darkness I've never seen before. It's hot, sexy. It's everything I need.

Like a rubber band stretched to its limits, I can feel his self-restraint snap. Still holding my face in his hands, he lowers his lips to mine. Carefully. Gently. Like there's no going back once our mouths collide.

When I feel the soft pressure of his lips, my veins light up with heat that almost knocks me over. I hold on to him to steady myself and lean into the whirling dizziness that comes from a kiss I've wanted so badly it hurts.

I don't breathe. I can't.

I let him kiss me until it's the only thing I feel, the pressure of his lips begging me for more.

My hands move into his hair, which is soft and silky as my fingers brush through the strands. Every part of my body aches to get closer to him, to feel him against me.

Our tongues tangle and taste. I feel myself running short of breath, but I don't care.

Finally, he breaks the kiss, his breath a rumble against my mouth. "God, Ella, I can't get enough of you…" I don't respond with words. Instead, I pull his face to mine again and kiss him hard, urging him toward something I can't articulate.

More.

"Morning." A soft voice startles us apart. Archer swears under his breath and rests his forehead on his fingers.

I look up to see a woman standing in the doorway of Archer's house wearing a short, hot pink dress. It's a definite walk-of-shame dress. No one wears that on a Saturday morning unless it's a leftover from Friday night.

My eyes stretch wide, but my brain is already directing traffic, telling me to turn around and get back in my car. I'm sure my mortification is written on my face.

"Ella, hang on," Archer says calmly, even though he looks caught like a deer on a hunting ground. "She's just a friend."

It still doesn't look good. My mind spins, and the lack of sleep and the oxygen deprivation I just experienced aren't helping. For all I know, he's just placating me with that story about taking care of a friend. The last thing I need is to pour my heart out to a man who's in the middle of a hookup or a date or whatever Archer Corbett does when he's not worrying about grapes.

Archer looks torn between my rapid dash away from him and the woman still talking from the doorway. "How did I end up here? Ugh, I'm seriously so hungover."

"Ella, hang on. Just come inside and we can talk."

"No thank you." I slide into my car and start to close the door, but Archer wedges himself in the space in front of it. "Do you mind? I need to drive my car, and I can't with your large body blocking my door."

"Actually, I do mind. I want you to come inside."

"Why in the world would I do that when you already have someone inside?"

"I told you she's a friend."

"Feels like I hear that a lot these days. Callum's tour manager was a 'friend' until I found him banging her last night. Why would I believe any guy?" I'm still dizzy over our kiss, and I'm trying to push away the image of him kissing her too.

Archer kneels in the space next to my car, still blocking the door. Expression serious and unwavering, he holds me by the forearms.

"She's a friend. I was at a bar last night with my brothers and she had too much to drink. No idea where her purse ended up, so I brought her back here. She slept on the couch." His voice is rough but soothing. I want to believe him, but walking in on Callum last night has me mistrustful of all men.

"I should go."

"Is that what you want?" His face is an unreadable mask, which helps because I need to make this decision myself, and not stay just because he wants me to.

I close my eyes and allow myself a moment to sort through the past twenty-four hours, when I've gone from dreaming about a future family to the present when I have no idea what lies ahead. But I nod.

"I'll come inside."

The presence of the woman in the dress has put a halt to whatever just passed between us, and now all I feel is cool air when Archer stands up and offers me his hand to pull me to standing outside my car. But he doesn't let go, and I take comfort in the strength of his large, warm palm and strong fingers wrapped around mine as we walk toward the woman still standing in the doorway, her dress looking even more sheer the closer we get.

I hope I'm not making another mistake.

rcher

THE SECOND CUP of coffee has Alicia talking a mile a minute, her legs crossed underneath her on my couch, while Ella looks on from an armchair in the corner.

I don't blame her for sitting as far away from the trainwreck of my personal life as possible. If it were me, I'd have driven away like she was planning. Especially after Alicia recognized her and went fangirl for a full two minutes until I could settle her down. I'm not sure how I persuaded Ella to stick around, but I'm grateful for whatever gods of manifesting convinced her.

Without her purse, Alicia has no idea how to reach her friends. All of their numbers are stored in her phone, which she doesn't have. "D'you want to log into your account on my phone and search for it?" Ella offers.

"Oh, good idea," she says. I meet Ella's gaze and press my lips into a sort of smile, hoping it conveys how much I appreciate her kindness to Alicia. I can't think of many women who'd take me at my word that there's nothing going on between us, especially after what she just witnessed with Callum. I feel even more lucky that Ella chose to come here this morning. That she chose me.

I also kick myself for not searching for Alicia's phone last night. I could've set off a chime to alert whoever had the phone, saving myself the whole nightmare of carrying Alicia from my truck to my house. In other words, I could be standing in my driveway with my hands on Ella's soft skin right now instead of staring at her across the room like I've been doing for the past half hour.

Ella and Alicia set about logging in, and after a minute, they've located her phone. "That's Carla's house." Alicia slaps her hand against her forehead. "Right. I had a clutch, so I stuck it in Carla's bag, and she hung it on the hook under the bar. Totally forgot about that."

A few minutes later, they've succeeded at reaching out to Carla on a social media messaging app and arranging for Alicia to pick up her bag on the way to her apartment. Relief washes over me as I see my errand coming to an end so I can pick up where I was with Ella outside. For the past half hour, I've been able to think about nothing else. I keep sneaking glances at her, clocking details I didn't notice when we were outside. Her rosebud mouth, devoid of gloss or lipstick. The way her eyes dance when Alicia tells her that I'm a big teddy bear underneath my "snarly exterior."

"I wouldn't go that far," I gripe, only to find Ella smiling at me from her chair, which is about as far away from me as she could be in this room. My muscles twitch, eager to pull her onto my lap and inhale a deep breath of her skin, her hair. I can't stop staring.

"So where was I?" Alicia asks, reminding us that she was in the middle of giving Ella "all the dirt" on me since we've known each other forever. So far, it's only resulted in a few stories about my football days and the cheerleaders I used to date. But then she started in on a story about a bear and I distracted her by refilling her coffee cup.

"The story about the bear," Ella reminds her. I shoot her a frown, but she returns a sweet smile that says she's eager to hear embarrassing stories about me.

"You should've seen his face," Alicia says, telling a story she drags out whenever she wants to relive the glory days of our high school friendship. Usually it's when she wants me to do something for her, some sort of man-power errand that requires a truck. She reminds me of how close we were once, which only serves to remind me that we're not close anymore.

"Pretty glad you didn't. Not my finest moment," I say, hoping Alicia will cut to the shorter version of the story of how I thought I was defending my friends against a bear on our senior retreat.

"On the contrary, it was adorable." Alicia sips more coffee.

"It was a normal testosterone-fueled guy response," I explain. "My knuckleheaded friends thought it would be hilarious to pretend to be a bear when it was my turn to tell a ghost story by the campfire, and when one of them yelled 'bear!' I jumped to my feet and put my hands over my head to make myself look big and menacing."

Alicia snorts coffee from her nose at the memory. "He looked like he was ready to shred the bear with his teeth." She does her best impression of a vicious-looking face, teeth bared and jazz hands, which I most definitely did not do.

"You look like you're auditioning to play the wolf in a bad Broadway musical," I say, shaking my head. I drain the last of my coffee and stand up. "Anyway...we should grab your stuff from Carla's and get you home."

Alicia looks from Ella to me and nods. "Right. Got it. Sorry." She stands up, straightens the hem of her short dress, and twists her hair into a knot on top of her head. "Okay, ready." She looks around us on the floor. "Did I have shoes?"

I walk to the back door and grab her stiletto sandals. "Ready?"

"So pushy," Alicia says, grabbing them from me and hanging them from her finger. "I'm kidding. I've taken up enough of your time."

"Do you want to hang here or come for the drive?" I ask Ella.

"I'll come."

"I was hoping you'd say that," I whisper when she walks past me to my truck. It earns me a smile and I tuck it away like a gold star.

Ella insists on sitting in the back seat while I drive the quick two miles to Carla's and then to Alicia's apartment. "It's on the border of Calistoga," she tells Ella.

"Never been there."

"Really? Oh, well, I guess that makes sense. Lotta locals hang there. Tourists mostly want to see downtown Napa or St. Helena. The more chichi places with the cute shops and restaurants."

I worry that Ella may take offense to the assumption that she's a fancy tourist, but she doesn't skip a beat. "Sounds like I'd like Calistoga."

I meet her eyes in the rearview mirror, hoping she can see my smile.

A few minutes later, Alicia gives me a wet kiss on the cheek and waves at Ella. "Thanks again." She saunters up the walkway of her apartment building with her shoes slung over her shoulder. A second after that, the passenger door opens and Ella slides onto the bench seat next to me.

"Where to, cowboy?" she asks, pulling the seat belt across her body. I unsnap it just as fast. She looks at me quizzingly, but I put one arm around her shoulders and haul her to my side. The warmth of her body ignites something deep within me, an ember that's been smoldering since I first laid eyes on her that day in the old brown barn. Now there's no chance of extinguishing out that flame. It's already consuming everything in its wake.

She takes a quick look around, but there's no one on the street at this early hour. We're safe from cell phone cameras. Then she gazes up at me, jaw slack, eyes hungry. Her tongue slips out to lick her bottom lip.

My cock jumps in my pants, instantly hard like it was when she showed up in my driveway this morning. It's taken all my self-control to wage war against it, and now I'm fucking done.

Turning in my seat, I face her more squarely, my eyes roaming over her face, my brain firing off a hailstorm of ideas about where to kiss her first, which part of her skin to taste. I shut all that down and focus on her lips. They're parted slightly. Pale pink. Wet.

I cup her jaw in my palm, finally emboldened to take what I've been denying myself for weeks.

Brushing my thumb across her cheek, I feel her face sink into my hand. I feel her heart beating beneath the surface. Her quiet sigh.

My hands are rough against her smooth skin. It's a warning. This is her chance to reject the farmer, the guy from the small town, the man who isn't her fiancé, even if he's proven himself barely a man. But she only moves closer to me, one bent leg sweeping across my lap to drape over me. I pull her in tighter, one hand firm against her back, showing her exactly how unwilling I am to let her go. One hand still tracing the graceful lines of her face, wanting to be gentle with her until she screams for something else.

She watches me, waiting to see where this will lead. I get it—even if Callum cheated, she's still engaged—she can't be the one to make the first move.

Fine by me.

I tip my head to her forehead, taking a moment to inhale the scent of her, all floral and citrus and fucking perfection. Her breath is choppy and shallow, and I want to steal all of it.

As my finger trails over the apple of one cheek, I memorize every curve. Every inch of her heart-shaped face.

When I bring my lips to hers, it's just a whisper. A promise of what I'll give her if she'll let me. I can barely stand to limit myself to just a gentle brush, but I've spent too many nights thinking about this moment to rush it.

"Princess," I rasp against her lips. "Just say the word and I'll stop."

It'll take every bit of self-control to do what I've just promised, but up until last night, she thought she was marrying another man. I don't want to take advantage of her vulnerability, don't want her to do anything she'll regret.

"I want the opposite of stop," she breathes. "I want it all."

It's all the permission I need.

I keep things slow, warming her up, guiding her to trust me, daring her to want me as much as I'm desperate for her. Guiding her into a kiss that I want more than anything in the world.

She responds in kind, deepening the kiss, pressing her body into me. Tracing her bottom lip with my tongue, I delve deeper. Her lips open and our tongues find each other. Desperate. Seeking. Satisfying beyond anything I could've imagined.

The heat in my truck blasts into the triple digits as our kiss goes on and on. Her quiet sighs and moans grow louder, and her hands roam over my shoulders and back before coming to the nape of my neck and pushing into my hair.

We deepen the kiss until I can't tell where each of us begins or ends. It goes on and on. Day turns into night, for all I know. What's certain is that I'm exactly where I want to be for maybe the first time in my life.

Briefly breaking the kiss, we stare at each other in disbelief. "God, Archer. If I'd known this was how it felt to kiss you, I'd have done it the first day we met."

This. This is how people fall in love.

It strikes me like a shock of lightning from a storm I didn't see coming. The obsessive thinking about only one woman. The inability to sleep. The anger about any part of my day that didn't involve her. I'm not saying I'm in love—that's crazy. It's just…that thing that always felt like other people could find it and I'd always somehow be on the outside…it doesn't feel so impossible anymore.

From one kiss.

That's when I realize how fucked I really am.

No matter what happens after this, I will never be the same. I'll know what it's like to feel this, and I'm never getting over it.

Ella slides over so she's fully on my lap and grinds circles against my cock. I groan, "Careful. You're playing with fire." She gives a sly smile on her face that says she knows exactly what she's doing to me. And she loves every second of it.

"Tell me what you want. Tell me and I'll do it."

I know she's just talking about sex, but I hear the words the way I want to—I hear her tell me she's mine.

"Not here," I grit out.

"Why not?" she breathes against my shoulder, grinding harder. Her breathing is ragged, and I know I could make her come if I shift my hips a little bit, move up against her. But that's not happening.

"I'll make you a deal, princess. Let me drive us back to my house and I promise I'll make it up to you."

She pulls back and I chafe at the space between us, not realizing until that moment how right it felt to hold her close. It's like she belongs there, pasted up against me.

It's only two miles.

I drive like hell.

CHAPTER 22

Ella

ARCHER PULLS the car to a stop as close to the house as he can get without ramming through the front door. Even then, we can't get inside fast enough.

Before I'm out of the car, Archer has already slammed his door shut and walked to my side in three long strides. He sweeps me up into his arms and carries me through the front door, which doesn't seem to be locked. I loop an arm around his neck, and he pulls me tight against his chest.

"I hope you didn't have anything planned for today," he says, taking the stairs two at a time.

"Nothing I can't cancel." I think I know what he has in mind, and I am there for it.

"Good. Because I'm not letting you do anything that doesn't involve my hands on your skin."

Cue full body swoon.

We reach the doorway of his bedroom, and I peek in at the

immaculate space that's mostly decorated in tan and off-white linen. Fierce sunlight streams through the open blinds of an east-facing window, and somehow, he had the wherewithal to throw the duvet cover over his bed before he left the room so that it looks well-made.

"Sounds like you have an idea or two for how I should spend my day," I tease, taking in the king-sized bed that seems extra luxurious with giant pillows.

"I have ideas for how you should spend all your days."

Laying me gently on top of the covers, Archer leans over me and drops his lips to mine, and the soft sweep of his mouth takes the breath from my lungs.

It's not like anything I've experienced before, not from a fling and not from any of the short relationships I've had since I first kissed a guy in sixth grade. I thought I knew what it felt like to have my body respond to a kiss, but this…this is every cell in my body lining up and chanting Archer's name, all calling on him to kiss me longer, harder, deeper.

He does, rolling his hips against mine and driving his erection right where I need the friction. My hips buck up to meet his and I wrap my legs around his waist to pull him closer.

"Better," I breathe. "Don't you dare move."

We pick up where we left off on the driveway, only with less hesitation. We've had an hour in the car to work up all kinds of heat and frustration, and now it's all roaming hands and desperate kisses.

He teases me, circling his hips against mine until I'm so hot and bothered I'm sighing and then he backs away, leaving me wanting. His smirk says he knows exactly what he's doing, exactly how he's torturing me. And it's the best kind of pain.

Pushing himself up to a kneeling position, he looks at me with the rapturous eyes of a predator who wants to devour everything in his wake. And I want to be devoured. After weeks of thinking about him, being near him, and walking away each damn time, I want him so much now it hurts.

Archer takes my hand and pulls me up to sit. "Come. Here," he growls, eyes darting from my lips to my breasts, like he can't decide where to begin. Lifting my shirt gingerly over my head, he sinks his lips into my shoulder, kissing his way up the side of my neck and making me shudder with each new area of skin he touches.

"God, Archer. If it feels this good when you kiss my neck, I'm gonna die when you're inside me."

It's like I've flipped a switch. His responding growl sounds like he's being tortured. "Don't talk like that, princess, or I'll have to punish you in all sorts of sensual ways that you will fucking love."

Game on.

He pulls down the straps of my bra and massages my breasts, making my nipples throb and beg for attention.

Reaching behind my back, I snap the clasp, and the bra falls to the bed. Archer stares at my breasts and licks his lips. He drops down to take one nipple into his mouth. It goes hard under the wet massaging motion of his tongue. So hard that it starts to ache.

He massages the other breast with his hand and keeps working my nipple with his tongue until I cry out from the delicious ache.

Lavishing the other nipple with equal treatment, Archer looks like a man feasting at a banquet. Starved and sated at the same time.

"I want you inside me," I rasp against his neck. "So badly. Having you so close to me in the wine cave and not being able to touch you made me insane."

"Fuck, princess. I warned you."

"I know," I breathe against his neck, licking my way to his ear until he hisses with pleasure.

We're quickly losing control, clothing flying off. I pull at his belt and unfasten it. He tears off his shirt. I push down his jeans, and he rips them down his legs and tosses them to the floor.

Now, clad only in silk boxer briefs, Archer looks like a marble sculpture, all abs and pecs and muscles I can't even name. "How do you look like that?" I gasp, reaching for the hot skin that stretches taut over his abs. Running my fingers up and down the rippling muscles gives me chills.

I notice him smirking at me, thoroughly enjoying how much I'm enjoying his body.

Win-win. I'm good with it.

I let my hands roam up over his pecs, which are chiseled and hard from who knows how many hours at the gym. I say a little prayer to the gym gods for stocking extra dumbbells or whatever is necessary for Archer to look like this.

He flinches when I run a nail beneath the waistband of his boxers, shivering as I feather his skin with my nails. I move my hand lower until I reach his hard cock, which feels so good in my hand I let out a sigh. "I mean, really?"

He chuckles and I push the waistband down, freeing him so I can get a nice good look. "Yeah, I'm really gonna need you inside me. Not kidding around here."

"Okay, that's it. Last warning."

With moves of a ninja, he flips me onto my back and peels my pants down so slowly I think I might die from anticipation. He inhales and gradually lets his breath out as he rolls my panties down the length of my legs.

"Well, we're both naked now. No time to waste," I say, trying to keep the nervousness from my voice because, well, I'm nervous about how big he is. I may come off like I'm ready for him to impale me, but…what if I can't take it?

He must see the trepidation on my face because his smile turns to a smirk. "We are not going to rush this, princess. No fucking way."

And he doesn't.

He slowly, torturously moves down on the bed until his face is between my legs, which he spreads gently apart. For such a gruff man, he's as gentle as a saint. Featherlight touches with his hands. His tongue slowly following. Up the sensitive skin inside each thigh.

Until he reaches my center. He blows a light breath against my wet flesh, and I shudder. Then his tongue sinks in for a long, slow lick.

I'm done with sassy banter now because it's all I can do to stay conscious. The things he's doing with his tongue are probably outlawed in several states. He's so attentive, so thorough. Every lick and suck has me writhing on the bed.

It's shameless how much I want him inside me, even as he's delighting me in so many other ways, bringing me higher, closer to orgasm.

He thrusts a finger inside me, curling it against me until I moan. It's the perfect combination of friction and soft strokes. Then he sucks my clit. Hard.

And I fall off the edge of the planet. Even though I know the Earth is round.

What I know and don't know becomes irrelevant because *this* I know: Archer Corbett is giving me the best orgasm I've had in my entire life, and he's not even done.

I've barely recovered from shouting his name and mewling for him like a kitten when he pushes his boxers the rest of the way off. Rolling to the side, he makes quick work of grabbing a condom from his nightstand, ripping open the package, and rolling it on.

Then slowly, gloriously, he pushes inside me.

Gone are my thoughts about his size because his size is perfect. We're two sides of the same coin. Yin and yang. Made for each other, or at least that's how it feels in this moment of extreme pleasure.

"Princess, you're so tight. So wet for me. I've thought about you so many nights when I was alone…"

His words come out in a rhythm, like a chant he's combining with the motion of his hips, circling and grinding against me. Thrusting harder. Taking me higher. Until…

He's shouting my name on an oath and I'm moaning and digging my nails into his back. And we're both coming apart, falling apart, losing our ever-loving minds.

"Holy shitballs."

Archer starts to laugh, and I realize I'm the one who just said that.

"Sorry. Unfiltered."

"No, princess. Never be sorry for that. That was the best thing ever." Our hearts are pounding, seemingly in unison, as he lays on top of me panting. I'm sweating and heaving indelicately beneath him. And all I can think to say is, "Let's do that again."

And we do. All night long.

CHAPTER 23

rcher

"I borrowed this. Hope it's okay," Ella says, padding into my kitchen wearing an old gray shirt of mine that was sitting on the folded laundry pile in my room. It's worn and nearly see-through in places. Her pert nipples are outlined in perfect detail by the sheer fabric and the hem is just short enough for me to see that she's not wearing anything underneath.

Standing in front of my stove in sweatpants, I finish beating a bowl of eggs and milk and let the mixture slide into a pan of sizzling butter.

"Princess, it's okay if you wear it every damn day. Nothing on the planet is sexier than you in my shirt. C'mere."

Ella seems tentative as she comes closer, but as soon as she's within reach, I pull her to me and wrap her in my arms. Her body relaxes and I bend to kiss her. Our lips fuse, bodies melt. In moments, we're both breathless. Ella puts a hand on my chest and pushes back a few inches to look at me. "So it wasn't my imagination."

"What?" I ask.

She gestures between us. "This. Our chemistry. It really is that good."

"It's that good." I kiss her again, slower this time, easing into the feel of her lips melting against mine, loving having her hands on my skin. I hear an angry popping in the pan and break the kiss. "Shit."

The eggs are stuck to the pan, dried out and browned in places. I scrape the mixture away to try to salvage what I can of my scramble. "Not sure this is edible," I admit, looking at the unappetizing plate. It makes me recall days back when I was a teenager and our mother had just moved out. With four younger siblings waiting for breakfast and our father upstairs working, I did my best to make eggs and toast for everyone, having never made toast, let alone cracked an egg.

A fair amount of eggshell ended up in the mix and the scramble burned because I didn't know to add butter to the pan. My siblings were content enough to have something resembling breakfast, but when our dad came downstairs, he sniffed the air. "Thought I smelled something burning."

"I made eggs," I said proudly, anticipating his appreciation for getting everyone fed without being asked.

He took a forkful from PJ's plate and crunched down on a piece of eggshell. Wincing, he spit the bite into the sink. Two days later, we had a full-time nanny who did all the cooking.

I sigh at the reality that all these years later, I haven't improved much.

"It looks great. Do you have some cheese? With enough melted cheese we won't even see the eggs."

A wave of warmth floods my body and the ache that lives deep in my chest eases a tiny bit. "Deal."

She goes to the refrigerator and finds the cheese drawer, returning a moment later with a block of cheddar. "We can put the eggs on toast and leave them under the broiler for a sec to melt the cheese."

"That's some next level cooking, princess. And here I figured you had a staff to fetch you green juice and twenty-dollar acai bowls."

She sticks her tongue out at me. "When are you going to stop doing that?"

"What?" I open a drawer and take out a cheese grater.

"Making assumptions about me. You think I'm this celebrity diva who doesn't live like a normal person." She takes the grater from my hand and starts working on the cheese, attacking it with such gusto that shreds fly everywhere and very few end up in a pile on the counter.

"Sorry." I kiss the tip of her nose. "No more assumptions. I like everything about you."

The toaster dings and I use the distraction to avoid answering her questions. Retrieving the toasted sourdough slices, I put them on a plate and start piling my ugly eggs on each piece. I slide the plates across the counter to Ella. "Here you go. Ready for cheese."

She sprinkles cheddar on top of the eggs, and I put everything back in the toaster oven to broil. Then I fill up a coffee mug and beckon her toward me. She moves around the island block, and I wrap a hand around her waist to pull her close. "I can't have you that far away," I say, nuzzling the sweet-smelling skin of her neck. She purrs and drapes her hand over my shoulder, fingers brushing the back of my neck.

With both hands on her hips, I lift her onto the tile counter and lean into her. She wraps her legs around my waist and dips her head down to kiss me. In less than five seconds, I forget all about our breakfast, completely sated by the taste of her. The ding of the toaster breaks our kiss, and I reluctantly move away.

"Don't think you're escaping that conversation. I want to know why you're so hung up about LA," she says, hopping down from the counter. I stay focused on the toast, calculating the odds that I can distract her in some other way. When she comes up behind me and wraps her arms around my waist, I decide my odds are good. I turn toward her and bend to kiss her again, but she leans away, wagging a finger. "Down, boy. No treats for you until you talk."

"Did you just reprimand me like a puppy?"

She shrugs. "Are you trying to misbehave like one?"

Bouncing my eyebrows, I can't resist the idea of misbehaving just a little bit more. She squeals as I scoop her up in my arms and start marching toward the staircase that leads back to my bedroom. "Princess, you have no idea."

Her arms loop around my neck and she giggles. "Fine. Be that way. But eventually, we're gonna talk."

I reach the top of the stairs, and my lips are on hers. It's a deep, searching, desperate kiss that I may not recover from. No more talking.

AFTER A SEX MARATHON that has us both splayed out on our backs panting, Ella rolls to the side and puts her cheek on my chest. "I'll melt cheese on toast for my man every day of the week, if *that's* the result." She sighs, and I've never felt anything better in the world than this woman claiming me as hers.

Twisting my fingers through the strands of her hair, I want to pinch myself to make sure this is real. Ella pushes herself up and faces me, cross-legged. "Okay. Is this where I get to ask you all the things I've been dying to know?"

I chuckle, wondering what she could possibly be dying to know. "Have you been idly waiting, just hoping to get me into bed so you could pepper me with questions? Is that your game, lady?"

"I told you I was a nerd. I like information."

I don't share things with people unless I have to, but all bets are off with her. Something about her openness makes me want to give as good as I get.

"Fine. What do you want to know?"

She sits up and rubs her hands together like she's hatching a plan. "What does the Great Grumpy Grape do for fun, other than roll heads and growl at passersby, of course?"

"You're never going to let that nickname go, I'm guessing."

"Not a chance. So spill, Triple G."

"I, um, I run." Tucking my hands behind my head, I feel like that went well enough. One question, one hobby.

But she shakes her head. "Nope, not good enough. What's something you like to do that not many people know about? Come on, Grape, let me get to know you better."

"Okay. Well…I…play hockey."

"Wait, what? How did I not find this out earlier? It's my absolute favorite sport."

I immediately regret telling her because a hockey fan will have expectations, and I'm just an amateur player in a rec league. So I offer what I can. "Well, if that's the case, I can probably hook you up. My brother-in-law plays for the Oakland Otters." I can feel my face redden. "I guess you don't need me pulling favors when you're a celebrity. You could probably get a seat at center ice anytime you want."

She holds up a hand. "Okay, first, I don't do that celebrity front-of-the-line shit…at least not very often." I smile at that. "And second, I want to see *you* play, not some team anyone could watch."

A muscle in my jaw ticks as I try not to smile even wider, but I lose the battle.

"If you want to watch, I'll get you the best seat in the house. Which means somewhere on uncomfortable bleachers with the wives and girlfriends of the other sad sacks I play with."

"Perfect. I'm in. Can I really come watch you?"

"Princess, nothing would make me happier."

rcher

THE ICE-O-PLEX FEELS COLDER than usual. Actually, I've never noticed the temperature before. By the time I put on the padding under my pants and jersey and slide on my gloves, I have so much extra layering that I can't wait to get onto the ice and move around. And once we start playing, I'm only focused on my teammates, my opponents, and the puck.

Tonight is different, though, because I can see Ella sitting on the bleachers in the middle of the WAGS—the wives and girlfriends that make up our unofficial fan club. A few diehards stick around after their games and watch us play, but they don't care who wins. They're as likely to be avoiding chores at home as they are to be interested in our team. But the WAGS, they're our diehard crew, they're there to cheer us on, whoop and catcall when we score, and generally make us feel like NHL all-stars. I've never invited a woman to come watch me play before, but there's always enough hyped-up adulation from the others to go around.

I've also never invited a professional hockey player to substitute for one of our regulars before. But that was before Dominick "Ren" Renaldi became my future brother-in-law and every guy on my rec team started pestering me to bring him out to a game. "He doesn't want to watch your sorry asses fumbling around the ice," I'd told them, even though I'm quite proud of our team and our ten-and-two record in the league this season. I wasn't even going to mention it to Ren because I didn't want to put him in the uncomfortable place of having to turn me down, but then Beatrix went and brought up this week's game.

"You should go," she urged him when I stopped by last week to drop off a taster of the wine we're about to bottle. So far, I've succeeded at keeping my involvement with Ella under wraps because I don't want my sister in my business, and she's already running around like a headless chicken now that Ella asked her to quietly put the wedding plans on hold. She didn't tell Trix the reason, and I can't explain that she has to work with her public relations team on what to say about splitting with Callum. It all has to be timed right, and she wants her lawyer to weigh in about her adoption prospects if she tries as a single parent.

I've tried to push down my fear that she'll work things out with that ass wipe for the sake of adopting a baby, but things have felt too fragile and perfect to rock the boat with what-ifs.

"I doubt he wants to see a bunch of amateurs bat around a puck."

"Better yet, you should play!" Trix said.

"You're hilarious," I told her, backing out of her kitchen before Ren had to make up some excuse for why he couldn't come.

"Hey, wait, could I do that? Would that break any of your rules? 'Cause I'd do it for sure."

I was halfway down the hall when I heard his response. At least, I thought I heard him correctly. No, he had to be talking to Beatrix about something else entirely. Poking my head back into the kitchen, I prepared myself to hear a discussion between my sister and her fiancé about some questionable sexual position. And I prepared myself to gag.

But Ren was nodding at me and pumping a fist. "Oh, yeah. I'm so in, man."

It had taken me more than four months after meeting Ren to mention quietly that I play in an amateur ice hockey league. Eventually, my sister outed me, and Ren has been nothing but gracious, offering to watch game tape—as though we have any— and give me pointers. I was so dumbfounded by his interest in joining our team for a game that I found myself nodding and giving him all the details of where and when he needed to show up. Only later did it occur to me that this was the same game I'd invited Ella to come watch. I somehow needed to keep Ren from noticing Ella and reporting back to Beatrix that I'd invited her there.

And here we are. Not only am I playing tonight for the woman I can't stop thinking about, but I'm doing it in the shadow of one of pro hockey's biggest stars.

Fuck. Me.

As we warm up and pass the puck around the ice, I sneak a look at where Ella takes a sneaky sip from an insulated coffee mug that I know is full of wine. The complex has a strict no-alcohol rule, and it's just as strictly ignored by the crew of women who coordinate their mugs of choice and fill them in the parking lot before each game. By the end of the first period, their cheers are always noticeably louder. I've never cared one way or another whether people drink at our games, but tonight, I'm kind of hoping Ella forgets her glasses or gets tipsy enough to have wine goggles when it comes to my playing. I want her to have a good time, but the macho idiot in me also wants her to think I'm as talented as Ren. Yes, I know that's impossible, but a man can dream.

Ella looks adorable with a pink wool scarf wound around her neck and a matching hat with a pompom. Her hair spills over her shoulders and her smile stretches her cheeks as she cups her coffee mug in her hands. The guys on my team and their wives and girlfriends assume Ella is there to watch Ren, which makes more sense than her coming with me.

My chest strains under my jersey as my heart thunders like a drum. I'm in decent shape from running and playing hockey every week, so I know I'm not breathless for lack of fitness. It's just the effect of her.

It's an unsettling feeling, one I like a little too much.

"Arch, look alive," Carson yells as a puck comes sailing toward my shin. I stop it with my stick and send it back where it came from, reminding myself to keep my focus on the ice. The last thing I need is to be caught in dreamland and get hit in the face. Even with a helmet, something like that could knock out a tooth, not to mention the humiliation I'd face.

Casting one more look at Ella, I hope she's not too cold or bored. The other women seem to be keeping her busy with wine and conversation, so I talk myself down and put on my game face. "We ready, boys?" I shout, looking up at the scoreboard, where the clock is ticking down to our final two minutes before game time.

My teammates bring it in, and we huddle near our team bench. Carson is the captain, but everyone is looking to Ren for direction. Defeat washes over me as I accept that my job tonight is to get out of Ren's way and let the limelight shine on the guy who deserves it. I'm just a bit player here, but at least I'm in good company with the rest of the guys on my team.

The ref starts our game and our opponent's entire defense mobs Ren before he can get near the puck. Their defensive strategy seems to be entirely focused on boxing Ren out of the game, which ends up working in our favor. I race to the crease and Carson sends the puck flying toward me. It's an easy shot on goal, but their goalie is quick, deflecting it back to center ice.

Their guys can't seem to settle down, leading to an offsides call and a high-sticking penalty within the first five minutes of the game. Our cheering section goes nuts when the clock starts on our power play. Carson passes to me, and I see a clean opening to take a shot, but I also see Ren, who's moving away from the pack of defenders. I mentally calculate whether my odds are better taking the shot myself or handing it off to a guy with some of the best stats in the pros. Much as I want to impress Ella, I take the safe bet, passing cleanly to Ren.

A defender backchecks him in a flash, and he loses the tiny opening he has. I fly past him on the ice, giving him a passing opportunity I doubt he'll take, not when he can easily outmaneuver the defender. I'm well-positioned, but it's pointless when Ren is faster than everyone out here and quickly finds an opening to move toward goal. All I can do is watch, awed by his grace and speed. It's what drew me to the sport all those years ago when I picked up a stick and played on roller blades.

But Ren's skill comes from doing the unexpected. Instead of taking a shot, he bats the puck around the back of the goal with a defender on him and moves back toward center ice. I watch his eyes flick to the stands where our little cheering section is going nuts, chanting "Ren, Ren," like a mantra. Then he looks at me, and something in his eyes tells me to start moving toward the goal. I do it and watch Ren take another loop around the rink with two defenders chasing him. Which means I'm open. He sees the opportunity, passes me the puck, and I see a clear shot on goal.

I take it. The goalie crouches and tries to block my slapshot, but the angle is too sharp. The puck glides into the net and the goal buzzer sounds, reverberating through the near-empty complex, making the small victory that much sweeter. Only then do I dare glance up into the stands, and there I see Ella jumping up and down, clapping against her coffee mug and screaming my name. Best fucking thing I've ever heard.

~

A COUPLE HOURS LATER, we're all gathered at the Dark Horse the way we usually do after games, but again, tonight feels different.

With Ella sitting next to me and holding my hand surreptitiously under the table, it feels like I've won the goddamn lottery. My one goal was followed by a Renaldi hat trick that made me look like the minor leaguer I am, but I don't even care. I'm the one with Ella Fieldstone's hand in my lap, even if I'm the only one who knows it. I'm not letting her out of my sight.

"I was so nervous watching you, but it was fun!" She's been chattering nonstop since the game ended and she raced down to the ice and fist bumped all the players. Only difference when it was my turn was the sly grin she gave me when she tapped my fist. "I'll be back in a sec." Wriggling off the bench, she trails behind two of my teammates' wives toward the bathroom and I watch her adorable ass waggle until I can't see her anymore. When I turn back to the table, I see Carson smirking at me like he's just won a bet.

"What?" I ask, grimacing into my beer.

"You've got it so bad for her. It's awesome to see, man."

"Whatever. I was just checking to make sure she knew where to go. It's her first time here."

"Bullshit," Ren coughs into his hand, making me realize for the first time that he's listening. Looking up over my shoulder, I see him standing behind me, gloating.

I shrug. "So, I like her. Not sure why that's so amusing to you all." I need to curtail this conversation before any more of my teammates get wind of it. They're always up in my business, asking why I don't ever bring a date to watch our games. This, right here. This is the reason. I like to keep my personal life personal.

Ren pulls a chair over from the next table and wedges it in next to Carson, swinging a leg over the seat and leaning his elbows on the table. "Because she's engaged to another guy, for one thing."

"That's…not my story to tell, but it's not how it looks," I say, wanting to protect her honor but also let her handle how and when she reveals her personal life to the public.

He gives me a knowing look. "Okay, I understand 'complicated.' And I know Trix has been going nuts over the wedding, so I'm living with it too. I'll let you sort out your own business. Just saying I like what I see." He downs the last of his beer with a smirk and signals to the bartender to bring us more drinks. "On my card," he instructs. "I've got this round."

"Don't think you can 'I've got this round' me into admitting anything else," I say, burying my face in my beer glass.

"You don't have to. It's written all over your damn face." He watches me, so I do my best to keep my face a mask of indifference. It's a test of wills I intend to win. I reach for my beer, but there's nothing left. "Nowhere to hide." Ren laughs. "Be careful. I don't want to see you hurt, man. And I won't tell your sister…yet. I'm giving you time to tell her yourself. But if you don't tell her soon, then I will. Trix and I don't keep secrets from each other."

I try to get my brain around the idea that the guy who's been nearly single-handedly steering his team toward the Stanley Cup this year is acting like we're bros—the kind he'll protect from the wrath of my sister. His fiancée. It surprises me so much that I don't have a ready response.

Fortunately, the bartender shows up with a tray of fresh pints for us all and starts clearing the empty glasses and replacing them with full ones. Ella has been sipping a glass of cider, which is still half full. I move it next to my full glass. Before I can respond to Ren, the women are back, and Ella reassumes her position next to me. She takes note of Ren, who is grinning like a loon.

"I don't think we've formally met." She extends her hand, which requires her to bend her elbow against her breasts. "I'm Ella."

"Ren."

"Nice playing out there. You guys all looked great."

"Ren's a real hockey player," I explain, filling Ella in on his career highlights like some kind of hockey groupie. "He's captain of the Oakland Otters," I finally conclude, noticing that Ren and Ella have the same bewildered look on their faces. "What?"

"Just that I already knew who Ren was before your greatest hits lecture, but seeing you blush over hockey stats is freakin' adorable."

"And I was just thinking you should be telling her about your own stats, not mine," Ren says, turning the full wattage of his smile on Ella with a wink. My fists ball and I nearly take a swipe at him before I realize he's still talking. About me. "Archer here is a lefty—he's got a slapshot that's as good as some of the pros. Did you know a lot of Canadians shoot left-handed because they grew up playing hockey and they use their stronger right hand on top of the stick, which makes them natural lefties. But here in the US, Archer has the advantage." Ella listens, attention fully focused on him like he's telling the most absorbing bedtime story. I can't help but sit with my jaw hanging open, wondering why he's bothering to talk me up.

I never get the chance to ask him because a bunch of my teammates ambush him and drag him to the middle of the bar for a series of selfies. "Just please don't post these on your socials, guys. My coach'll have my head if he knew I just risked injuring myself in a non-league scrimmage."

Ella leans her head against my chest, and I see the weight of her eyelids fan her eyelashes over her cheeks. "You tired, princess?" She nods.

"I can rally, though, if you want to stay out with the guys." She can barely keep the yawn from her voice and it's all I can do not to bundle her up on my lap and pet her hair until she falls asleep like a kitten.

"I don't want to stay out with the guys. Not when I could stay in with you. Let's go."

I follow her to the door of the bar without saying goodbye to anyone. On the off chance anyone notices, I turn and give a salute to the bar as a whole before I ghost the place. They'll either chalk it up to me being grumpy or they'll realize that for the first time in my life, I have somewhere I'd rather be than in a bar talking about hockey plays. And someone I'd much rather be with.

CHAPTER 25

rcher

ELLA'S FOOT taps nervously on the floor where she sits in an armchair in my office. At least I think it's nerves. Maybe she's tapping the beat to a song only she can hear.

"I don't want to tell her. Is she going to hate me?" she asks, her forehead etched with worry. Nope, nervous.

"C'mere," I say, standing up behind my desk and going to her. I walk her to the large paned window and stand behind her, looking over her shoulder. "Look at that view," I instruct, pointing at the miles of vines creeping up Buttercup Hill to where they disappear in the morning mist. The sun shines through the watery air in silver sheets, lighting up the grape leaves and casting a glow on everything in view. "You can't be upset about anything in the world when you look at that view, right?"

She laughs and turns in my arms. "Are you honestly asking me that, Grumpy Grape? I seem to remember you scowling your way through the fields with this exact view when we met. More than once."

"What can I say? I'm a changed man. And I'll admit, the view is much, much better when you're standing here in my arms, looking at it with me." I lean down to kiss her. It's a can't-get-enough-of-her kiss.

A throat clears behind us and Ella looks over my shoulder and grimaces. I turn around and we both face Beatrix, who stands with her arms crossed and a quizzical look on her face. "You called a meeting," she says, not moving from the doorway.

"I did." I beckon her in, but she doesn't move. Neither does Ella, feet rooted to the floor by the window. I walk slowly around to my desk and take a seat. "Do you want to come in?"

"No," she corrects, pointing at Ella. "*You* called a meeting. I was headed to the restaurant to see you, but I had a question for Archer."

"Right. About that. I was about to go to the restaurant too."

"What is this?" She points between the two of us.

Ella steps forward and smooths her hands down the front of her skirt. Holding her shoulders back, she speaks slowly, unapologetically. "I'm no longer engaged to Callum, so I need to cancel the wedding here. There'll be a press announcement about Callum, but I wanted you to hear it from me. Whatever you need to charge me for time already spent, or losses if you can't re-rent the venue, I'll cover. And I so appreciate all the time you put in on details. I know it would have been the loveliest event, but not with the wrong man." Ella gives her a polite smile and turns to me.

I beckon her closer with a nod. She walks over and hugs me around the shoulders, before walking to the door of my office. "I guess we don't need to meet at the restaurant," she tells Trix. "Thanks for understanding. I wanted to tell you in person." Nodding again, she looks at me before walking out.

I turn to my sister. "Obviously, we'd have preferred to talk to you before you saw that," I say, pointing at where we were standing by the window.

Trix looks like her brain might explode. She shakes her head and wags her finger at me. "Is this why the wedding was 'postponed indefinitely'? You're the reason it's now canceled?" Her gaze flits from the doorway to me. "I told you not to torpedo this for us, Archer, so why did you?"

I hold up a hand. "It's not what you think."

"No? So what is this? You *not* trying to torpedo the wedding by sleeping with the bride?"

"Hey, cool it." I point to the chair in front of my desk. "If you sit down, I'll explain."

Slowly, stubbornly, she walks to the chair and drops into it. "Explain."

"I love her." I can't keep the smile from flooding my face. "I know what I said about hating her and not wanting the wedding here, but then my stubborn ass got to know her. She's so different. So special." I can't believe I'm confessing these feelings to my sister, who will undoubtedly give me shit about them later, but I feel how I feel. "I've never met anyone like her and she's... changed me. I feel myself getting lighter, being easier about life. Starting to reconsider things I was never willing to think about before. And if I could have avoided falling for her, I would have. But it was impossible. She's amazing."

I wait for my sister to yell at me some more about screwing up her plans for the magazine spread about the wedding of the decade, but instead, I find her smiling at me.

"Really?"

"Really, what?" I'm confused.

"You're in love? My grumpy brother is in love?" She stands from her chair and comes around the desk. "Screw the wedding of the decade. I'm just so happy for you."

I'm too stunned by her reaction to say anything.

"Really. So happy. Will you bring her to hang with us? Bring her to Dash's taco fest."

"I'll...I can see if she wants to go."

"Bring her." She wags a finger. Then she leans down and whispers in my ear, "And I'm going to keep that wedding date open. No pressure because I know you're a guy and you have to do your guy brooding about everything. Just saying...it's there if you should happen to know anyone in need of a wedding." She hugs me and practically skips out the door of my office.

CHAPTER 26

lla

"I'm a little bit embarrassed for dragging you here," I tell Tatum, who sits on the love seat at the foot of the hotel room I rented so I don't overstay my welcome at her house. She sits patiently as I wheel an entire rack of clothing that my stylist sent over.

At first, after I broke up with Callum, our publicists resisted, and Callum begged me to reconsider. I refused, but it's taken a while for everyone to agree on how to frame our uncoupling. Until I talk to my adoption lawyer, I don't want to say anything that might derail my plans. It's meant that Archer and I have spent our time at Buttercup Hill, out of public view. I don't need prying eyes wondering what we are to each other. Especially when I'm not sure myself. I just know I really like him, which means I want to make a good impression on his family members at their taco fest later on.

Behind Tatum, my bed is unmade, and the bright morning sun feels like it's pointing a finger at the messy beige blankets after a poor night's sleep. I adjust the blinds so it's not quite so glary, but nearly everything in the room is white or cream, so it still screams *bright* in here.

"Don't be. I had to be over here anyway. I have something to tell you."

My eyes go wide. "Pregnant?" I ask, looking at her flat belly.

"No, not that. But close. You know Becca."

"Your sister? Yeah, I think we've met a few thousand times."

"Don't be a pill or I won't tell you. I brought my mah jong tiles. We can just play quietly." She gestures to her purse, and I stare at it, worried it may actually contain a mah jong set.

"Sorry. What's up?"

"There was a baby left at the Safe Surrender in the hospital where she works."

My eyes go wide because I know where she's going with this. Becca is an obstetrical nurse at Alta Bates Hospital in Oakland. I rush to the love seat and hug Tatum. "Oh my God, oh my God."

"I know. I don't know how adoptions work, but your lawyer should work on it. Maybe you can adopt her."

I'm already dialing my cell phone, pacing in circles. When my lawyer answers, I put her on speakerphone and spew information and questions at her for ten minutes straight until she assures me that my chances are very good if she gets moving quickly. "Don't get your hopes too high, but let's be cautiously optimistic. All your paperwork looks great so there's every reason to think you're a good candidate here. Let's set a meeting for this week and we can get into it."

I hang up and hug Tatum again. "Oh my gosh." I feel stunned at the idea that I might be able to adopt this baby, but also heartbroken about the circumstances that led her to be left at a Safe Surrender. "I've always imagined this moment, but I didn't expect to feel so sad. I mean, I'm cautiously happy, but…this is a baby who was given up by her parents. She may never know them. It… breaks my heart."

"Maybe not, but she'll know you. And you will give her an amazing life. You'll give her all the love she needs."

The weight of it slams into me. The responsibility. The reality.

"What if the adoption courts are hesitant about me as a single mom? I thought I'd have time to put out a statement about breaking up with Callum and let the dust settle, but now…will I look unstable if news hits about our breakup right now?"

Tatum offers a sympathetic smile. "I don't know, sweetie."

I drop into a chair. "I think I'm kind of in shock."

"Understandable. Just…sit with it a while. Let your lawyer do her job and give yourself time. It's a lot of change all at once."

Nodding, I try to focus on picking an outfit, but it feels so frivolous in light of this. Tatum, who doubles as a best friend mind reader, nods. "I know. And everything is so new with Archer, and I can't even get my brain around where that could lead."

"Just…try to stay in the moment. It's okay to focus on the dress. And who knows, maybe you're seducing the future father of your child."

"No, nope. Not happening. He's not into having kids. I don't think that's even on his radar."

"Are you sure? People change their minds when they fall in love."

"Not sure it's love either."

She laughs. "I'm just going to ignore that because I've never seen a glow on you like this. Deny it all you want, but you, my friend, are in love."

I feel the blush creep across my face. Tatum doesn't suffer fools and it's silly to pretend in front of her. "I might love him," I whisper. "But that only complicates things because he doesn't want kids. He was serious about it."

I haven't wanted to broach the subject with Archer, and I'm still not sure I'm ready. "Like you said, I'm going to stay in the present," I say, running over to where she's relaxing on the couch. "Right after I hug you one more time. Thank you for being here for me. For everything."

"Honestly, since you ordered breakfast, I feel like I'm the one coming out ahead," she deadpans. She picks up one of the lattes from the low table in front of the love seat and takes a sip.

"Still, you'd think I could pick out an outfit on my own."

"This isn't just any outfit. This is a romantic meet-the-family outfit."

"Isn't that kind of an oxymoron? I want the family to think I'm sweet and appropriate for their brother. I don't want to romance them.

She waves a hand and takes a bite of a blueberry muffin. "They already know you're sweet and perfect for him. They'll love you. This is for your man. It needs to be casual but also seductive. It has to make Archer salivate and stare at you, just as he's picturing how you'll look later when the outfit hits the floor."

"That's a lot to expect from an outfit. Maybe I should just wear a sandwich board with instructions."

"Sure. Like 'Stare, Drool, Fuck'?"

Tatum has already eaten two croissants, half a bowl of berries, and now the muffin. I haven't touched a thing, other than the coffee. I'm too nervous to eat, which is silly because Archer and I have already been on plenty of "dates." They just weren't planned. Somehow, having a plan makes me feel like I need to prepare, but I'm not sure how. And now I'm wishing I hadn't brought Tatum into my circle of confusion. She still likes and respects me, but after seeing me go to pieces over outfits, she may decide I'm a mess.

"Might be simpler."

She brushes croissant crumbs from her sweater into a napkin and crumples it into a ball. Then she stands up and starts rifling through the outfits on the rack. "No. Too formal. Too cutesy. Too slutty..."

"Hey!"

She pulls out the dress in question and holds it against her body. I have to admit the plunging neckline and high slit up one thigh is probably appropriate for any kind of date Archer has planned. "I figure I should have options."

"Sweetie, if you wear this, the only option will be getting railed within five minutes of walking in the door."

"Tatum!" My mousy computer nerd of a friend isn't usually this direct.

"What? I'm not wrong."

I sigh. "You're not wrong."

"Fine. Not that dress, but I think I need something in case we're going to a nice dinner later or something."

She pulls out an ankle-length silk sheath that hugs every curve. "This one. Red lips, a bit of skin, a hint of the curves that lie beneath. It will drive him nuts. More of a tease, less of an overt invitation."

Nodding at the red dress, I have to admit she's right.

"Pretty much a sandwich board, after all."

rcher

AT FIRST, I don't recognize the woman who walks onto the sprawling wood deck at the back of Dash's house. I look away initially because I'm not about to ogle another woman, even if I'm curious who the woman is who walked confidently out the back door in a fire-engine red dress that's way too fancy for a backyard shindig.

Then I hear her laugh and my head jerks up, eyes hungry for the woman it belongs to. My heart thunders in anticipation of seeing Ella in that fucking red dress, which I can now see hugs every curve of her body. And she has curves galore. The red dress is like a flag and I'm a goddamn bull.

I put my margarita down on the picnic table in Dash and Mallory's yard and take long strides toward the deck, feeling the denim pull at my legs, keeping me from getting there as fast as I want to.

She reaches the bottom of the stairs and wobbles in her

sandals just when I get there, her hands extending toward me as I hold up my forearm for her to grab. Her fingers sink into the skin of my forearm, and I wrap my other arm around her shoulders, pulling her in tight. I lean in and inhale the sweet jasmine scent of her perfume and vow to myself that I'll never let her go.

"I never knew what it meant to take a person's breath away, but when I saw you in that dress, I forgot to breathe," I growl against her ear. I feel her shiver and stare down at the goose bumps on her bare arms, wanting to make her feel so much more than chills.

Her cheeks pink up at the compliment, and she leans her head on my shoulder. Her hair is untamed and curly, tickling my cheek as I breathe her in once more. I want to consume her.

I lead her to the table where I was sitting moments ago. "I just met Dash. What a sweetie. And very serious about his tacos," she says, casting a glance to the deck where Dash mans the barbecue in a green apron that says, "I cook as good as I look."

"He is indeed serious. The chicken has to be barbecued and hand-shredded, and he makes his own salsa and guacamole."

"Well, sure. You've gotta make those from scratch."

She's still gazing in my brother's direction, so I bring my fingers to her chin and turn her head back toward me, unapologetic about the need to have her looking only at me. "Spoken like a woman who knows her way around a kitchen?"

"Oh, yeah. I can make guac like the best of 'em, but I won't divulge my recipe."

Taking her by the hand, I walk her back toward Dash's house, where Mallory is in the kitchen putting together a crudité platter. "Wow. These family barbecues don't lack for food," Ella says.

"Yeah, it's a good thing that all of us live on the property because after the amount of food and wine we consume, we can barely waddle to our respective homes. And lucky me, I have the shortest walk," Mallory says.

I start to introduce them, but both women stop me with a

wave of the hand. "We met," they say in unison. They laugh and high-five each other, and I feel warmth spread in my chest at the idea of Ella blending with my family.

"I'm an only child, so this is like the family of siblings I never had," Ella says, accepting a margarita from Mallory and taking a sip. "Ooh, these are strong."

"Yeah, I put half a bottle of tequila in here," Mallory says, holding up a juice pitcher of margaritas.

"I'm all for you getting drunk and not being able to keep your hands off me, but that's not why I brought you in here," I say, calling for Dash to come inside.

He pokes his head in the door. "Yeah?"

"I think we've got ourselves a little guacamole competition." I point between him and Ella and watch the smile spread across his face. He's just slightly competitive about his cooking skills and I'm dying to see if Ella can show him up with some ingredient he never thought of. "Oh, wait," I realize, pulling Ella aside and whispering in her ear to ask what ingredients she needs.

She gives me her list, which requires me to run back to my house for a few ingredients, but by the time the rest of my siblings arrive, they're presented with two perfect-looking bowls of guacamole on the picnic table and one bowl of chips.

"Two guacamoles?" Fiona nods, impressed. Being the only nine-year-old at the barbecue, she's the odd one out, so I always like to give her a little extra attention.

"How's third grade, Fi? Any boys you like?"

She twirls her hair and thinks about it. "Only one, but he's into basketball, like, all the time, so that's not super fun."

"I could teach you some basketball if you want to give him a run for his money."

Nodding, she gives me a high five. "Let's do it. Now?"

"How about after we eat?"

I catch Ella smiling at me. I give her a little salute.

Margaritas are poured, and then Dash comes down the stairs

to make sure everyone's briefed on the rules before a single chip is eaten.

"Taste them both and decide which one is best. Loser has to do the dishes."

"Better get ready for dishpan hands, mister," Ella says, fluffing her hair and jutting a hip to the side.

I study both bowls, certain I've seen Dash's version enough times that I can figure out which one is Ella's, but they both look pretty much the same. "Which one's yours?" I lean in and ask Ella quietly, but Dash sees me do it.

"No way, no cheating," he says. "Mallowmar is the only one who knows which is which, other than Ella and me, so don't even think about trying to get an advantage." I cringe at his nickname for his wife, but then figure people would probably think Princess is just as bad.

Jax and Ruby each take a chip and taste the first bowl, chewing slowly. They wash down the taste with a healthy swig of margarita and taste the second version, nodding solemnly as though this is a royal competition.

The rest of us do the same, and Mallory hands out slips of paper, so we can vote secretly.

Then she shuffles through them and reads the results. When she's read the last one, her gaze turns to Dash, an upside-down smile on her face. "Sorry, honey."

Ella jumps up and down and extends her hand to Dash. "Good game, sir. Honestly, I loved your version. I think the cumin in mine is what tipped it."

"Damn cumin," Dash grumbles, making his way back to the house to assemble the rest of his dinner. "Whatever. Tacos in ten minutes. Save some guac to go on top."

Conversation erupts around the table, and everyone digs into the appetizers. Ella grabs a handful of baby carrots, but when she turns back toward me, her face falls. "Did I just kill his vibe? He's hosting us all, so I don't want to make him feel bad." She looks to where Dash is stomping up the steps to the deck.

"You did not kill his vibe. We Corbetts are a competitive bunch, so if anything, you just made him like you a little bit more."

I wrap my hand around hers and pull her close until she collides against my chest. She looks up at me, brow furrowed. "Are you sure?"

I nod, my eyes greedily taking in her milky skin, the apples of her cheeks, her rosy lips, which beg to be kissed. "I'm very sure."

Her smile tells me she understands that I'm no longer talking about Dash. I lower my lips to hers, barely brushing against them, barely tasting what I want from her. But I'm not going to grope her in front of my whole family.

"Aw, how cute are you two?" PJ asks.

There was a time when hearing that from my youngest sister would have annoyed me, but I'm too content right now to bother with any other emotion. "Very cute," I say, leading Ella away from the picnic table.

"We could get lost in the vineyards for a while. I'm sure no one would notice."

"Ha. I'm sure everyone would notice."

I shrug. "I'm the last single guy in the family. They know what these vineyards are for. Let 'em notice."

Ella's laugh fills the air as I take her by the hand and pull her toward the outer edge of the grass and beyond Dash's yard to where miles of vineyards take over. She drops my hand and starts running down a lane of vines, tossing a look back at me, daring me to chase her.

Don't have to tempt me twice.

And don't have to ask me if I really want to strip the red dress from my rom-com princess in the middle of a vineyard. The answer is always, "fuck yes."

CHAPTER 28

rcher

ELLA STRETCHES her full length like a cat taking in the sun's rays, only she's so petite that there's a full foot of space at the end of my couch. So I slide in beside her, tugging her feet to bring her closer, and drape her legs over my lap.

She settles in with a carefree hum, doing nothing to dispel the image of a contented feline. For a moment, I allow myself to sit with the image of the two of us here, as though it's real. Just a normal couple in love on the couch—not a woman who was engaged to someone else mere weeks ago and a man who loves her more than he should. Do they make Hallmark cards for that version of a couple?

"Do you have to drive back down to the Bay Area?" I ask, already knowing the answer. Ella told me she has an early meeting in San Francisco, so I know she'll need to sleep at home.

"Nope."

I can't have heard her correctly. "Wait, what?"

"I can stay." She pushes herself up onto her elbows so she can look at me. Sparkles dance in her eyes.

"You were planning this all along?" I ask, thinking back on how hard she made me work to figure out when I could see her again. She nods, her smile edging up the corner of her mouth, hair glowing in a messy halo around her with the afternoon sun that streams through the window.

"But I have conditions." She sits up, her face serious now.

"What are those?"

"I want to talk."

I nod. "Is this one of those 'we need to talk' discussions or just a regular conversation?" I can't help feeling like each time I see Ella could be the last. One of these days, she's going to get over her wine-boy fantasy and find a man who will father the children she wants to adopt.

"It's a regular conversation, but I have questions for you."

"Questions?"

"Yes. Those are the things people ask when they're unclear on something and want more information."

"I'm familiar."

"Good. All you need to do is answer. I ask, you answer. Easy. Like Ping-Pong." She mimes the motion of a Ping-Pong paddle returning a shot.

I lift her legs and scoot out from under them in order to get up. Making my way to the kitchen, I call back to her, "In that case, I'm having a beer. D'you want one?"

"Sure, if you have pretzels or chips to go with it." As usual, she surprises me with her response. I rummage through my pantry and return a minute later with two beers, an opener, and a bag of Baked Lays. I pop the caps off the beer bottles, and she rips open the bag of chips.

Sitting up on the couch now, she swivels to face me when I drop down next to her. "This looks serious," I observe, taking a sip of my beer. The bitter ale feels good on my throat, and I realize that I'm uneasy because I have no idea what she might ask me.

"Your dad," she says, leveling me with a stare. "Tell me about him."

I shrug and give my usual description. "Hard worker, driven to make this place into something." I gesture toward the vineyards out the window. "Clearly he succeeded."

Taking another sip, I wait for Ella to agree. Then I plan to move on. When I hear nothing, I look at her and find her resting her chin on a fist, waiting me out. "Okay, that's a nice story. Put that on the back of your Buttercup Hill brochure if it's not there already. How about the rest?"

It's too nice of a day to be inside doing this. I glance around my living room, searching for some shiny object I can use to distract her from asking questions about my dad. Instead, I lean forward and capture her lips with mine. She acquiesces instantly as I cup her cheek and my hand glides into her hair. There was no reason to look far and wide for a distraction.

Except that a moment later, she pushes me away with both hands against my chest. "Nice try, big guy. What else can you tell me about your dad?"

"You mean the dementia?"

She shakes her head. "No. Before that. What was he like?"

"Why do you want to know this so badly? Are you secretly doing research for a biopic about a winemaker?"

"No, but interesting idea." She folds her legs beneath her and shakes out her hair, sending the ribbons of curls skating over her shoulders.

I hem and haw and think about ways to avoid this conversation until it finally dawns on me that I want her to know me better. Which means I need to share this part of myself I'd rather keep hidden.

"My dad was tough. Hardworking, unforgiving of weakness, a real ballbuster...but I loved him. Still do."

"Does your feeling about not wanting to be a father have anything to do with him?"

I open my mouth to answer but no words come out. "No one's ever asked me that."

"I'm asking."

Running a hand through my hair, I try to harken back to the first time I concluded that I shouldn't have kids. It was some time around when I came back to Napa to take over for him. "I guess, partly. I just saw how limited he was as a parent when he was running the business. I never wanted to do that to a kid, never wanted to be a half-assed dad. And I have no choice about running the business, so…" I put up my hands. Discussion over, as far as I'm concerned.

"So that's it? You just sign up to be a working stooge and give up on your dream of having a family?"

"It's not like that, exactly. I guess I…never really had a dream of having a family, so it's not really giving anything up. My dad always saw me as a younger version of him, but drawing the line here is a way I can be better."

I wait for her reaction, assuming she'll try to argue me out of my stance. Instead, she nods and looks away.

"You're great with Fiona. I'm sure you'd be an awesome dad, but I understand how an idea can take hold and grow roots. Then, no matter what, no one can talk you out of it." She nods sadly. "Just like no one could talk me out of wanting to be a mom."

I can't tell if there's more she isn't saying, so I wait, but she curls up against me again, so I decide that maybe she's satisfied with my response. I thought it would be hard. I thought sharing my feelings about my dad would make me feel exposed.

With her, it feels like an unburdening. And when I watch her face, soberly taking in every detail, reaching for my hand when I have trouble articulating a feeling, nodding in understanding, not judgement…it feels like love.

So I keep going.

"I didn't want to be him. Desperately wanted to go my own way, prove I could do it differently. Be less of an asshole in the process, have a family I'd actually get to spend time with, find a world that wanted me for me, not just because of a legacy built by someone else."

"What kind of start-up?"

I shake my head. "It's not a great idea. I don't know what I was thinking back then. Now it sounds dumb, even to me."

Her hand tucks under my chin and she swivels my face to look at her. "Hey. Don't assume I'm going to reject your idea before I've even heard it. Try me."

Our faces are inches apart and I could close the distance and kiss her. That would end the discussion and I'd be spared seeing the look of disappointment on her face when she realizes I'm not as smart and innovative as I thought I was when I packed up and moved to LA. I like the idea that she thinks I'm a somewhat savvy winemaker and would really prefer to leave it at that.

"Come on, tell me," she urges quietly. Her accepting, patient eyes make me want to make her happy.

"Fine. It's basically a wine encyclopedia in an app. Kind of like the ones where you scan a leaf or a flower and the app tells you what kind of plant it is and where it grows, this would give you all the tasting notes for a bottle of wine based on scanning the label."

I wait for signs of boredom or disinterest, but she nods. "Go on."

"The app would tell you the best window to drink whatever bottle of wine you scan, and there are ecommerce opportunities with food pairings, so you could order grazing boards or full menus to go with specific wines and have it all delivered. There's more to it—other co-branding opportunities and revenue streams, but those are the basics."

Ella's expression goes blank. She shakes her head, and I worry that I've lost her in the details or maybe she realizes it really isn't a very good idea.

"Holy shit," she says finally. "I want that app."

"You do?"

"Um, yeah. It's a great idea. You didn't find investors for that? I'm surprised."

Pulling in a long deep breath, I debate whether to tell her the one bit of information I've withheld from everyone in my life, especially my siblings. Ella reaches over and picks up my hand. The warmth of her fingers intertwining with mine dissipates whatever resistance I have. If anyone is going to know my deepest secrets, I want it to be her.

"I did have one offer. A good one," I admit.

"That's amazing."

"But I couldn't take it." It hurts to say the words out loud. I explain how discouraged I'd been after every investor had reconsidered, how disheartened I'd felt that night at the party in the Hollywood Hills. I neglect to mention her part in it—how I'd almost folded my cards after she blew me off, how she somehow came to symbolize everything I'd never achieve in LA. But I don't want to pollute what feels so good now with detritus from the past.

The truth is that after she'd blown me off, I'd had a firm talk with myself and considered leaving LA, but I couldn't do it. Somehow the rejection by her and all the investors fueled me to seek out one more meeting with a venture capitalist who was even more flush with cash than anyone else I'd met with. It felt like a hail Mary, the kind you throw when you have nothing left to lose. She'd been the final push that got me there, and the next day, I reached out to a contact of a friend of a friend and got the meeting.

"My dad had a stroke. This was before the Alzheimer's diagnosis, but the end result was the same. I had no business pursuing some dream in LA when my dad needed me here to run the business for him. I had to come home, and the investor insisted that I be in LA to build the company with him or there was no deal."

I'd been looking at my lap while the words rushed out, trying to convey the information without having to think too long and hard about it. It was painful then and it's just as painful now, only now the situation with my dad is so much worse.

I feel Ella's hand softly graze my cheek and look up to find her looking as crushed by my story as I feel. Her eyes search my face as if trying to find evidence that there's more to the story, a happy ending that I'm holding out on her. I shake my head.

"I'm so sorry," she says.

"Thank you." I can barely get the words out, suddenly choked up by how much she cares. It's such a relief to have the truth out in the world finally, even if she's the only one who knows it. Especially because she's the only one who knows it.

"So that's it? You just had to walk away?"

"Yeah. It's been a fire drill twenty-four-seven since I've been back. Keeps getting worse every day, somehow, so there's no time to work on it."

"There has to be a way. It's too good of an idea to let it go to waste."

I lean toward her and kiss her temple. She's so good and sweet, so optimistic. It's hard to be the one to tell her there's no Santa Claus, but I need to make her understand.

"I have a responsibility to my family. I needed to take over for my dad, so here I am. I'm him."

"You're not him. You're doing his job, but you're a completely different person."

She hasn't even met him, but she says it with such certainty that I want to believe her. I want her to be right. I don't want to be my dad.

But it may already be too late to prevent it.

rcher

"I HAVE AN IDEA," Ella says, indicating that I should get off the highway at the next exit. "Field trip time. And no, it's no 'wine-tasting experience' but it's something fun we can do.

"I'm just going to ignore your mocking of my wine tasting."

"At your peril."

She points at where I should turn next. We're not near anyplace I can think of that has entertainment venues. This part of town is mostly businesses. There's a car repair place, a mini mart, and a gas station, but not much else. I wonder if I should offer Ella some help since she probably doesn't know the area.

"We could drive to St. Helena. Have you been there?"

She laughs. "Of course I have. Your sister took me there for lunch after one of our planning meetings."

"Seriously? She cheated on Butter and Rosemary and took you to a place in town? Wow, she really must like you."

"It's what people do for rom-com princesses," she deadpans.

"Fine. I deserve to be mocked for that."

"Multiple times," Ella emphasizes. "The mocking will continue, let's be clear."

I roll my eyes. "Great."

Ella looks delighted as she directs me down a street that has nothing but warehouses lining both sides. Not a car drives down the street. The desolation screams crime scene. "Keep going. It's down there."

I turn the wheel of my truck down the one-way street she indicates, worried she'll be disappointed when she sees nothing there where we can eat or do something date-worthy. "Are you sure? There's not much—"

"Turn here," she says, pointing to the dilapidated bubble carwash next to a gas station. I do as instructed, taking in the sagging roof on the place and looking at the gas station in hopes that it has a mini mart where she can use the bathroom. I assume that's why we're here.

"If you had your heart set on sex in a gas station restroom, I'm game, but I should warn you that it probably hasn't been mopped in a bit and guys don't always have the best aim."

"Ew and double ew. Are you serious?"

"Some guys don't pay that much attention, especially in public—"

"No, I mean, do you really think my fantasy date would be sex in a gas station bathroom? Dude, not a rom-com princess move."

I look around, wondering what else she could possibly have in mind. "Something involving gas station snacks?"

Shaking her head, she points to the bubble wash at the end. "Drive in there, buddy. I've got lots of quarters." She holds up a change purse and presses her lips together in a no-nonsense expression. I do as instructed.

Once my car is parked, Ella starts loading coins into the machine. Lots of coins. Way too many for a simple wash and rinse. "Slow your roll there. You only need a couple quarters for each cycle. You've programmed that thing for, like, a half hour."

Her eyebrows bounce. She pushes the button for the spray nozzle. And aims it straight at me.

Before I know what's happening, I'm being pelted with a spray of water. Through the mist, I see Ella holding the nozzle like a rifle, joyously soaking me. "What the hell?" I yell, more shocked than irritated. On a blazing hot day like today, the water feels good.

"Good date, no?"

She's grinning like the Cheshire Cat and I fucking love it.

"Oh, it's great. But you're way too dry." I rush her like a football tackle, and she dodges me, squealing as she moves to the side. The water sprays the ground, and she tries to use my truck as a shield. I'm too fast and too big for her to defend herself for long.

Wrenching the spray nozzle from her hand, I turn it and aim it at her bare legs, drenching them with water as she dances from foot to foot. "Wow, that's cold."

"Uh-huh, gotta give as good as I get," I remind her, holding the nozzle over my head so she can't reach it. It doesn't matter. The roof on top of the shed ensures that all the water spraying out rebounds back at us. We're both soaked. Ella's hair twirls in corkscrews around her face, curlier and longer than when it's dry. I'm sure I look like a drowned puppy myself.

I start spraying the roof again, letting the water fall on us like summer rain, but Ella goes to the wall and starts pushing buttons. A moment later, she has the bubble brush in her hand and my spray nozzle stops shooting water.

Ella comes closer to me with the bubble brush. "We haven't really washed down the truck. Let's not soap it yet," I say.

"Haven't you figured it out yet?" she asks. "We're not here to wash your truck."

The mist clears around us and the image of Ella with her sly smile and that bubble brush in her hands sends a jolt of heat through me that dead ends at my dick. I'm hard before she sends the first spray of soap from the brush to my chest.

"Oh, my little rom-com princess is actually a naughty little housemaid," I say as she mimes scrubbing the floors like Cinderella.

A moment later, I'm covered in a froth of bubbles. Ella points at me to turn around. She sprays more bubbles down the length of my spine and rubs circles with her hands. I've never felt anything hotter, never wanted a woman more than I want her.

Spinning around, I take the brush from her hands and squeeze out a stream of bubbles, painting her with them from shoulders to knees. I don't touch her with the brush. Instead, I hang it up and return to where she stands waiting to see what I'm planning. I stand in front of her and let her wait.

And wait.

Dripping with suds, she waves a hand in front of my face. "You sleeping there, big guy?"

Slowly, I shake my head. I take a step toward her. Then another. When I'm close enough to put my hands on her, I reach for her waist, spreading the bubbles up and down as I stroke her skin through the soaked T-shirt.

The sheer cotton of the wet shirt hugs her curves, accentuating the swell of her breasts. That's where my hands go next, lathering her up until her nipples harden beneath my hands. She sighs and presses into me.

The beauty of her choosing this random carwash in the middle of nowhere is that there's no one here, and the idea of someone driving past and seeing us soaping each other up only adds to the forbidden thrill of what I'm already planning to do with her here.

It's only out of the corner of my eye that I notice an eighteen wheeler that has positioned itself between us and the street, effectively blocking the carwash from public view. "Did you hire a giant truck for privacy?"

She laughs. "I sure did. Perks of the job."

That's all I need to hear. Tipping Ella's chin up with my index finger, I keep one hand on her breast, massaging circles into the foamy soap. She groans against my mouth when I kiss her, and it takes all of two seconds for me to lift her up and turn her, so her back is up against my truck. Her legs grip my hips, and her arms wrap around my neck.

Our kisses grow deeper and more intense. The water mingles with our lips and tongues. Soap squelches between our bodies, making them slick.

Ella's hands grip my hair, pulling my mouth against hers as the space between us vanishes entirely.

My hands move to cup the ripe cheeks of her ass and hold her so she's moving directly against my cock. I can't distinguish between our respective moans, and I don't care.

Her hands grip the hem of my shirt, pulling it up so she can rub suds on my chest and abs. Grabbing the back of my collar, I yank the wet fabric over my head. Then I strip off her shirt, gazing down at the incredible swell of her breasts, rising and falling with each breath.

"More," she pants against my neck, kissing a trail up to my ear. "More." Her need is more insistent this time.

I loosen my grip and let her slide down my legs until her feet hit the ground. Then I kneel in front of her and unbutton her denim shorts before peeling them down her legs. Ella's skin is still soapy, and my hands slide along the skin of her inner thigh as her head falls back against the door of my truck.

I lean in and plant a row of tiny kisses from her jaw to her ear. "Princess, this was a very good idea," I rasp as she hums her agreement.

The motor of the bubble brush rattles against the wall, and water hangs in a mist around us. It's a ramshackle situation of imperfect car door angles and a sudsy, slippery flood. Fucking perfect.

Ella's hands work at my belt, unbuckling it and pulling it open. She pops the button on my soggy jeans and shoves them down my thighs. The water makes them stick like a wetsuit, so I bend down to push them off, and before I stand back up, I spend some time wiping the soap away from Ella's legs with my hands, taking special care as I move up her inner thighs to the spot I'm dying to taste.

"You sure about this, darlin'? It's pretty public," I say, looking around at the empty street. Not a soul is using the gas station, and the walls of the carwash stall block the view from two sides, so I'm feeling pretty good about our public display. Still, I want to be sure she's comfortable before my tongue touches her skin and I lose all sense of where I am.

"I'm sure," she breathes.

I don't need any further permission, diving in and lapping a long stroke between the wet hot folds of her flesh, ending at the hard bud of her clit. I pay extra attention there, sucking and circling her with my tongue until I hear her moan. It's become the sound I love more than anything else, as she gives over to feeling everything I want to give her.

Her hands flex at her sides and come up to grip my hair. Drips of water roll into my eyes and I close them against the sting of soap.

Ella's hips jerk as I insert two fingers inside her, curling them so I hit the spot that makes her go crazy. Her back arches and her hips jut forward, begging me for more. I give her all of it, feeling her start to shake beneath my hands.

"Archer, oh God."

Hearing my name on her lips brings me close to the edge myself, but my focus is her.

"Yeah, princess. Come for me," I growl against her before I take her clit into my mouth again and suck.

"Archer, oh…" She trembles beneath me, and I feel her release on my tongue, but she doesn't say another word. I feel more powerful and more necessary in the world than I ever have in my life. This is why I was put on this Earth. This one moment—Ella coming apart beneath me and screaming my name.

When her breathing slows a bit, Ella pulls me to my feet and her lips ravage mine. It feels like she's giving me a piece of her soul.

It's seamless how she moves her body against me, still backed against the side of my truck. Her hands move down my torso, rubbing the last bits of soap into my skin.

Someone honks a horn as the car drives by. Ella laughs and fills up my soul with the soft musical sound. It's a balm to my senses. I want to make a recording of her laughter and play it like a mantra, reminding me that I was this happy in this moment.

Even if it disappears someday like I fear it will.

For now, I have everything I want, and I tell myself to focus on that alone.

Ella slithers from her spot between me and the truck and goes to the wall. She punches the button to turn the water sprayer back on and carries it back to the truck. It takes a bit of maneuvering and my longer arms to do what she wants—and it takes me a minute to figure out what that is—but together we get the arm of the spray nozzle to drape over the roof of my truck.

Ella resumes her position with her back against the car door and pulls me toward her with one hand. Her fingers run the length of my torso, pausing to appreciate my pecs and abs. I watch the delight on her face as she rubs circles over my skin.

With her other hand, she turns on the water spray and holds it there. The shower of drops flies up toward the ceiling and cascades down on us in a cool shower that chills my skin just as Ella reaches for my cock and gives it a few good strokes.

I don't think I've ever been this hard in my life. Never been so hot for a woman. Never been so in love.

The thought snags in my brain, but I push it aside, needing to focus on the intensity of the feeling of her when she guides me between her legs. I've never unwrapped a condom so fast. She rolls it on, and I thrust inside her.

Ella lets go of the spray nozzle when I lift her hips and bracket her face with my forearms. I hammer into her body and stare into her eyes through drips of water and mist in the air.

"This is the hottest fucking field trip in the history of time," I rasp against her temple.

It's all lips against skin. Hard absorbed in softness. Goose bumps and rivulets of water. The best goddamn hour of my life.

When I can't hold out any longer, I cup Ella's face in my hands and our eyes lock. She nods, knowing what I need and giving me even more.

Her hips buck against me and I thrust once more. Deeper. Harder. And then I can only yell her name on an oath and a prayer.

I collapse against her, grateful to my truck for holding us upright. Grateful to the universe for not giving up on me.

Maybe this is what my sister meant by manifesting what I wanted because I sure manifested the hell out of today.

Slowly, our breathing slows. Slowly, we peel ourselves away from each other.

Ella turns on the sprayer and shoots it around the space like a wild hose. I'm not even sure it hits either of us. Then she opens the passenger side door and retrieves two towels from the tote bag she brought with her.

"And here I thought you'd packed us a picnic lunch," I say, taking a towel and using it to carefully dry her skin, every inch of it.

She smirks. "Would you have preferred that?"

"No fucking way."

Laughing, Ella digs into the bag again, producing two

wrapped sandwiches and handing one to me. "One's turkey, the other's vegetarian. Preference?"

I shake my head. Then answer, "Turkey."

She hands it over and we walk to a bus stop bench where we sit on the damp towels in the sun until our clothes are dry and our sandwiches are gone. Then we drive home.

My truck isn't clean. If anything, it's worse for the wear than before—streaks of soap on the hood, spots of water mixed with dirt on the windshield. But I feel like I've been cleansed from the inside out.

Gone are my ideas about not risking my heart on a woman who might not stick around. I know we're different, but right now I don't care.

We drive down the Silverado Trail toward Buttercup Hill, and I drop my hand onto Ella's thigh. She puts hers on top of mine. Everything about us feels right. For the first time in my fucking life.

It's what gives me the courage to tell her the one thing I know for sure. "I love you, Ella Fieldstone. So much."

I don't have to look at her to see her smile, but there's no chance I'm missing an opportunity to do so. "Wow." I need to watch the road, so my gaze shifts back and forth between her and the highway.

"Wow?"

"I mean, if I knew I could get you to love me by washing your car, I'd have done it weeks ago."

I let out a long breath, not sorry I confessed my heart to her, but worried I misjudged whether she might feel the same way. But it's okay. I still want her to know how I feel, even if it's one-sided.

"That's not why—"

"I'm kidding." She takes off her seat belt and scoots closer to me on the bench seat of my truck. "Sorry. I was trying to lighten the mood because I got nervous."

"I didn't say it to make you nervous. I—"

She puts a finger against my lips. "I meant I was nervous to say it too. But it's true. I've fallen hard and fast for you, Archer Corbett. I love you." It makes me the luckiest man alive.

lla

"Mmmm," I hum, liking everything about my surroundings—a soft quilt, cool sheets, a quiet room. I'm splayed on my stomach, with my arm flung across Archer's chest. My cheek rests against warm skin over a hard plane of muscle, and I feel the subtle rise and fall of Archer's chest as he breathes. His hand comes to my forehead, and he smooths my messy hair away from my face. His fingers tangle in the strands, which he twists and rearranges. As he gently tugs, the nerve endings in my scalp respond like they've been tamed by the most decadent hairbrush. Every part of me that he touches has the same response, asking for more. Forever.

My eyes pop open at that thought. There can be no forever with this man. He doesn't want kids, which makes him my polar opposite in one very important way. I have no business thinking about anything beyond right now. And right now is oh, so good. Maybe I'm destined to be the girl who never has a happily ever after, at least not in my romantic life. I decide not to think about that too much right now.

I haven't heard from my lawyer, and I'm almost afraid to call her for fear of bad news.

"Hey," I say, looking up at him.

"Hey yourself."

"Haha. Do you want to come to a movie premiere with me next month? Walk the red carpet and do all the things. I promise the after party will be next level."

"Yeah? You want me to be your date in public? Won't people talk?"

I think about it. "Yeah, you're right. See, this is the problem—I make impulsive decisions when my heart is involved. Story of my whole romantic life. A movie star scandal might help wine sales, though."

He tickles me mercilessly. "You think I'm only in this for wine sales?"

"What are you in it for?" I tease.

"The phenomenal sex." His face turns serious. "The beautiful woman I can't stop looking at. And a hundred tiny meaningless moments that fill me up because I'm experiencing them with you. Listening to you slurp your coffee to cool it down instead of blowing on it. Watching you tame your hair into a knot without using a hair band. Feeling you lean closer when I stroke your hair. I'm in for all of it."

I lift my head and stare at him, floored by his thorough answer and endeared by his honesty. "Wow."

"Keep asking questions, princess, and I'll keep answering 'em."

"God, I love you."

He smiles and shifts beneath me, pulling me closer and tugging me onto my side, so my stomach meets his hip and one of my legs rests on top of his. Now, we're a tangle of limbs. I look at his face again and find a small smile playing on his lips, like he might not realize he's doing it. I like catching him in these unintended moments of honesty.

"Why are you smiling?" he asks.

"Because *you're* smiling."

I expect the hint of happiness to leave his face in an instant, but instead, his almost-smile grows into the real thing. "Impossible," he says, trying to turn his smile into a frowny face. He doesn't try that hard.

"This is pure heaven," I say, lowering my cheek to his chest and letting my eyes drift shut again. Even without knowing the time, I can tell it's late morning by the way the sun tilts in through the window, already high in the sky in late fall.

"You can stay for as long as you want," his voice rumbles beneath me. "You can stay forever."

And there it is again—*forever*—that word that sounds all cute and fun, but it means something neither of us really means. Right?

I can't help feeling a little devastated that he doesn't want the same things that I do. I can imagine waking up next to him every morning, telling him my secrets every night before bed.

I want him for all of it.

Story of my whole romantic life.

But there's a baby out there without a family and that's my destiny, I just know it. I can't give up on my dream, even though it means Archer can't be my forever. Plus, he lives at Buttercup Hill, which is not my reality. It's been great to be here between films, but soon enough I'll be on location or back at my house in LA. It's hard to imagine how his life could mesh with mine.

"You're sweet. I'll be right back." I roll away from Archer's naked body and off the bed, even though every fiber of my being is begging me to go right back where I just was. *Don't go, give us one more hour,* my cells seem to be imploring. But I can't. It will just make it harder to remember where my boundaries lie if I keep pushing them farther away.

Once I'm off the bed, I yank my tee from the floor and struggle it on while I walk to the bathroom. Shutting the door behind me, I look at myself in the mirror. "What are you doing?" the woman looking back at me seems to say. She's asking why I'd leave a hot, amazing man naked in the bed and shut myself in here.

She's also asking what I'm doing with a hot amazing man who is never going to be my future. I try to ignore her as I brush my teeth. Then, I ignore her some more and slide back in bed with the man I can't resist.

 rcher

ELLA'S PHONE RINGS, but she ignores it. I tip my head in the direction of her purse. "You want to get that?"

She shakes her head and snuggles into my chest. "Not if it means getting up."

"I'm not gonna argue with that, princess. You stay right here." I kiss her temple and tip her chin up so I can claim her lips. She tastes like ripe berries and honey, addicting me with every new time I sink against her mouth. I'll never get tired of this feeling of her curled against my body.

Her phone rings again, a new chorus of beeps and bells, which sounds more insistent this time. "Someone really wants to reach you." I bristle at the idea that it's Callum, even though she's made it clear they're finished. I can't help thinking that if I were him, I'd try harder to get her back. And they haven't announced their breakup officially, so I don't think I'm simply paranoid.

She sighs as the phone beeps with a voicemail. "Seems like it, huh?"

Shifting in my arms, she seems resigned to getting the phone, so I reluctantly loosen my grip. My skin feels cold and my chest protests with a hollow ache when she rolls off the bed. She compensates with a waggle of her perfect ass, and my senses settle down, knowing she'll be back in my arms in a moment.

"So, uh, has Callum reached out at all?" I ask, needing her to spell it out.

She stops moving, phone in hand. "What?"

"He just let it go that easily, the arranged marriage? What about his image and his tour and all that?"

"That's his problem. He should've thought about his image before he slept with his tour manager. And God knows who else?"

I nod and look away.

She sits back on the bed. I feel her hand beneath my chin, guiding me to look at her. "What aren't you saying?"

A knot of stress in my chest loosens a little bit at her touch, but I'm still wound up. "I guess I wonder…if he hadn't cheated, would you have broken up with him? In other words, would this pull between us have been convincing enough to make you choose me?"

Her eyes soften and she shakes her head. "I can't rewrite the past. But I know how I feel, and I'm in love with you. I choose you now. Without question."

My heart floods with love for her and I tip my face down to kiss her hand. "I choose you too."

Ella looks down at her phone and her eyes go wide. "It was my lawyer." She dials without listening to the message. I can hear the phone ringing as she settles into the crook of my arm and tucks her knees against me. "Everything okay?" I whisper.

"I hope so." She nods as the person on the other end picks up.

There's a lot of "uh-huh" and some excited questions on Ella's end. "Really?" "Just like that? "When?" "What do I need to do?"

When she hangs up, she rolls over in my arms with a grin that spans her entire face. I get the full effect of America's sweetheart, all sparkling eyes, pink cheeks, and dimples, only it's not made for the silver screen. I'm the only lucky son of a bitch in the world with a front-row seat, and it's in that moment that I realize I don't want to give it up. I want her for more than something temporary. So much more.

From the gleefully shocked look on her face, I can tell there may be a hiccup in that plan.

"You're not going to believe it, but I think I'm going to adopt a little girl." Her face can barely contain the span of her smile, and it floods my heart with warmth to be here with her as she digests the news.

"Tell me." I brush the strands of hair from her cheek so I can see her face better.

"My lawyer wants me to come to her office in the morning… there's a baby. I didn't say anything before because it seemed like such a long shot and I didn't want to jinx it, but I can't…I've been waiting so long for this." Her eyes fill and she blinks back the tears, swallowing hard.

"That's amazing." I really do mean it, though it feels like the first step in her path away from me. Even if she and Callum are over, there isn't necessarily room in her future motherhood scenarios for a guy who doesn't want kids. But I push those thoughts aside. This is too important to her, and I want to be one hundred percent here for her.

"I mean, I guess I didn't really believe it would happen, which is why I didn't say anything to you, but I have this friend with a sister who's an obstetrical nurse." She goes on to tell me about Tatum's sister Becca, who let her know about the baby who'd been surrendered to the hospital.

The fact that she didn't mention it shouldn't be a big deal. She just said she didn't think it would happen, but it still feels like a blow. Like she's taking back tiny pieces of herself and her future one moment at a time. And in total, they'll add up to her leaving and going on with her life without me. Of course she will.

Two months ago, I wouldn't have cared. We were having fun. I didn't want more than that. But now…I want more. A lot more. And I see the writing on the wall telling me I can't have any of it.

"What happens now? I want to hear everything." I hope she doesn't notice how my voice cracks on the last word as I try to maintain joy and enthusiasm for what is probably the most exciting news of her life.

She takes a deep breath and shakes her head. "It's so wild. I'm so glad I was here when I found out. There's no one I'd rather share my news with. There's a lot that still needs to happen, home visits and evaluations, and I think there's a probationary period before the court will grant custody…I guess I'll find out more tomorrow, but right now, it's looking like I'm gonna be a mom." Her shoulders go up and she gives me a small guilty smile like she's watching a soap bubble, and she doesn't want to move too abruptly lest it burst.

I open my arms, and she snuggles in. "Congratulations, princess. I'm really happy for you." She nods against my chest, and I dip my face into her hair, inhaling everything I love about this moment—her safe in my arms, her sharing important news with me, her loving me the way I never thought I deserved.

When I exhale, I try to hang onto it a little while longer.

lla

"Are you sure you don't want company? Moral support? I won't say a word. I'll just sit there." Archer sounds more nervous than I am, but I don't stop to consider why that might be. I assume he's just excited for me and doesn't know how to help.

"No, I'm good. You're sweet. Thank you."

We drove to San Francisco together and now we're sitting in Archer's truck outside my lawyer's office building. "I'll just hang here, get a coffee or something. Then I can drive you back."

"No, really. You were so nice to drive me all the way down here, but it's the middle of the workday. Go back and take care of the piles on your desk. Tatum said she'll meet me. She works nearby."

Archer lingers, and I'm not sure what else to say. I don't think he should come into the adoption meeting with me because I don't want my lawyer to think I'm bouncing from one man to another. I told my lawyer on the downlow that I'm not going through with the marriage to Callum and expressed my fears about how that will look, but she said we'll cross that bridge when we come to it. Having Archer there will just complicate things.

"I'm staying."

"Fine. I'll see you after."

I race down the hallway of Cindy's office with a spilling cup of Starbucks in my hand, hoping I don't slip on the shiny floors. Spoiler alert, it's happened before. I'm wearing penny loafers and a navy-blue pencil skirt that ends well above my ankles, reducing my chances of getting tangled up in myself. My purse strap slides down the arm of my suit jacket as I run, so the purse whacks my thigh as I struggle not to drop the folder in my other hand or lose the coffee cup entirely.

In other words, I'm a hot mess heading into what feels like the most important meeting of my life. Forget auditions for starring roles or sit-downs with A-list producers. I don't think I've wanted any of those meetings to go right as much as this one.

I know it's just a meeting with my lawyer, and there's no one there from the adoption courts to judge me, but I dressed up and tamed my hair into a low chignon as though I'll be video recorded and assessed for parental fitness. I've been waiting too long for this opportunity to risk anything going wrong.

Yanking open the glass door to my lawyer's office, I'm greeted by the receptionist, who acknowledges me with a tip of her head as she finishes a conversation on her headset. I wait at the water-fall desk, trying not to convey my nerves by tapping a finger on the slick, glass surface or shifting impatiently from one foot to the other.

Finally, she ends her call and smiles at me. "Ella Fieldstone," I tell her. "I have an appointment with Cynthia Cannon." She types information into her computer and nods at me.

"She'll be right with you. Would you like some water? Coffee?"

I hold up my paper cup. "I'm good, thanks."

Perching on the edge of a fuzzy couch covered in off-white boucle fabric, I peer at the display of magazines on a low marble table. They've been arranged in a fan, and *Town and Country* magazine happens to sit atop the pile. I flip through the issue but don't really focus on any of the headlines or pictures. My hands need something to do, so I fan through it a second time, trying harder to take an interest in anything on the pages that shuffle by.

After what feels like three hours, Cindy breezes into the lobby and extends her arms toward me like I'm a long, lost cousin who survived passage on the *Titanic*. "Finally," she says, backing away and holding my arms. "We're there."

"I still can't believe it," I tell her as we walk down the brightly lit hallway to her office. I barely notice the assistants' cubicles and partners' offices that we pass on the way to our destination, the large corner space at the end of the hallway. When I walk into Cindy's office, I notice the spectacular view of the Golden Gate Bridge and feel grateful for her exorbitant hourly rate that affords her this vista. It's all worth it if we really are "there."

Cindy points to a chair, which is when I realize I'm still standing in the middle of her office, gawking at the landscape, as though I've never been here before. Or been anywhere. "Have a seat." She goes around her desk to sit in her chair and looks up at me. "Ella?"

I move toward a chair and drop into it on a wobble that almost lands my ass on the floor. I have to steady myself with both arms of the gray wingback chair, and when I look over the desk at Cindy, I notice her grin. "Are you okay?" she asks.

"No, I'm really nervous."

"That's normal. But this is exciting, Ella. It's going to happen."

I nod, still in disbelief. "I've wanted this for so long."

"I know. I know you have, and I'm so excited for you." She takes a folder from the top of a stack on her immaculate wood partner desk. On the side facing me, a vertical row of drawers with gleaming brass handles taunts me to slide them open just so I have something to do with my hands, but years of doing TV interviews have taught me to keep them in my lap. I inhale a cleansing breath and let it out like I do before every scene, which reminds me of the day Archer laughed at the face I make when I do it.

The moment Archer's face enters my mind, I can't shake it. The only thing that would make this moment better was if he were here with me. No, that's not right. It's not just his presence here in the room that I want. It's his presence all the time.

Much as I've tried over the past few days, I can't deny the fact that I wish it were the two of us getting ready to adopt a baby and start a life together.

Shaking myself back to the present, I plaster a smile on my face and try to push Archer from my mind. The idea of a tiny baby girl reels me in.

"I have so many questions. What can you tell me about the baby? Where is she? How old is she? I want to know everything."

Cindy opens the folder and shuffles through the pages inside before she starts reading the details. "She's four weeks old. She was dropped off at a Safe Surrender site at Alta Bates Hospital, as you know from your friend, and she's currently in the care of a private, pre-adoption agency. I don't have the identity of her parents because it was an anonymous surrender, but her mother left a family health history and she's been examined by pediatricians. No health issues, no red flags. And she's adorable."

Cindy slides a photo over the surface of her desk, and I grasp it in my hands, staring down at the face of my future daughter.

"I mean, it's not over until it's over, but I don't see anything on the horizon that gives me pause. Unless there's something I don't know, I can't foresee any roadblocks to prevent this from happening."

I realize I've been holding my breath while she said the last part, needing to hear the words, but also worried about what would happen if I added a roadblock she didn't see coming. I let the air out slowly and summon my nerves.

"I have a question," I begin, giving myself a moment to rethink the wisdom of asking it. I don't need to rock the boat, do I?

"Sure. What's that?"

"The elephant in the room… Is there a chance that I won't be able to adopt if I'm doing it as a single parent? Be honest with me."

Cindy's mouth pulls down into a frown. "I wish I could say that it doesn't matter. I wish I could say that perception is irrelevant, but I've seen things go south more than once. It's not fair, but it is what it is. I wish I could offer you the guarantee I know you're looking for."

I twist my hands in my lap, unsure how to get out of the mess I'm in and coming up empty. "So…even though we've done everything right, there's a chance I'll be denied."

"A chance. I'm not saying it'll happen, but you should be prepared in case."

Cindy blinks but not a muscle in her face moves. Her expression stays passive with a practiced indifference like a doctor forced to convey bad news. I fixate on her lashes sweeping down over her cheeks each time she blinks and wait for her to say something. Finally, her lips start moving.

"Is there a chance you might still marry him?" She's as calm as if she's asking if I want fries with my lunch order.

"I—no. I've actually been seeing someone else."

She nods. "This would have been good information to know." She sounds disappointed, but I can't believe she's actually serious. I'm tired of being judged over my dating choices.

"Okay, well, I'm telling you now," I snap, feeling judged and defensive. After all the work I've done over the past year to get my old reputation behind me and paint a new picture of myself as a responsible future parent and all the happiness I feel in a relationship based around love, I don't appreciate the implication that I'm doing something wrong.

She holds up a hand, still blinking. "I'm not saying you need to stay with the wrong man for the sake of the adoption. I'd never tell you that. And I'm on your side here. I just want to make sure we do everything right to give you the best possible chances."

A breath chokes in my throat, and I realize how fragile I feel with my future in the hands of other people. I assess Cindy from where I sit, noticing her dark hair pulled tight into a clip at the nape of her neck. I don't think she has to undergo quite the struggle I do to tame her hair into place. Her red blouse with its jaunty bow at the neck softens the austere look while still communicating power. I feel like an impostor in my navy suit, like someone from a movie wardrobe department dressed me up to look serious. My hands fist in my lap as I try to control my emotions.

"So you're saying my chances of getting a court or adoption agency or whoever to approve me as an adoptive parent aren't as good if I do it as a single parent?"

I already know the answer to this question. It's why I've been so careful about my reputation for the past year. It's why I overlooked red flags long before Callum cheated.

"All I'm saying is that I've seen it go the wrong way in the past. I don't want that for you. If you really want to make this ironclad, don't go in as a single parent. I've seen these things fall apart, and there's been a lot written about your dating life that could be seen as unstable for a vulnerable child."

I nod, my mind scrambling to come up with a plan for how to make everything work. "I'm not going to do anything to jeopardize my chances, not when there's a baby girl who needs a mom. I want to be her mom—just from seeing that picture, I know it's what I want."

Cindy looks relieved, and I should feel the same way. But as I sign the paperwork she pushes my way, I can't help feeling uneasy.

I know how Archer feels about having kids. He's made it abundantly clear, and I'm not about to try to convince him he's wrong when I understand where his fear comes from.

It seems crazy, though, when I see him with Fiona. He's so great with her. He absolutely lights up like the favorite uncle he is, the man she knows him to be. It's like she sees something he doesn't—that he'd make the best dad in the world if he just allowed himself to try.

I have to at least talk to him about the possibility. Because maybe, just maybe, there's a chance of him seeing it too.

rcher

LOOKING at my phone for the fifteenth time, I see no calls or texts from Ella. I'd give anything right now for an emoji. Anything.

I've been pacing on the sidewalk for the past hour, my stomach in knots, wondering how it's going. And also thinking about what it means for the two of us if she can adopt a baby in the next few months or even weeks.

Walking back and forth on the same block, I've decided one thing for sure—no matter how much I love her, I can't be the one to stand in the way of what she wants. She wants a baby. Which means she probably won't want me, the man who can't be a father.

I just can't.

With my family obligations and work situation, I'd be exactly the kind of dad my own father was, and I refuse.

As I'm twisting my brain trying to come up with any other conclusion, the door to the skyscraper opens and Ella walks out.

I can't tell from her expression whether she's happy or sad. She just looks…concerned.

I jog over to her and grab her shoulders in case she needs steadying. "How'd it go?"

Her expression doesn't change. "Well, I guess. No, it went well. I think I'll be able to adopt her."

"That's amazing. I'm so, so happy for you." I pull her in for a hug but find her stiff instead of the usual way she melts against me. I want to be the guy who says the right thing. More than that, I want to be the one who does the right thing.

She backs out of my arms, still looking dazed.

"Hey," I say, rubbing her arms. She feels cold. "What's wrong? What aren't you telling me?"

Ella shakes her head as though she's knocking sense into it. She blinks a few times, but I'm not expecting what she says next.

"My lawyer says…there's still a risk I could be denied as a single parent. It could work, but my past reputation…it could blow up. She actually asked if there was a chance I'd get back together with Callum and go through with the wedding."

"Like hell you will." My alpha male wants to beat his chest and stand on that asshole's neck until it snaps.

"I know, it's just…" Her brow creases, and it hits me.

The anguish on her face isn't just disappointment. A part of her wonders if getting back with Callum is a good idea. She's actually considering it. At least, that's what I allow myself to believe.

My brain fills with conflicting thoughts, some about killing Callum for hurting her in the first place, but most of them about how I could be the hero in this scenario. Be the guy she needs.

Could I?

"Maybe there's a way for me to help. We could get married. I could be the guy." The words rush out before I have time to consider what I'm offering. Because I don't just want to be a suit filler on a wedding day. I'd never want to be just that to her. But

I'm not sure I could be more. I know my limitations. I'm my father's son, as he spent my life telling me, and I'd only be an absentee father like he was, given my responsibilities to Buttercup Hill and my family. Ella and her baby deserve better.

She gives me a closed-mouth smile that looks more sad than happy. "Archer, no. I don't want you as just a stand-in husband in my plan. I'd want…more. With you, I'd want it all. And I know I can't ask that."

Ask it. Please ask.

My inner voice begs her to want me for more than a stand-in. Maybe knowing she sees me as capable of more would push me to… No. I can't.

"I know," I say, resigned.

"It wouldn't be fair. We're so new and we haven't built enough of a foundation yet. There's no way I'd ask you to take this on when I know it's not what you want," she says, tears filling the corners of her eyes.

She closes her eyes for a moment, but when they open, there's a question behind them. An invitation? Here is where I should tell her I've changed my mind, that I do want to have kids, that everything I thought I knew about myself is wrong.

But is it?

So much of me just wants to hear her say that we should do this together. I need to know how she feels about me as a part of her future, as the father of as many children as she wants to have with me. Not just as any port in a storm who would give her adoption application the best hope of going through. I can't be a placeholder.

I also don't want to lose her, so I offer what I can.

"I know I love you. And I know I want to help you."

"I'm not sure that's reason enough—"

I interrupt with a finger over her lips. "I could. Even if we don't know where this is going, I could give you that bit of security to help the adoption go through. I want you to have what you've always dreamed of." I almost want it more than I want my own happiness. Almost enough to push aside my fears.

But not quite.

"Archer…" She gives me the barest of smiles. Like it's hard. "I don't want to be one more person in your life who needs you to be someone you don't want to be."

Her words break something deep inside me because she sees me more than anyone ever has.

Right now, it feels too tender and too painful for me to understand the full significance, but I do know I'll never be the same from this point forward. I stare down into a deep abyss of the truth she's already accepted—that this is the end of us. It causes the fight to leave my system. I feel a dull ache in my heart and a searing pain behind my eyes as I hold back the sting of tears I can't let her see.

There's no way for her to understand how deeply it hurts that I can't be what she needs. So I stand here, stuck. "I love you. So much." I want that to be enough.

Ella takes a step back and puts her hand up as though she's blocking anything else I have to say. I feel the distance between us like a chasm neither of us can bridge. "I love you too, but we have no future. I have a baby to think about and I need to put that child's needs before my own. Even if it breaks my heart. So maybe it's time…to walk away."

My animal brain can't make sense of what she's saying. Once again, I want to kick myself for being so bad at expressing my feelings because I'm not getting this right and I know it's going to cost me.

"I don't want that."

"Archer, you know it's the right thing to do."

"The right thing?!" Of course it is, but I'm hurting too much to accept it. I don't mean to raise my voice, but my emotions are ruling me the same as when I'm on the ice. I've never been good at controlling my anger, and right now I don't have the benefit of a puck I can smack with everything I've got. "There's nothing right about saying goodbye to you."

I don't know what to do with my sadness and frustration, so I do what comes naturally—I act like a dick.

"I'm not going to fight you, if that's what you're hoping for. I'm not going to beg you to stay." I want to beg. I want to push back against the idea of her leaving with every ounce of strength I have. Or at least, that's what my heart wants. My brain has other ideas. It digs in, stubborn as always.

She turns her back and for a moment I think she's going to walk away without saying more. I'd deserve it. I know I'm being a dick, but I don't know how to sugarcoat my feelings, never have. When she turns to face me, I see the hurt—it's in the way her shoulders slump. The beautiful features of her face sag in sadness. That's when I know I've gone too far.

"This. This is why I need to go."

The sadness is etched in her features and I'm itching to wipe the lines away with the pads of my thumbs, like if I can smooth out her skin, I can erase the pain I'm causing. But I say nothing. I do…nothing.

"Okay," she says softly.

"You want what you want, and you should have it," I tell her, not seeing a path forward.

"Right…" She cocks her head to the side as though there's more to my declaration than I'm saying.

"We've talked about this. I'm not having kids."

"You don't have to keep saying it. I get that you don't want to have kids with me," she says, voice hoarse. She nods and takes a step away from me.

My hands come to my face to try to block the anguish that wants to pummel me for my shortcomings. But it's useless.

"I don't want to have kids with anyone." I hate that it's true and I hate myself for not doing a damn thing to make it untrue. I feel myself pull away, almost as though I'm hovering above the two of us and watching the interaction unfold. Like I'm not a part of it. Like I have no ability to change trajectory.

I hate myself for that weakness. I hate my father for dooming me to be like him. Then I hate myself again for not having the spine to change those very things about myself that are keeping me locked in a cycle of unhappiness. Especially when I have the chance for something different, and I'm about to let her walk away.

"I'll mail the clothes and stuff you left at my house, so you don't have to come back there. Just easier that way. For both of us," I say, feeling slightly better about being pragmatic.

Ella shrugs. "If that's what you want."

"It is."

It's not.

Not at all.

But if I'm going to give Ella the chance at her dreams, I need to get out of the way. And maybe I want that more than I want my own happiness. It sure seems that way.

As she turns to leave, I let out the breath I've been holding, releasing the last tether that's been attaching me to hope. It breaks with a snap I feel deep in my chest—and what's left of my heart crumbles with it.

CHAPTER 34

*A*rcher

One Week Later

"Come on."

I look up from my desk, where I've been sitting since I last had to use the bathroom, approximately four hours ago. Other than that, I have no idea what time it is. Darkness fell on the vineyards outside my window hours ago, and once day turned to night, I didn't much care about the time.

In fact, it felt like a relief from the relentless sunny day, which challenged me to be in a better mood. Fuck that.

For the past week, I've spent every day at work for twelve hours at a stretch, and I've spent every night alone in my house nursing a glass of whiskey before passing out from sheer exhaustion.

Lather, rinse, repeat.

The ritual has done little to keep my mind off Ella, but it's the best I can do. Beatrix hasn't rebooked the venue to host Ella's wedding but maybe she still will. Every day or so, I log in and check the events schedule. So far, nothing.

Then I let my mind wander to Fiona and how much I love being her uncle. It wanders further to what it would be like to be a father, to take care of Ella and a baby. A part of me wants to do it. That part is my heart.

It wants me to call Ella my wife. Be a father to *our* kids, adopted or not. Build a life with them. Take care of something so small and give it the kind of love and attention my siblings and I never got. Teaching a kid to play ice hockey. How to grow grapes.

Another, louder part, is still telling me I am no different from my father. I work all the time, and I have a responsibility to my family to keep the legacy of Buttercup Hill alive. I've always listened to that part—my head—and so far, it hasn't steered me wrong.

Has it? Is this really where I want to be?

"Come on where?" I grumble, not bothering to look up at Jax. The rumble of his voice is almost as surly and gruff as mine, so I recognize it without laying eyes on him. He sounds annoyed, and annoyed is the last thing I feel like dealing with right now. "Actually, never mind. I'm not going anywhere."

To prove that, I start moving piles of papers around on my desk, still refusing to look at my brother.

"Field trip." This voice is unmistakably Dash's, and I growl with annoyance.

"Oh great, now you're ganging up on me?"

But when I look up, I see my brothers standing in the doorway of my office, joined by Ren and a few guys I don't recognize initially. Jax takes a step inside closer, and I get a better look at who's behind him—none other than Grimm and Yancy, the starting defenders on the Oakland Otters.

"What the hell is going on?" I ask, trying to recall whether I accidentally agreed to accompany Ren and his teammates on a trip someplace. As though that's something I'd do. Just proves how out of sorts I am right now.

"Like he said, field trip." Jax points to Dash, who I then notice is standing next to the Otters' enforcer, Skinner.

"Fine." I push the papers to the side and stand up from my desk, lacking the energy to argue with them. Jax can be as stubborn as me if he wants, so the easiest path will be to get this little outing over with so I can go back to brooding at my desk in peace.

Outside, an Otters' team bus idles in front of the old brown barn. Suddenly, this seems more like a kidnapping than a field trip. I shoot Ren a look. "What's this about?"

"Team captain called a last-minute training session. You're coming. Get on the bus." Given that Ren is the captain, I know he's up to something, but my brain is too exhausted to conjure up ideas about what it could be.

"Seriously? You're kidnapping me?"

"Seriously. We're inviting you to join us."

Shaking my head, I walk toward the open door of the bus, feeling a gust of cool air from inside blast into the dry Napa heat. "Fine." If they feel like dragging me to a cold rink to watch the Otters practice, fine. I can think of worse ways to spend an afternoon.

Ren gets on the bus in front of me and points to a seat near the front of the bus. "All yours."

I start to protest because I can find my own damn seat, but he blocks the aisle until I sit. Shaking my head, I grumble and take the seat nearest the window, half expecting him to drop into the seat next to me like a babysitter, but he drops a brown paper bag on the seat instead and goes to another seat further back.

The rest of the guys file onto the bus, not paying particular attention to me, which puts me in a marginally better mood. Jax sits across from me and gestures to the bag. "You gonna open that?"

Looking at his seat, I notice he has his own bag. As I unroll the top of mine, he does the same. I lift a cold six-pack from my bag and a can of Pringles.

Ren leans over the headrest on my seat and explains. "In case you need some sustenance."

I'm about to get up and walk off the bus because my lack of sustenance is none of his damn business, but my stomach growls in protest. "Thanks," I mutter, determined to be a moody son of a bitch in the face of my captors.

An hour later, we reach the practice rink, which hides behind a fenced parking lot in Oakland. Despite my sour mood, I can't help feeling a small thrill when the gates open to let the bus through, and the ice rink rises up in front of us. My mood lifts at the sight of the complex, its holy gates open to me for the first time in my life.

Ren and I have become friendly since he and Beatrix started dating, but he's on the road a ton and I'm always busy trying to bail Buttercup Hill out of trouble, so it's not like we spend much time hanging out. It makes me all the more curious about this outing and what's behind it. I'm sure my brothers have something to do with it, but I'm too tired to question them.

The door to the bus opens right outside the entrance to the Otters' locker room and we file off the bus. I follow Ren inside with my head on a swivel, taking in a wall of framed action shots of players from over the years. Once we reach the locker room, I blink in silent reverence for the sacred space.

For the first time in weeks, my mood lifts and I feel something resembling a pathway forward. Maybe this is how my life could look as I move on without Ella—a bunch of guys playing sports, drinking beer, and eating bad chips. The way my life used to be. Maybe it's enough.

Ren hands me an oversized bag of gear, which I assume I'm

supposed to distribute to the team players for this impromptu session. "Just let me know who needs what," I say, pawing through the jerseys and padding in the bag.

"This is for you."

"O-kay…what do you want me to do with it?"

"I want you to put it on and get your ass on the ice." Ren points over his shoulder with his thumb and pops the release on his locker, which is full of clean practice gear.

I look around. All the players seem to have plenty of their own gear and jerseys to wear, but I'm still not understanding because it sounds like he just told me to suit up and go practice with a pro hockey team, which is nuts.

"Sorry, what?"

"Bunch of sizes in here, and there's a lefty stick over there." He points at a rack of sticks and my eyes land on one that glows like a perfectly polished sword being given to the newest knight before battle. I get dressed in the padding and a white Otters practice jersey, noticing that half the guys out there are wearing black jerseys.

My eyes land on Jax, who holds up a pair of skates I recognize as my own. "I believe these will fit you."

As I turn toward an empty locker and put away my street clothes, I'm still a little confused about why I'm being invited to practice with the Otters, but I can only conclude that I must be just that pathetic in the eyes of everyone around me. And since a hockey rink is one of the few places where I can forget about everything else in my life, I decide not to question it.

When I'm done putting on my pads and lacing up my skates, I'm surprised to find that both my brothers along with Colin are all dressed for the ice, even though none of them plays the sport.

"Okay, I feel better knowing I'm not the only rookie on the ice," I tell Dash, stomping past him in my skates and deciding this might actually be fun.

Wrong.

Well, wrong if a person's idea of fun is getting his ass handed to him. Over and over again.

Instead of my brothers and my nerdy billionaire friend being the rookies, they skate around getting easy passes and assists from the Otters players, who protect them from injury and make them look good on the ice in our scrimmage.

I, on the other hand, seem to be the designated punching bag.

Ren comes at me, skating faster than I've ever moved on the ice, dribbling the puck until he nutmegs me for an easy score. But not before another forward on his team shoves his shoulder into me and knocks me onto the ground. Without any referees around to call fouls, I have to take every punch thrown and high stick shoved my way.

By the end of the third period, I limp off the ice for a necessary water break. Heaving up a lung after skating like the wind, just to avoid extra pummeling, I look up at Ren. "What the fuck?" I pant.

He shrugs. "Sometimes we're a little extra fired up."

"Bullshit."

Squirting water in his mouth, he skates back onto the ice, signaling to me. "Get your ass out here. Teams are switching up. You're with me."

At first, I breathe a sigh of relief knowing that the Otters' team captain won't have it out for me if we're on the same team, but I quickly learn I'm wrong.

A minute into play, I narrowly miss getting checked by a defender when someone gives me a shove from behind. I land on the ice, skidding to a stop by the sideboard. Ren skates over to give me a hand up, but I don't take it, not when I can tell from his cheeky grin that he's the one who hit me.

"No thanks, asshole."

"Oh yeah, forgot to tell you that I might headbutt you just for sport."

Skinner, the Otters' enforcer, checks me hard and I wince,

feeling like my shoulder may have popped out of its socket. The guys give me a second to pull myself together before they start in again.

No one else is taking a beating like I am. All the other guys are having a normal scrimmage, batting the puck around to improve skills, stay fit, and avoid injury. I'm the group punching bag, and at the end of the next period, as I nurse a bleeding lip, I punch Ren in the arm.

"What the hell? Why are you all trying to kill me?"

"It's called knocking sense into a person." Ren flashes his team-captain-winning smile, and I almost fall for the persuasiveness of it. Then I remember he's been pummeling me.

"Do I seem particularly devoid of sense?"

"Yes, if you think walking away from the first woman who makes you happy is the right thing to do," Colin pipes up as he slides into the spot next to me on the bench. Turning to look at him, I almost laugh. He's never played hockey before, much less put on a pair of skates. He's been clinging to the siderails of the rink the whole time we've been out there, and now his helmet is askew and he's blinking sweaty hair from his eyes.

If he came out here willingly, it has to be about something more than dude bonding time. "You're on Team Ren too?" I grumble, feeling grateful for this bunch despite the pain in my shoulder, my shins, and my jaw. And we still have another period to play.

"I'm on Team Archer. We all are." The other guys skate over and crowd around us.

"What are we chatting about, ladies?" Jax asks, giving me a jab in the gut with his stick. I jump to my feet and wrap him in a headlock, and he throws a few punches. In typical hockey fashion, the other guys let us go at it for a couple minutes before they pull us apart.

"Jesus," I huff, gasping for breath. "What the fuck is wrong with all of you?"

"You," several guys say at once. "Guy who doesn't respond to reason needs a more obvious lesson."

"I'm not some dumb caveman. If you've got something to say to me, use your fucking words!" I'm this close to skating back to the locker room and throwing my skates against a wall. "I don't need another period on the ice with you assholes," I say, standing up. But the guys crowd around me and don't let me move.

I'm so goddamn frustrated, I feel the hot sting of tears threaten to spring free. It takes everything I have to push them back, and I swallow hard, unwilling to let these guys see weakness, even if they've just spent the past hour turning me into human pulp.

The worst part is they're telling me something I already know —my life is far worse without Ella in it, and I'm the only one with the power to do anything about my sorry situation now.

I figure that I have a choice. I can start throwing punches, take a beating in the process, and fight my way to the locker room so I can lick my wounds in peace. And sure, I used to be the guy who threw punches first and asked questions later, but that was before I met Ella. Now I want to ask the right questions the first time around. Like why did a pro hockey team take the time to beat the living shit out of me? Because I need to clear my mind, feel the fear, and play the game anyway.

Because I need man up and at least consider what my heart has to say. If I fuck things up after that, it's my own damn fault.

CHAPTER 35

lla

I HAVEN'T BEEN able to stop crying for seven days.

It feels like I have a giant hole ripped in my gut and my heart aches more than I ever thought possible. "I shouldn't feel like this," I tell my mom, who drove to Santa Monica after I couldn't take a long enough break from my tears to have a conversation with her. "I've had relationships end and it's always been fine. We walked away and went on with our lives, and I didn't look back. I don't know what's happening."

My mom puts a teakettle on the stove to boil water and signals for me to sit in the banquette under my kitchen window. I used to like having a cup of coffee there and looking out at the view of the Pacific Ocean, but after Archer showed me a completely new way to make use of a window seat at his house, sitting here feels hollow. Everything does.

I gaze at the view, which drew me to buy this house two years earlier. Now I long to stare at the miles of grapevines laden with fruit ripening in the Napa sun.

My mom bustles in my kitchen, pulling mugs from my cupboards and opening my fridge to look for creamer. Her light brown hair is pulled back into a ponytail and she shuffles around in workout pants, a long sweater, and Ugg boots. It's clear where I get my fashion sense.

By the time the kettle whistles, she's fished a box of Girl Scout cookies from the freezer and assembled the Thin Mints on a plate. She brings this to my round marble table, along with two mugs of tea. I can smell the lavender mingling with the decaffeinated black tea, and it makes me long for Buttercup Hill. Everywhere I turn there are memories of Archer, and each one makes the tears spring forth anew.

"Oh, honey, come here," my mom says when she sees that I'm crying again. She pushes the mugs and cookies aside and comes to sit next to me on the bench. She puts her arms around me and pulls me close. I let her smooth my hair and rub my back, all things I believed I'd outgrown when I became an adult. A part of me is relieved to know I'll probably never outgrow these mom moments.

I didn't think I had any tears left but they keep coming. We sit there for so long that the tea goes cold. When my sobs subside, I sip the lukewarm beverage.

My mom pushes the plate of cookies to me, but I shake my head. "I have no appetite."

"You're in love. And heartbroken. I can see it on your face. So whatever is going wrong with Callum, you'll work it out. I know you will, and the wedding date isn't for months," she says, popping a cookie into her mouth.

It's then that I realize how much I've withheld from her. I shake my head. "No. Mom, I'm not going to marry Callum. And that's not who I'm crying over."

She gives me a bewildered look and tucks a strand of hair

behind her ear, ready to listen to whatever I plan to say. "Oh, my girl is never far from drama." I know she means it to sound sweet, like she's on my side no matter how scandalous my behavior is, but for once, I push back at the perception people have of me—including my own mother.

"It's not drama. Callum cheated on me. He and I are done. I don't love him. But the engagement was a sham to begin with. I never loved him. It was cooked up by our publicists to solve our respective image problems. I'm sorry if I'm not the perfect daughter with the perfect husband, but I did it so I could adopt. At least I was going to be the perfect mother. Or try." It pains me to burst my mom's bubble, the idea she had for me as a glowing bride, but she might as well know the real me.

"Oh, honey. There's no such thing as the perfect mother." She points to herself. "Case in point. And I'm sorry if I've made you believe I'd ever question your choices. And good riddance to someone who'd do that to you or my future grandchild. I'd like to call him up and tell him exactly what I think of his cheating cowboy self."

"Be my guest."

I attempt a hollow laugh, so I'm not expecting my breath to catch as I inhale. Or the tears I try to blink back. My mom reaches out to hug me and I gratefully embrace her. When she lets me go, she puts her hands on my shoulders and nods as though something has been decided.

"I'm sorry you're so sad about how things went with Callum. But you'll find your way, and when the time's right, you'll be an excellent mother."

I shake my head. "It's not that. I met someone else who's amazing, but we have no chance at a real future, so we ended things. That's why I'm sad. I miss him."

"Tell me about him, this man you're in love with."

"I don't think I want to talk about it." I take a sip of tea, unsure if I want to tell her about Archer. It will probably just make me sadder.

My mom throws up her hands. "Why are you being so stubborn?"

"Fine. His name is Archer, and I love him. I do. For the first time in my life, I actually feel like I've found the fairy tale prince. He calls me princess, if you can believe it. But so what? He doesn't want kids and I'm going to be a mom, so it's a non-starter."

She stirs some cream into the lukewarm tea but doesn't drink it. I can tell she's thinking by the way she fixates on the motion of the spoon. "You're certain of this?"

"Mom, when he found out there's a baby I have a real chance of adopting soon, you should've seen the look on his face. He looked happy for me but resigned to letting it be the end of us. There was never any discussion about us staying together for the long haul and doing this together. He offered to marry me to help keep the adoption going through, but I know now that I don't want a marriage of convenience. Especially with him."

My mom takes a long inhale that seems to speak its own language, as only my mother could. Problem is that I don't know what she's saying. Face stern, she taps a finger against her chin.

"If he feels the way you do, that doesn't sound like convenience. It sounds like love."

"No. He said he didn't want kids many times. Why would that change just because I'm in a pickle?" I think about it. "He only offered after my lawyer suggested I stay with Callum, so it wasn't so much that he had a change of heart. He was just trying to be a good guy."

"Or maybe that good guy really loves you more than he loves his plan to be childless."

I want to believe her, but I can't carry that responsibility for changing his plans. Eventually, he'll resent me for it.

"No. He wants what he wants. Or doesn't want, in this case."

She looks thoughtful. "A lot of people don't think they want to be parents until they're faced with it."

I shrug. Archer has made it clear how he feels.

"Listen, you know I love you more than anything, but I wasn't ready to be a mother until that pregnancy test came back positive. First, I freaked out, then I was in denial, and then I started to come around to the idea of being a parent. Probably a reason Mother Nature gives us nine months. Some of us need it to wrap our brains around the idea."

"Not being ready to be a parent is different from not wanting kids," I clarify, unwilling to let her be right when she doesn't know Archer.

"All I'm saying is that he might not know what he wants until he wants it with a person he loves. And based on how you're wallowing, I'd say whatever you have between you is different than anything you've felt before in a relationship."

"It is."

"Then talk to him. You owe yourselves that much."

I take a sip of my tea, which is so cold I wince. "Why are we drinking this?"

"Because crying makes you dehydrated. Listen to your mother." She puts an arm around me and hugs me tight.

CHAPTER 36

rcher

IT FEELS good to go for a run around the property, mainly because it forces me to breathe.

In, out.

In.

Out.

I never spent much time thinking about why I like to run. It's not a contact sport like hockey, so I'm not getting my ass handed to me like I did the other day. But maybe it's the solitude and the steady drumming of my feet on the pavement. A different kind of contact sport—me and the earth, each step letting me know I'm alive.

I round the bend behind Sweet Butter and stop to stretch my calves before going inside for a quick latte to drink on my walk back home.

Same routine as always—workout, coffee, shower, twelve-hour day. I don't even question it anymore. I just show up and get things done.

Latte in hand, I walk slowly home, enjoying the quiet chirp of birds in the surrounding vineyards. The picking season is over, and it's almost time for bottling. I can tell we're within a week or two of the wines being ready. Then all hell will break loose. For once, I'll welcome the distraction.

Even after the beating I took on the ice and the thinking I've done, I haven't been able to shake myself free from inertia. Haven't picked up the phone. Haven't responded to Ella's texts, the few she sent.

Her words were sweet, and she seemed forgiving of my limitations, which made me feel like even more of a bad guy. Why in the world would I deserve love, especially hers, when I've turned it away and hurt her? Am I really the only one who sees that?

All she asked was to talk things through. But I still don't see a way forward for us, so what's the point of talking? Or seeing her and opening up the wounds that have barely had a chance to scab over?

Better to acknowledge that I can't do what everyone is asking of me and try to move forward.

I drop the coffee in a trashcan and walk faster. Then I run, pushing until my lungs burn with the pain I feel like I deserve. My lungs throb from the cool air ripping through them. Before I realize it, my route takes me around the back of the restaurant and the inn and I'm coming up on the lake. It's impossible now to go anywhere without thinking about Ella.

The swans are back, floating along with me as I slow my pace to a jog on the path. "You too?" I ask, certain that they're here to tell me all the things I'm doing wrong with my life. Fortunately, they can't talk. Grateful for their silence, I stop running and take a seat on the bench that faces the lake, not feeling a need to rush back to work right away.

A light breeze filters over the hills, chilling the sweat from my skin. I take a deeper breath and let it out slowly, closing my eyes against the pale early morning sun.

"You're not him."

The voice comes from behind me, but I recognize my sister's no-nonsense tone. A broad shadow looms over me from behind, now that she's standing there.

I shake my head. "People have got to stop sneaking up on me and dropping ominous one-liners about my life."

"Ha." The shadow shifts as she drops onto the bench next to me, but it doesn't disappear. Clouds, I guess. "It wasn't meant to be ominous. I had half a conversation in my head first. The last part just came out loud."

"What was the rest? You might as well tell me, since everyone seems to have opinions about what I'm doing wrong these days."

Beatrix sits next to me and takes a sip from a coffee cup without a lid. Steam rises from the top of the light brown beverage and twirls in the breeze. "Honestly, what I said is really the gist."

"I'm not him… Who is him?"

"Dad."

I roll my eyes. "I know that."

"Do you?" She turns to face me, but I stare out at the lake, willing myself not to get riled up. I've run myself to exhaustion this morning trying to keep the negative thoughts from taking over my mind.

"Of course."

"You don't."

I try for a cleansing breath, but I only manage half an inhale before my frustration gets the better of me. "I would really like it if everyone would stop lecturing me."

"Then stop acting like a child who needs a lesson."

"What the—?"

"You're not Dad and you don't have to be Dad." Beatrix starts talking again before I can get words out.

"Someone has to do the job."

"Sure. Someone. Best case, someone who wants the job. Not you."

"He picked me."

"Because he respects you and knows you can carry on his work and grow the business, but guess what? It's not up to him to decide your life for you."

I'm about to argue back, but her words hit me differently than all the other well-meaning lectures I've been getting lately.

"I know that. Or at least, I thought I did."

"Go on."

This time, I get a full breath in and let it out slowly. "It's complicated. You know that."

It's really not.

"And all this crap about you not wanting to be a father, what's that?"

"It's the truth, or at least it was." I say the words, but I feel like they lack the conviction they had before I met Ella. Before I let the idea of being a parent—with her—edge its way into my thoughts and stick there.

Maybe I do have hopes and dreams.

"Right. Past tense. Now you have someone worth changing your mind, someone you love." Beatrix was never one to mince words. "I see how you are with Fiona. We all do. You were meant to be a dad. I can't understand how you don't see it yourself."

I swallow hard, not wanting to say the words out loud, even though they've been swirling in my brain for as long as I can remember. They're as true as anything I know about when grapes are at the perfect time for picking.

"He wasn't there for us. Work always came first. And when I look at how I am with my job—always chasing deadlines, always a day late and a dollar short, always worried about letting you guys down—I don't see how I could possibly be everything Dad was and also be a good father. As Dad was not."

Now it's Trix's turn to inhale a deep breath. She nods as the air leaves her lungs in a cloud through the morning chill. "It's why we want you to leave the winery."

Her words hit me like a shard of glass through my gut. "What? Why? You think I'm fucking it up?"

"No! We think you've saved the place from ruin six times over. But look at what it's doing to you. You're miserable and you've walked away from the one person who clearly makes you happy. You're giving up on love because you think you'd be letting us down?"

"Pretty much."

"Well, hear this. The only way you're letting us down is by walking away from the chance to be happy. Do you think any of us wants that?"

"We need to keep the winery going."

"Fuck the winery."

I startle at her harsh words. She's never seemed to want anything except our family business and the inn and the restaurant. Surely, she doesn't mean it.

"Seriously. Dad isn't aware, and you don't owe him anything. You've already preserved and grown his legacy in ways that would make him proud. So now, you owe yourself. Go back to LA, get your start-up going again. Or fanboy my husband around the country and be the Otters' equipment manager."

"Thanks, but no thanks."

"Then talk to Ella. Give the idea of a life with her a chance. Open yourself up to the idea of being a dad. You'd be amazing, which is a pretty big feat, considering who you had as a role model."

Her words hit me in a way they haven't before. "He was tough on you too, huh?"

"He was toughest on the ones he loved the most. Guess maybe that tells you something."

I nod because she's probably right.

And because life—or our dad—has an ironic sense of timing, both our cell phones start beeping at the same time. We look down to see the same message from Dad's nurse, telling us she called the doctor to the house. Dad's taken a turn.

rcher

WHEN WE GET to the house, the nurse is there waiting for us. She hands me a letter with my name on the envelope in my dad's messy scrawl. "His instructions were to give you this if he reached a point where he couldn't hand it off himself. I'm betting he still has many days ahead, but I'm not psychic, so here it is."

"Thank you, Betsy." I take the letter and turn it over in my hands before shoving it in my pocket.

Betsy starts up the stairs. "The doctor is still examining him. He may want to brief you before you all go in to see him." She gestures to the second floor, where I hear the hushed voices of Dash and Jax talking with PJ.

I start to follow Betsy, but Trix lays a hand on my arm and gestures with her head toward my pocket. "You don't want to see what it says?"

"I dunno. Do I?" I can only imagine what kinds of "take care of the family" pressure my dad wants to impart.

She shrugs. "Open it anyway."

I'm too worn out to argue, so I pull out the letter and read it aloud.

ARCHER,

By now, you're probably pretty pissed at me, both for leaving you to manage the winery I built and for not giving you an explanation for my shenanigans. And maybe you're also a little mad at me for dying, if I did that, or getting sick enough for this letter to be sent. Maybe it's because you miss me, but I don't want to presume too much. I know I was not a very good father.

"HE ALWAYS CUTS right to the chase." My voice comes out like a croak, and despite the situation, a hollow chuckle escapes me at my dad's pithy recap.

"So, are you?" she asks.

"What?"

"Pissed at him?"

I start to nod because yes, of course, I'm angry. But my response comes from a different part of my brain. "No."

She nods and leans her head against my shoulder. "Good. There's nothing to be gained by it now."

"Maybe he knew he had limitations, even if he never admitted to them."

We keep reading.

BELIEVE IT OR NOT, **everything I did was with my kids in mind. I felt I owed something to Graham after the way I left his mother and denied him a family, even though you were all living right nearby. Maybe you won't see it that way, but I** hope you'll come to realize that family is family, even the ones you stumble into because your dad has ransacked your company to buy him land next door. He's a good man in a world where we need good men. I hope you'll all find solace in each other.

I CLOSE MY EYES. "It's unbelievable but so typical of him, somehow," I say. I can't even get mad because there's something sweet about the way he thought things through. If completely misguided and nuts.

As TO THE FIRE, I hope everything worked out the way I planned. Our insurance policy was meant to reimburse you for the damages and give you a choice. Rebuild or take the money and go live the life you want. No strings attached. When a person builds a family business, there's always the hope that a son or daughter will find the same passion that went into growing it in the first place. My hope is that you'll want to keep Buttercup Hill alive for another generation. But I'm aware it was my dream, not yours. So now you have a choice. Build it your way, or go the way your dreams take you. Either way, I hope you can do it without too many hard feelings about your dad and the way I made sense of the choices I had.

BE WELL,
    Dad

A SMALL SLIP of paper falls from the envelope and flutters to the ground. "What's that?" Trix asks, bending to pick it up.

We open the folded square and look at it together. It's a list of letters and numbers that I recognize as positions in the bottling racks. I've spent so many years there sweating over our various vintages, there's no mistaking what it is. And in my dad's slanted handwriting, a few final words, "Cheers, kids."

"Guess my work around here is never really done. Probably some last bit of business he wants us to take care of in the cellar. Even now, he's giving me a to-do list."

Betsy beckons us upstairs where the doctor is waiting to talk to us. "He had a mini-stroke, nothing fatal, certainly, but not good for someone in his condition," the doctor tells us. "He's suffering partial paralysis on his left side. You'll notice his facial muscles are a little limp on the left."

"Is there anything you can do?" Trix asks.

The doctor shakes his head. "He just needs to rest. The paralysis could abate over time. You can go in and talk to him quietly. He might hear you. Good to have love around him."

My siblings and I look at each other and Jax points to me. "You go."

I nod, having no idea what to say to my dad, and fearful that he won't even recognize me like last time. I take the stairs two at a time toward his room.

My dad doesn't move or give any indication he knows I'm in the room. His meal sits untouched on a tray by his bed, which confirms that he hasn't lifted his head off the pillow. Even in his most confused and agitated state, he always had an appetite.

Betsy wheels the ergonomic desk chair over to me and leaves the room wordlessly. I sit in the proffered chair and stare at my dad, who looks like he's sleeping peacefully, which feels like a relief after so many interactions when he was angry. It also feels like a sad surrender for a man with his kind of strength and loud voice to be still and quiet. It's not the real him.

I'm not sure what I'm supposed to do right now. Talking to a man who probably can't hear me seems like something people do in movies—an unburdening, a forgiving.

The TV is turned to an animal documentary channel without the sound, and a cheetah on screen is walking through the African tundra hunting its next meal. I wonder if my dad expressed an interest in animals at one point or if his nurse just decided it was a safe thing to have on in the background. If it were me, seeing animals gnaw at the carcasses of other animals would not be relaxing, but my dad seems relaxed, so I don't question it.

Walking over to the bed, I look for signs that my dad is uncomfortable with me coming closer to him. Sometimes he holds up a hand to keep me out of his personal space, but not today.

I take a seat on the end of his bed so I can talk with him out of earshot of Betsy, who knows enough to walk outside and give us some time alone. "Dad," I say, watching him for a glimmer of recognition that I'm speaking to him. Even if he thinks I'm one of my brothers, it's something. He doesn't move. "I read your letter."

Moving a bit closer, I think about what I want to say. I used to know when my dad was ignoring me. There were always subtle signs that he was annoyed—the furrow of his brow, the set of his jaw—the same things Ella says she sees in me.

Now, he doesn't flinch.

"I don't understand why you did what you did with the money and the fire," I tell him. Even if he doesn't acknowledge that he hears me, I tell myself he does. "But, Dad, we've got this. We have your back. We'll keep this place going because it's our legacy. You built it and that's worth something to me. I know I haven't always said so. I mean, I guess I've pretty much said the opposite, but that's just me being grouchy. It's not that I don't love it here." I take a long, deep breath. "I do love it here. And I love you. But I think this place isn't for me. Maybe it never was. And as much as I want to keep your dream alive, I think my time

—my *life*—would be better spent doing something else. I'll be happier, and that's gotta make for a better situation here. So…I guess that's it."

I close my eyes for a moment because I feel the hot sting of tears and I will not cry in front of my dad, even if he's not aware I'm even here. He raised me to keep my shit together. The bed shifts, and my dad's hand reaches out and covers mine. My eyes pop open, but he looks exactly the same as he has the whole time I've been talking. Serene. Expressionless. Void of personality. But his hand stays on mine—I didn't imagine that.

Then the tears come. And I don't care if he knows it.

lla

Two Weeks Later

Klieg lights sit beneath the marquee of the movie theater in Westwood, still one of the best places for a premiere, as far as I'm concerned. The word *Shimmer* is exactly that in large lights adorned with flashing sequins.

A red carpet runs down the middle of Broxton Avenue, which is closed to traffic and blocked off by fake ivy-covered walls covered in sparkly lights. Overhead, an arch of champagne-colored balloons bounce against the darkening blue sky. Night can't come soon enough for me. I need to get through the gamut of photographers and fans and slip into the dark movie theater, where I don't have to smile and pretend I'm not coming apart on the inside.

When I invited Archer to be my date to this premiere a month ago, I never imagined the weeks that would follow, the ripping out of my heart, the sadness it's taken all my acting training to hide.

"Ella, who are you wearing?" "Ella, I'm hearing relationship rumors. Can you comment?" "Ella, who are you dating?"

I've steeled myself against these questions and politely given a well-trained Mona Lisa smile. "I'll be happy to talk about the film during the Q and A afterward."

I pose for a few pictures against the movie backdrop, all glitter and flowers to conjure the rom-com vibe that hasn't changed since my first starring role. I've made this walk from town car to theater entrance down dozens of red carpets in dozens of cities around the world. I barely need to think about what to say now, and I can focus all my attention on not tripping on the carpet.

Same old, same old.

But tonight, everything feels different.

I went back to my lawyer's office after Archer walked away and told her she needs to lobby hard for me as a perfectly competent adoptive mother. I'm done apologizing for bad judgement calls I made in the past, and I've stopped berating myself for them as well.

Everyone does dumb shit when they're young. It's unfair for me to be held to a different standard just because of my career. And because I'm a woman.

Archer was right, even if I haven't heard from him in weeks, and my lawyer has been doing her best to move forward with the adoption. I can do it as a single mother. No one will love a baby more than I will.

I glance up at Nancy, my publicist, who is waiting by the door of the theater to intercept me on the way in. She nods, letting me know I've posed for enough photos and can slip in beside her, so she can escort me to a private room. I'll wait there while the film is screened and enter the theater at the end for the question-and-answer session with the director.

Tonight, it all feels harder than usual. Normally, I like seeing fans who've come early to stand outside the velvet ropes and take photos. They wave and shout and I wave back, always grateful that they support me and my career. I'll never take them for granted. But sometimes, a girl is just worn-out, and tonight I'm finding it hard to hide behind my smile and pretend my heart isn't broken.

It's not that I expected to hear from Archer after I left. And I know the last thing he has time for is to surf social media looking for tabloid stories about Callum and me, so he probably hasn't even seen the photos that seem to be plastered everywhere and our joint statement about how our careers put too much strain on our relationship for it to work out. Evidence for all the world to see that I want more than what we had.

"Excuse me." The voice is deep, gruff, and sexy as hell.

I whip around to find Archer standing behind me looking like a cover model in a dark suit that hugs his broad shoulders and tapers at his slim waist. Underneath, a crisp white shirt is open at the collar, showing off the tanned skin of his neck that I'd like to lick right here in the middle of the crowd.

He holds a chilled bottle of beer in one hand and a glass of white wine in the other, which he offers to me. "Can I offer you a drink?"

I feel my cheeks pull so hard that my face erupts into a smile, even though I'm still sad about how we ended and mad that he hasn't reached out at all.

"It's good to see you," I whisper, knowing he can barely hear me in the noisy crowd, but somehow he does.

"You too."

I take the proffered wine and sip from the glass. The cool liquid slides down my throat, and at first, I'm just grateful for something to do because I still don't know what else to say to him. But something strikes me as very familiar, and I take another sip. "Is this...?"

No. It can't be.

"Special edition vintage. Buttercup Hill Pebble and Clay. Just bottled this week."

"Aw, I missed the bottling."

"There's always another bottling season. The bigger news is that if you do a little searching, you'll probably find a business license for a new start-up. It's going to build an app to tell you exactly when you should drink it. But spoiler alert, today's the day."

My smile pulls at my cheeks so hard they hurt. "You did it."

He looks satisfied with himself. He lighter. He looks free. "I took the first step."

"Congratulations." I press my lips together, so proud of him and sad at the same time because I miss him and I love him. And I can't have him.

"Thank you."

"So you...came down here to...pour me a glass of wine?" I blink at him, trying to make sense of what he's doing at my movie premiere.

"Not just that. Can we go somewhere to talk?" He gestures to a private trailer he shouldn't know about. Nancy is sitting on the couch inside, and I start to explain to him that we can't use the trailer because it's serving as Nancy's office tonight. This whole event is under her oversight, and she needs to work.

But she stands up without a word and nods at Archer before exiting the trailer and disappearing into the party. "How did you...?" I'm still speaking in partial sentences because I'm so confused about what he's doing here and how he managed to commandeer Nancy's trailer.

We climb up the stairs of the trailer. Archer goes first, and then he extends a hand to me. I follow him inside and close the door. We sit next to each other on the small couch and put our drinks on a side table. Archer stretches his legs out and his feet touch the wall on the opposite side. "Not a lot of space for a big guy," I remark.

"Plenty of space for a grumpy grape," he says, which makes me smile all over again.

"I reached out to your lawyer and submitted a background check. If I'm going to be in your daughter's life, I don't want there to be anything that stands in your way when the judge looks at your adoption application."

I stand there, stunned, digesting what he's saying. "You want to…be in her life?" I'm almost afraid to ask because he's been so adamant about not wanting to be a father.

He nods and kneels in front of me. "I want to be in *your* life. Every damn day. I want to share the parenting journey. With you and only with you. I never thought I'd want to be a father because I was convinced I'd be awful at it. Like my own dad. But maybe it's time to stop blaming him for everything. I can still make my own choices. And I choose you. I choose us. I want it more than anything because I love you more than anything."

My heart swells with overwhelming love for this man who's shown me the difference between going through the motions like I'm playing a role in a film and the way it feels to do it for love. I never want to do things any other way.

"I choose us too. I just never wanted you to feel forced."

"I don't. I feel lucky."

From across the parking lot, I can hear that the crowd noise has died down, which probably means the movie is starting. That gives Archer and me two hours to sit here and figure out where we go from here.

"I need to be sure, Archer. You really want this with me, right? You're not just trying to be a good guy?"

Still kneeling, he reaches for my hands. "I am trying to be a good guy. The kind of guy you deserve. I'm not doing it because I feel obligated or because I'd still love to ring Callum's little goddamn neck. I want to be a good guy—the best possible guy—because you are the best possible woman I could imagine being with. And if I'm lucky enough to have you, I want to give you everything—kids, a beautiful life, and all the things a princess deserves. Will you be my forever, Ella Fieldstone?"

My heart leaps into my throat. "Wow, are you…?"

"Asking you to marry me? Yes."

I start fanning myself because I suddenly feel hot and dizzy. Without a word, Archer scoots over and tilts me so my head rests in his lap because he knows what I need. Like breathing.

From his lap, I look up at the man I want to look at every day for good, and I nod. "Yes. I will be your forever."

He smiles. "Do we need to make a big media announcement after the movie since you'll be up there for the Q and A and all that?"

"Do you want me to do that?" I sit up and assess him.

Archer brings both hands to my cheeks and kisses me. It's not just an ordinary kiss. It's a movie star kiss. It's deep and thorough and it makes me dizzy in a whole new way. But I know he'll catch me if I wobble, so I lean in for all of it.

Tipping his forehead against mine, he shakes his head. "No media. Just us. Let's enjoy being us for a while."

"Let's enjoy it forever."

CHAPTER 39

rcher

Three Months Later

Weddings at Buttercup Hill have always been special events, and not just because they take months to plan. It's the over-whelming beauty of the vineyards which stretch for miles under warm sun and perfect skies, to be sure. But there's a different kind of magic that settles over the venue when the bride walks down the aisle toward her forever partner.

I never understood that until today, the day when I'm standing under an arch of roses, nervous as hell, waiting for the most amazing woman I've ever met to walk down the aisle and marry me.

If there isn't some amount of fairy dust, fortune, and magic involved in me finding a woman like Ella Fieldstone and getting

263

her to agree to spend her life with me, I don't understand anything about the world.

My siblings walk down the aisle with their husbands, wives, fiancés, girlfriends. All of them managed to get themselves paired off before I found someone, even though I'm the oldest. I never expected to be standing here at all, let alone the last of the pack, so I'm grateful.

PJ walks down the aisle first in a short black dress with a full skirt that flounces as she moves. It suits her—playful and appropriate at the same time, which she manages to be at work and in her life with Colin, who I have a new respect for, now that I've seen him make an ass of himself on the ice. He gives me a little salute before taking his post to my left, and PJ kisses me on the cheek before moving to my other side.

Jax strides down the aisle, faster than he should, and faster than the music that's supposed to give him his cue. I watch Ruby pull on his arm to slow him down. He looks down at his feet and takes measured steps as she looks at me and smiles.

Dash escorts Mallory, gripping her elbow as she holds her flower bouquet in her hands. Her black dress is strapless and loose-fitting—to me, it looks like a long black sack, but Ella has already explained that it's made by some designer who Mallory loves, so what do I know? All I can see is that my youngest brother looks as happy as I feel, which is all I care about.

I will always wear the mantle of family caretaker, even on my wedding day. It makes me feel goddamn peaceful seeing that my siblings are paired up, looking happy.

Trix looks especially tall in her heels and a long black silk dress that winds around her ankles as she walks on the arm of Ren in a dark suit. He catches my eye before going to stand with the other groomsmen, and maybe it's bromance talking, but I swear he winks at me.

Finally, our half brother Graham walks in with Fiona, who seems to be keeping a rather large distance between them. Fiona is at an age where she does not like boys, and apparently that applies to relatives too. They both wear plastered-on smiles and walk twice as fast as Jax. I'm not the only one who notices. By the time they reach me at the altar, half the guests are giggling at their awkwardness, but neither of them seems to care.

Dad sits in the front row in his wheelchair. He has a far-off look on his face, and the doctors warned us he may not know where he is, but I want to believe he does. And that he's a little bit proud.

Our mom made excuses for why she couldn't be here, with promises to visit in a month or two, but I'm too happy today to think too hard about it. I realize now that it must have been pretty awful for her to live with Dad if it caused her to move across the country from her kids and never come back. It's not something I'm willing to think about on an otherwise perfect day.

The only thing missing is the woman I need by my side so badly that I've started to sweat up here. Dash hands me a handkerchief, and after I finish mopping the sheen from the back of my neck, I look down and notice it's monogrammed with the letter C. *It's Dad's*, he mouths. My heart leaps into my throat and threatens to strangle my breath.

And that's when the string quartet ends their jazz medley and starts playing the song Ella chose for her walk down the aisle. She wouldn't tell me what she chose and swore she'd never admit it even if I guessed it right, so I didn't bother to try.

As soon as the first notes sound, I know it's "Little Wing," the Jimi Hendrix song that was playing at the party where I thought I was cool enough to introduce myself to Ella Fieldstone. As I listen to the string rendition of the song, the lyrics come back to me, and I realize how appropriate they are.

A hush falls over the crowd and I struggle to pull air into my lungs, not wanting to be the groom who sees his bride for the first time and fucking falls over. Ella appears at the end of the aisle, which seems so much longer now than it did when each of my siblings walked down it just minutes ago.

Her hair is wild in that way I love it, trailing down her back with flowers woven into the strands. Her dress, a whisp of silk that hugs every curve, is beautifully simple, letting her radiance shine through. Her flowers are a loose bouquet that I picked with Beatrix this morning and left on her doorstep. She's holding them against the back of Polly, our sleeping daughter, who's nuzzled against her mom's chest, as she has been nearly constantly since the adoption went through a month ago.

Ella says she feels like she was magically transformed into a mother, and it's true that being a mom seems instinctive. But really, no transformation was needed. She already was an amazing mother—she just needed someone to take care of. Two of us, really.

Ella's parents wait for her at the last row of guests, and when she reaches them, they each grasp one of her arms and guide her the rest of the way down the aisle, where Ella seems to glide between the white chairs and rows and rows of friends who've shown up for us today. When they reach me, they each kiss Ella on the cheek and give me a hug. I've gotten to know them a little bit in the months since we decided to keep Ella's original wedding date, and they've already become family.

Ella looks directly into my eyes, and the certainty and love I see in hers allows me to let out a long breath. I feel steadier. The nerves disappear when she hands Polly to me, and I feel the warmth of our daughter against my chest.

I lean in and whisper something that isn't part of my vows. It's not for anyone else. Just her. "I didn't think it was possible to have love more than I already do with you, but this girl…" I kiss Polly on the head. "I realized that I have even more to give. And so much to be grateful for."

"You were made to be a dad," she whispers back, eyes tearing.

I wipe away the solitary tear that rolls down her cheek. "I adore you both so much."

"You okay?" she whispers, always in tune with how I'm feeling, even when she's only been next to me for five seconds.

"I'm a little wobbly," I admit.

She laughs. "Oh no, you too?"

Ella hands her flowers to Beatrix and finally turns to face me. I take her hands, and it steadies us both. As far as I'm concerned, there's nothing else to say or do. This is the kind of homecoming I never dared imagine for myself. I don't need anything else.

But for the first time, after barely taking an interest in the hundreds of weddings on our property over the years, I understand the reason for saying the vows aloud in front of the people who love us most. There's something about having them bear witness.

I glance out over the vineyards at Buttercup Hill and back at my gorgeous, soon-to-be wife. Then I look down at our daughter. *Our* daughter. And it's all I've ever wanted.

I lean close to Ella and whisper something that has just occurred to me. Once more, it's not part of my vows, just something I want her to know. "I didn't think instalove was real, but then I met you."

She smiles. "Look at you using rom-com language."

"I'm in love with the rom-com princess. Seems appropriate."

"Your rom-com princess is in love with you too."

And the ceremony begins.

EPILOGUE

rcher

Two Weeks Later

The whole family walks down to the cellar, and as I'm comforted by the casual chatter of the group, all paired up with the ones they love, I notice Graham following behind. I signal for him to join Ella and me at the front of our family herd, my dad's words echoing in my brain. "Family is family." We've never treated Graham much like family, but there's still time.

"How'd bottling season go for you?" I ask.

He looks momentarily surprised by my interest. "Good, actually." I see the hint of a proud smile. "I'd love to have you taste some of the new wines if you're down for it."

"I'm down."

Ella slips her hand into mine. I don't need to see her face to know she's grinning at me and my slight progress toward being less grumpy.

The wine cave runs nearly a mile underground, so it takes us a good ten minutes to reach the area that corresponds to the numbers on the slip of paper.

Trix insisted we wait until after the adoption went through—and then the wedding and the honeymoon—to follow our dad's instructions and come down here. "Just in case it's something stressful. I want to give you two at least a little time to be a happy family," she said. The idea that I have my own family still takes some getting used to, but it's the best fucking thing in the world.

It's dark, lighted only by small path lights on the ground and sconces every hundred feet or so that illuminate the lot numbers of the various bottles.

"Now we know why Archer likes it down here. It's dark and quiet like your personality," Jax teases.

"Hilarious. Actually, I rarely come to this area. It's all the really old vintages that mostly sit here unless collectors or high-end restaurants order cases of them." In other words, they're bottles that can run in the hundreds and thousands of dollars because of their age and rarity.

I use the flashlight on my phone to lead us to the area specified on the paper and find the section of bottles in question. When I pull the first one out and look at the label, I notice something familiar about the date, which is over thirty years old.

"Trix, you were born in ninety-six, weren't you?" I hand over the bottle so she can inspect it, already anticipating what I'll find when I pull out the other bottles. Sure enough, they all correspond to our birth years, including one for Graham.

"You never noticed these were here, Arch?" Dash asks, looking at the label of his bottle of cabernet.

"There are sixty thousand bottles down here. I don't look at every one of them," I say.

"Maybe you should."

"Maybe *you* should, since you'll be taking over the wine-making operations." I let the words land in the dark room and wait for my siblings to pick up on the conversation. It takes a moment for their chatter to die down, but one by one, they stop talking and look from one of us to the other.

"Hang on, did you just say—?" PJ tilts her head as though it will bring my words back for her to hear them again.

I nod. "Yes. I'm stepping down, as soon as I can get Dash trained. He's going to run the show here, and I'm going to…I've been working on something else." It feels good to say it. "Something I like." I give them the broad strokes of the wine app, which is fully funded and almost ready to launch, and everyone seems fine with my change of direction. Happy, even.

"Well, cheers to that," Beatrix says, holding up her bottle. We each bring ours up and clink them against hers and each other's.

"I know I knew our dad the least, but I'm pretty sure we're not just supposed to be looking at these bottles," Graham says.

"Smart man," Jax says, his arm around Ruby who is geeking out on the various vintages she never knew we had.

"If we're opening these, we need some fat and salt. Palate cleansers. Good glasses," she says, her voice getting higher in excitement. Jax beams at her and nods.

"Let's do it."

The chatter is louder as we make our way back out of the cave. The mood feels lighter, at least mine does. With the final piece of our dad's cryptic puzzle in place, I let out a sigh of relief. "I know what my first toast is going to be," I say, my voice booming in the cavernous space. "To no more weird charges on our balance sheet, no unexplained fires on our property…" I trail off before putting my foot in my mouth, but Graham punches my shoulder.

"It's okay, you can say it. No new surprise family members."

"Hey, if they're all as great as you, I'll take 'em," Jax says.

"Hear! Hear!" Dash agrees.

A few minutes later, we exit the cave, returning to the lazy afternoon sunlight filtering through the vineyards. Out of sheer excitement, Ruby practically skips down the path toward the outdoor patio next to the tasting room. She busies herself with glassware and snacks while the rest of us pull out chairs and push three tables together so we can sit together.

Colin pulls PJ onto his lap, and I revel at what a great couple my oldest friend and my sister make—and how I never saw it coming back when they were sneaking around Buttercup Hill and trying to keep their relationship under wraps.

Beatrix sits and keeps a chair open for Ren, who's busy talking to Dash about hockey. My poor brother actually thinks that after our scrimmage with the team he might have a chance at trying out for the Otters. Ren is humoring him, but I can see a future beat-down on the ice, similar to what I endured, if Dash persists.

Polly is at Trix's house with her daughter, Daisy. It's nap time for both of them, and Fiona takes her job seriously as babysitter.

Graham and Jax have been locked in conversation during the entire walk out of the wine cave. I've caught bits and pieces, but mostly it seems like they're strategizing how to connect the two pieces of adjacent land we each own and turn them into one large property. "We can keep yours under the Duck Feather brand and do limited-edition wines, but we should still share our labor pool and resources," Jax says. It makes me feel better about leaving the family business when I know that he's minding the bottom line. More than that, he likes what he does. It makes all the difference, as I've come to understand.

"I'm game for that, but do we want to do a big rollout in the media to announce the merger, maybe do some open house days with tastings?" Graham is the most animated I've ever seen him. Jax nods, rubbing a hand over his chin in that way he does when he's thinking.

"Totally. PJ will eat that up."

"What are you saying about me?" PJ calls from her perch on Colin's lap.

Jax waves a hand. "Fill you in later."

I can't help but think that Dad would be happy about Graham and Jax joining forces. It seems like that's what he wanted all along, but he was too afraid to connect us in person while he was able.

Ella comes over from where she's been talking to Mallory. "Hey." I pull her into my side and drape an arm over her shoulder. "That looked serious. You two planning to take over the world?" Mallory and Ella have really connected in the time Ella's been spending at Buttercup Hill, and it makes me happy to see Ella at home here. Even if I'm no longer running the winery, we're still going to live on the property for part of the year—one big family.

"Oh, yeah. She says Dash wants me to do another guacamole taste-off. He's determined to win," she says with the wink of a woman who knows that's impossible.

"Of course he is."

"Do you have some tricks up your sleeve to keep your title as reigning avocado champion?" I kiss her temple and feel her whole body melt against me. I'll never get tired of the feeling.

"You better believe it. Gotta keep a man on his toes."

I lean back and regard her smile. "Feels like you might mean someone other than Dash."

Her eyebrows bounce. "All to be revealed, Wine Daddy."

Before I can ask her to be more specific, Ruby comes back with wine openers and glasses, and I can see a few of our tasting room employees busy behind her putting together cheese plates with bread. "Whose are we opening first?" she asks, holding up the corkscrew.

We all look at each other, no one offering up their bottles. "You want to hang onto them, keep 'em as a reminder of Dad?" I ask the group.

"I dunno. I feel like he wants us to drink them," PJ says, offering hers up. She shrugs. "We're a winery, after all."

One by one, each of my siblings agrees and hands the bottles over to Ruby. She opens the first with a flourish. "This is the oldest vintage." Ruby pulls out the cork and hands it to me. I roll my thumb over the end of it and smell the fruity residue on the cork. I think of my dad putting the bottle aside the year I was born, and I wonder if he knew he'd have five more kids. The thought of him as a young man with big dreams makes me feel wistful that I didn't know him better when he was healthier, but I don't feel sad. I may not know him, but after walking in his shoes at the helm of Buttercup Hill, I feel like I understand him.

"You know what they say, oldest is best," I point out.

"I think they say oldest is just really fucking old," Jax says, earning a fist bump from Dash.

Ruby pours a taste and hands it to me. "You should do the honors."

I swirl the deep red liquid in my glass and watch it drip down the sides, the sugars stretching the legs of the cabernet. I dip my nose into the glass and inhale the heavy scent of the full-bodied wine.

Then I take a sip. Again, I imagine my dad doing the same thing before he instructed his team to bottle the vintage up. Just like I did a month ago when our cabernets were ready.

"It's amazing. Dad knew his wine," I say, tipping my head toward Ruby to pour glasses for everyone. She metes out small pours so we can all taste it, and everyone chimes in to agree that the wine is among the best we've ever had.

Jax holds up his glass and clinks it with a butter knife. "Feels like we should toast him." He looks at me and I nod, standing up. I wish our dad could be here with us, but he's not well enough. He's regained some function in his left side after the stroke, but his cognitive abilities are all but gone.

"To Dad. And all the half-baked ideas he had, and also to the really good ones. We're standing here together because of them, and I couldn't ask for a better bunch of people to call my family. Love you guys."

Glasses clink all around and everyone takes another sip of the wine.

I look at Ella, seeing everything I never knew I wanted in my life. "My heart knew all along."

"Knew what?"

"That you were the one. Back at that party when I tried to meet you, I think my heart knew you were it for me."

She smiles. "I'm glad you didn't give up on your heart."

I lift her up and hold her tight, transfixed by her beautiful pink cheeks, the light shining through her wild hair, her lips, which she lowers to mine. "I'm never going to want more than what I have right here in this moment. You are everything."

"You're my everything too," she says.

I look down at her flat stomach in disbelief that there's a baby growing in there. My baby. Against the odds, we're going to have another child in seven months. We're waiting a couple more weeks to tell anyone, but no one will be more excited than PJ. After all, she taught me everything I know about manifesting.

I think about all the years I convinced myself I couldn't be a father because I was too afraid to be the wrong kind of dad to kids who deserved better. "I'm going to give this baby the best possible life."

Ella nods, tears rolling down her cheeks. "I know you will. I've always known."

Wrapping her in my arms, I hold her tight, aware that there are three of us in this embrace. In less than a year we'll be a family of four. After that...who knows?

～

DEAR READER: Thank you for reading Love You Always! I hope you enjoyed Archer and Ella's story!

And...I have a new series in the works. We are traveling to Southern California for a group of smoking hot soccer stars play on a rival soccer team to the San Francisco Strikers! The first book, PLAYING THE FIELD, is a sizzling hot enemies-to-lovers story that will charm your socks off! You can preorder it NOW!

ACKNOWLEDGMENTS

I love my readers. That's it. That's the post.

It's also the truth. I could not write books for a living without you, and for that I will be forever grateful.

Jesse and Oliver, you make every day brighter, funnier, and just better by being you.

Thank you to Nicole and Erica for top-notch edits and for always making my words sound better. Leah, you have a gift for helping me find what's missing—thank you.

Echo Grayce I love the gorgeous cover x 2—you're amazing.

Valentine and the VPR family—you are the absolute best!

Bloggers and bookstagrammers—thank you for embracing my books and exposing my writing to readers. I couldn't do it without your help.

And to every writer who was afraid to put pen to paper for fear of rejection, I see you. You've got this.

ABOUT THE AUTHOR

Stacy Travis writes sexy, charming romance about bookish, sassy women and the hot cinamon roll heroes who fall for them. Keep the coffee coming, and she'll keep writing.

When she's not on a deadline, she's in running shoes complaining that all roads seem to go uphill. Or on the couch with a margarita. Or fangirling at a soccer game. She's never met a dog she didn't want to hug. And if you have no plans for Thanksgiving, she'll probably invite you to dinner. Stacy is the mom of two boys and two poorly-trained rescue dogs who keep her on her toes in Los Angeles.

Facebook reader group: Stacy's Saucy Sisters

Super fun newsletter: https://geni.us/travisNL

Tiktok: https://www.tiktok.com/@stacytravisauthor

Website: https://www.www.stacytravis.com

Email: stacytraviswrites@gmail.com - tell me what you're reading!

facebook.com/stacytravisromance
instagram.com/stacytravisauthor
bookbub.com/authors/stacy-travis
goodreads.com/stacytravis
tiktok.com/@stacytravisauthor

ALSO BY STACY TRAVIS

The Summer Heat Duet

1. The Summer of Him: A Mistaken-Identity Celebrity Romance

2. Forever with Him: An Opposites-Attract Contemporary Romance

The Berkeley Hills Series - all standalone novels

1. In Trouble with Him: A Forbidden-Love Office Romance (Finn and Annie's story)

2. Second Chance at Us: A Second Chance Romance (Becca and Blake)

3. Falling for You: A Friends-to-Lovers Romance (Isla and Owen)

4. The Spark Between Us: A Grumpy-Sunshine, Firefighter, Brother's Best Friend Romance (Sarah and Braden)

5. Playing for You: A Sports Romance (Tatum and Donovan)

6. No Match for Her - An Opposites-Attract, Friends-to-Lovers Romance (Cherry and Charlie)

San Francisco Strikers Series - standalone novels

1. He's a Keeper: A Grumpy-Sunshine Sports Romance (Molly and Holden)

2. He's a Player: A Second-Chance Sports Romance (Jordan and Tim)

3. He's a Charmer: A Brother's-Best-Friend, Forced-Proximity, Sports Romance (Linnie and Weston)

Buttercup Hill Series - standalone novels

1. Love You More; A Single-Dad, Grumpy-Sunshine Small-Town Romance (Jax and Ruby)

2. Love You Anyway; A Small-Town Billionaire-Next-Door Age Gap Romance (PJ and Colin)

3. Love You Truly; A Fake-Fiancé, Small-Town Romance (Dash and Mallory)

4. Love You Too; A Small-Town, Accidental Pregnancy Sports Romance (Beatrix and Ren)

5. Love You Always: A Small-Town, Grumpy-Sunshine Forbidden Romance (Archer and Ella)

www.ingramcontent.com/pod-product-compliance
Lightning Source LLC
Chambersburg PA
CBHW061655190726

48289CB00006B/1890

9 781956 749304